A Spirited Engagement

Book 2 of the Hesitant Mediums

Belinda Kroll

BRIGHT BIRD PRESS

A SPIRITED ENGAGEMENT
A Hesitant Mediums novel
Copyright 2024 by Binaebi Akah Calkins
All rights reserved.

ISBN 978-1-7369213-3-3 (pb)
ISBN 978-1-7369213-6-4 (e)

Published by Bright Bird Press at prices that enable the creation of future works. Thank you for respecting the immense energy expended to create the work in your hands.

BELINDA KROLL
HERE COMES THE GHOST BRIDE...
A
SPIRITED
Engagement
A Hesitant Mediums novel

Dedicated to my fellow mixed chicks who loved *Buffy the Vampire Slayer*, wished they could be a Sailor Scout, and read everything Jane Austen wrote. This is for you.

ONE

MARYLEBONE, LONDON, JULY 1887

IN WHICH THE MEDIUM ARRIVES

MISS TESSA PRESTON DROPPED her travel-worn satchel, dismayed by the ghosts sailing about the stately London townhouse intended to be her new home. Already out-of-sorts from the Marylebone Spiritualist Association's rude rejection letter burning a hole in her purse, Tessa found herself at a loss. That letter was supposed to have been her entrée to Society as a preeminent medium. That letter was supposed to have set her up for life. Her warm brown complexion took on an olive tone, reflecting the nausea roiling in her stomach.

Tessa pondered the comfortable and modestly upscale townhouse while twirling the errant black curl above her ear that always defied coiffure. Once upon a time, too many years ago, she had left this house and had been glad of it. To now return as the resident medium, and with so very many ghosts seizing her attention, wasn't exactly how she had imagined events resolving.

"A happy facade, don't you think?" Sir Hubert Preston, her uncle, said. His dark travel suit, well-tailored and well-patched, hid that it was a couple of seasons out of date. Still, he cut a fine figure despite or because of his healthy, tan, and entirely bald head, and drew the attention of admiring eyes as servants rushed along with their morning duties. "I must admit I hadn't noticed last night, but I daresay this shall be a fine stop for us."

They stood perilously close to the curb, along with their trunks. Their hansom driver had dispatched everything with great speed, muttering how he wanted nothing to do with this house and couldn't afford his horses getting spooked for the third time this week.

Tessa made a noncommittal noise, too distracted to engage her uncle's small talk. A spirit brushed past her, rustling her skirts and tickling the tiny black curls at her nape. "Well," she huffed.

"Given how you're staring, I can only imagine Dame Hartwell didn't exaggerate, and she does indeed have an overwhelming influx of ghosts calling?" Sir Hubert said.

"She didn't exaggerate," Tessa confirmed, "and while I know she's providing us room and board, I can't help but think we're being underpaid."

Sir Hubert shushed her with an annoyed click of his tongue. "You know I dislike such blatant talk of business."

Tessa gave him an amused sidelong glance. "An unfortunate truth, since you're supposed to be my guardian and manager."

Sir Hubert smiled. He brought forward an intricately carved walking stick, his nonchalance belying his intense study of the house. The stick itself was rather mundane in the hands of someone like Sir Hubert, who hadn't the Sense to see or hear ghosts. It was for this reason he wielded it.

"I don't think we need that quite yet, but thank you," Tessa murmured, not taking her dark brown eyes off the house, yet knowing her uncle would yield the stick at the flick of her wrist.

She counted ten distinct ghosts entering and exiting the home. They seemed a rather benign-looking group. But after last night's excitement, which had ended with Tessa exorcising two ghosts and Dame Hartwell extending an offer of employment, she didn't intend to let her guard down.

None of the ghosts seemed violent or emotional. Had they not been translucent, one might have thought they were simply visiting Dame Hartwell for a rather early cup of tea and a bit of gossip. They did not pretend to rely on gravity, however, and floated in and out of the residence with a peculiar sort of glee. A woman in full Elizabethan court dress caught Tessa's eye, mostly because a ghost of that age should have seemed . . . softer around the edges, faded with time.

Recalling how Dame Hartwell had begged them to stay to protect her family from the increasing number of spirits insomuch as she could discern for herself, Tessa realized a half-truth informed them.

She straightened her shoulders and tapped the little hat perched atop her artfully piled braids and curls. She tugged the short peplum of her once-smart traveling suit, and out of a dismaying habit, brushed the backside of her bustle for good measure. "We've spent quite enough time cooling our heels. We're expected inside."

"Are we?" Sir Hubert said. He removed his hat, ran a handkerchief along his bald head, and replaced the hat in a smooth, practiced move. "No one's come to get our things, and the curtains remain shut."

Tessa's frown deepened, her thin upper lip tucking into her full lower one as both flattened with displeasure. "I'm certain Dame Hartwell said to come early in the morning to avoid disrupting the family."

"Hm, yes. And who did she mean, exactly? She is the matriarch, is she not? Who could she possibly wish to avoid by our early arrival?"

Tessa immediately pictured Dame Hartwell's handsome son, Alexander Hartwell. He had deplored this "sensationalist ghost talk" all those years ago. Seeing how his mother had only furthered her interest in spiritualism to the point of hosting séances and hiring mediums-in-residence, Tessa could only imagine the reaction Dame Hartwell was avoiding.

"I've no idea," she lied. Sometimes it was best to not share every detail with her uncle.

Sir Hubert harrumphed. "Even so. Someone should collect our things. We're gaining too much attention standing out here."

Just as he was about to ascend the short stair to the front door, a woman in an elegant, dark lavender dress with a dainty bustle and black trim slipped outside. She was careful to close the door with both hands to reduce the noise of the latch catching.

"Hello! You must be our welcoming committee," Sir Hubert said, deceptively cheerful.

The woman spun around, clutching the bit of lace at her throat. Her violet-gray eyes, already wide with surprise, widened as she looked them over. She touched the little hat, similar in style to Tessa's, atop her dark hair. "Oh! Good morning. I didn't realize Dame Hartwell was expecting guests."

Tessa appreciated how the woman assumed they were Dame Hartwell's guests rather than employees. She wondered belatedly whether they should have arrived at the back entrance. Habit from a lifetime ago had landed her on the front stoop instead.

"We don't mean to be a burden, my dear," Sir Hubert said, taking a fatherly air, grating Tessa's already strained nerves, "but we're supposed to be moving in, only no one's come for us or our things despite our prompt arrival. Could you send word to the lady of the house on our behalf?"

"Moving in?" the woman echoed. "You must be the new medium."

Tessa and Sir Hubert glanced at one another. "*New* medium?"

"I suppose it's better to meet this way, on our own terms. My name is Mary Trentwood." She pried her gloves off, slapping them into her fringed purse as she descended the steps. "Dame Hartwell goes through a medium every couple of days, it seems. She's seeking someone to teach me."

"Teach you?" Tessa said. She accepted Mary's hand, annoyed at having taken so long to figure out the dame's scheme. "Dame

Hartwell said she wanted me to protect her son and his fiancée by ridding the house of ghosts."

Things were far worse than Tessa feared. She winked one eye shut, allowing her Sense to shift the sight of her open eye. The world wavered before snapping into place. The ghosts moving about the townhouse took on a startling sense of solidity, while Sir Hubert faded and seemed ghostlike himself. Mary, however, glowed with all the cool beauty of blue-black flame.

It was no wonder the house attracted ghosts. Mary was a beacon of the brightest sort, surpassed only by Tessa herself, it seemed.

Mary's pinched smile hinted at her displeasure. "I'm certain she means to explain everything, but in short, I'm the fiancée of which she spoke."

Sir Hubert harrumphed, shifting his weight.

Tessa resisted the urge to rub her forehead. She really, really ought to have known better.

Mary pulled a key from her purse. "Let's head inside for some tea. I'll send Pomeroy for your things."

"We daren't disturb you," Sir Hubert said. "You looked to be on an errand."

Mary shook her head. "Only a morning walk to clear my head."

"Alone?" Sir Hubert said, scandalized.

Tessa coughed. Her uncle was always so easily surprised by any form of independence in other women, despite having seen and even aided her in some rather physical battles with unwieldy spirits.

Mary searched for a response. "I'm accustomed to my morning walks in the country. But I must admit, the morning air here isn't half so fine."

Tessa noted how Mary flinched as the suspiciously well-defined Elizabethan ghost sailed past her into the house. With a Sense that strong, it was only natural Mary Trentwood saw ghosts. Clearly, she wasn't adept at pretending otherwise. "Are you well, Miss Trentwood?" Tessa asked, glancing at Sir Hubert with a knowing expression.

"Oh, yes, thank you. Merely a headache." Mary's eyes flitted nervously to the sight of the Elizabethan ghost sticking her head through the front door, wondering aloud what kept them remaining outside. "Headaches that, on occasion, make me see things."

Tessa let the silence hang between them. "Is that so?"

Mary shoved the key into the lock, opening the door as she said, "A trifling matter. Join me in the library, won't you?"

Tessa couldn't help rubbing her hands together as soon as Mary turned her back. This was exactly what she needed to distract her from the narrow-minded Marylebone Spiritualist Association. If she could help Mary control her Sense, she would finally have a case study on English soil to present as evidence of her right to be a member of the venerated association.

"You must wipe that smirk from your face," Sir Hubert said as he took her arm to lead her in the house. "You'll reveal your mercenary nature too early in the game."

"Is it mercenary to make the most of an unexpected and unfortunate situation? I prefer pragmatic," she quipped.

"Whatever you need to tell yourself," he said. "Just be careful. Dame Hartwell is a well-connected Spiritualist, and this is her house and future daughter-in-law you're playing with. Don't forget, the Spirit World has its own warnings for you."

Tessa touched the high neck of her dress, uncomfortable in the summer morning heat. She had decided on the dress because it hid the deep bruises left by the angry ghosts she exorcised from Dame Hartwell's parlor last night. "They're coming for you," had been the warning. Who was coming, and why, Tessa didn't know.

She smiled sweetly at her uncle. "One crisis at a time, if you please."

Two

In Which One Discovers

The Elizabethan ghost hovered in the foyer, clearly waiting for Mary.

Mary cleared her throat, trying to appear as though she wasn't avoiding the ghost as she inched past the entry table.

Ghosts couldn't help but gather near mediums who couldn't control their Sense out of denial, ignorance, or inability. After all, a hesitant medium is to a ghost what a moth is to a flame. There are certain bragging rights that come along with breaking in, or breaking down, a new medium.

Tessa shook her head at the ghost, letting a bit of her Sense to flare out in warning.

"Thou shouldst mind thine betters," the ghost said, advancing on Tessa. "Shakespeare may have written of a Moorish king, it doth raises thou naught."

Mary stopped, looking as though she wanted to ask a question, but didn't dare. Instead, she said, "The library is this way." She moved down the square-shaped hall to the door on the right. As with most townhouses in the area, the library sat on the ground floor just beyond the hall, with the dining room beyond that to entertain guests. Tessa let Mary guide them as if she hadn't lived a year under this roof.

Everything was as it had been. The same wallpaper, rugs, drapes, and family portraits. Hartwell House felt lived in, but not shabbily so. The wear and tear over the years imbued a sense of familial comfort rather than destitution. Tessa wondered at Sir Hartwell's fortune that he could leave such a comfortable living for his widow, Dame Hartwell, even after all these years.

Mary stopped abruptly when the Elizabethan ghost stood in the library's doorway, blocking her entry. Sir Hubert, having placed his hat on the table in the absence of a butler, frowned at Tessa.

Tessa took her uncle's arm, whispering, "She has the Sense, badly managed. One minute she's bright as the sun, another dark as night. I'm exhausted watching her. And we have a friend teasing her, knowing she doesn't want to admit anything to us."

"Why ever not, if she knows Dame Hartwell hired you to help her?" he whispered back.

"Perhaps she doesn't want someone else to know," Tessa mused, more to herself than to her uncle.

"You don't think she would keep such a thing from her future husband, surely?"

Tessa shrugged, taking the walking stick from her uncle. The moment she touched it, the energy in the room shifted such that the Elizabethan ghost focused solely on her. Whatever it was about Tessa holding the cane, it seemed to make her an immediate threat to any and all spirits nearby. The ghost moved out of Mary's way, her narrow gaze speaking volumes.

"Whether he knows," Tessa whispered as Mary entered the library, "I agree Miss Trentwood could use my help."

"So Dame Hartwell wasn't exaggerating when she said her son's fiancée required protection?" Sir Hubert replied, his tone suggesting Tessa could find a conspiracy in an empty corner.

The sight of a familiar face in the library stopped Tessa's retort.

A low voice, achingly familiar and reminding Tessa of simpler, if heartbreaking, days, greeted Mary from the worn settee. "London air not suit you this morning, my dear?"

"I hadn't the opportunity to find out," Mary said. "It seems your mother invited yet another medium to stay with us." Her calm demeanor dropped as she settled her hands to her waist and said with some acidity, "When I came to London, I never thought I'd have such a rotation of roommates."

"The devil she has!" Alexander Hartwell sat up from his lounged position to engage Mary on the topic. Upon noticing Tessa and her uncle, he leapt to his feet, dropping his book. "Tessa!"

"Hello, Alex, it's been an age." Tessa kept her eyes on Mary and Hartwell, mostly to avoid the knowing grin she knew was spreading across her uncle's face.

Hartwell was a man of moderate height, with dark hair and eyes. His distinguishing feature was the scar that ran from his left eye and down his chin. It was what could have made him dashing, but honestly, made him seem a questionable Gothic hero. Tessa had often, in her girlish days, imagined Hartwell as a Mr. Rochester to her Jane Eyre, silly as it was.

It was supremely unfortunate that, clearly, Sir Hubert remembered Tessa's former *tendre*.

Hartwell moved to stand beside Mary. "I'd no idea you'd returned to London, though!"

Mary looked from Hartwell to Tessa, brows raised. "I see I've no need to make introductions?"

"No indeed," Hartwell said, a smile breaking across his scarred face as he offered his hand to Tessa's uncle. "So Mother finally got you back. I never thought I'd see the day."

"Nor I," Tessa said, hoping no one could tell how her heart beat against her stays. She should have assumed Hartwell would be in the home when Dame Hartwell invited them to stay. Her son and his fiancée, indeed. Were they all to stay in the house until Tessa removed the ghosts, or simply until Hartwell and Mary married?

"And you, Sir Hubert," Hartwell said as he wrapped an arm around Mary's waist. She looked embarrassed, yet pleased. "I suppose you're staying with us as well?"

Sir Hubert nodded. "You're a sight for sore eyes." He motioned to the scar running down Hartwell's face. "Damn shame that didn't heal."

Tessa pinched his arm. "What my uncle means to say is we're glad to be among friends again."

"Quite," Sir Hubert agreed, rubbing where Tessa pinched him. "We may let down our hair, as it were." He chuckled with Hartwell at his joke, touching his bald head only somewhat self-consciously.

Tessa noted how Mary kept glancing in the corner, where the Elizabethan ghost now hovered, glaring at Tessa. Rolling her eyes ever so slightly, Tessa handed the walking stick back to her uncle. "It's easier if you acknowledge, rather than ignore, the benign ones."

"Much that you know," the Elizabethan ghost said, dropping her affected tones. "I've been haunting this one for nigh onto two weeks, and as masterful an actress as I've ever seen, with how well she ignored me!"

Mary spun on her heel, and Hartwell jumped back, startled. "You're not Elizabethan!" she accused the ghost.

The ghost crowed, bending as she laughed. "So now she pays attention! I'm but a poor actress myself, miss, with the bad luck of dying in my costume between sets."

Mary covered her face, half-laughing, half-groaning. "This is so much worse than being haunted at home."

"You swore last night the ghosts had stopped bothering you," Hartwell said.

Tessa exchanged a look with her uncle. Something indeed must have happened, for the Alexander Hartwell of old did *not* believe in ghosts.

"Your dearest doesn't wish to alarm you," came Dame Hartwell from behind them. She was a slight woman, persistently dressed in gray fabrics that complemented her silver hair, ivory complexion, and cool blue eyes. "But as I keep telling you, not only does Mary see them, she's attracting them to the house. Tessa, my dear, so glad you came early. You must join us for breakfast. We must debrief about last night's séance."

Hartwell's expression turned stormy. "You mean Tessa was here last night, and you didn't tell me?"

"Well, who else do you think could exorcise three ghosts in a sitting? Madam Sylvia? I should think not." Dame Hartwell took both Mary and Tessa's arms, pulling them from Hartwell and Sir Hubert. "Stay in the library and stew if you must. We shall be in the dining room. Coming, Sir Hubert?"

"I've never missed the promise of breakfast before. Seems foolhardy to start now," was Sir Hubert's jovial response.

Tessa felt her cheeks and neck grow warm. With all the excitement after their visit to the association that morning, she had put aside last night's excursion. "I should correct you, ma'am. I only sent two spirits Beyond. The third left of his own accord," she said as Dame Hartwell dragged her and Mary to the dining room, with Sir Hubert and Hartwell following close behind.

"Oh, no one cares of such details," Dame Hartwell replied. "Only think, you made such quick work, we shall be rid of these spirits in no time at all."

Tessa doubted that very much indeed. She kept the thought to herself, however, for she could see how dispelling a house of ghosts was certainly one way to impress the Marylebone Spiritualist Association to gain entry to their membership.

Tessa pressed her lips together, noting Mary do the same. A roof over her head, and an opportunity to prove her worth,

Tessa reminded herself. This was why she submitted to Dame Hartwell's incessant managing.

However, teaching someone to control their Sense, now that was an entirely different matter. Though her ears still burned with the derision and laughter that someone like her, of mixed heritage, would dare sully the hallowed halls of the Marylebone Spiritualist Association, Tessa still wanted—no, needed—their acceptance. With their sponsorship, she could work anywhere in England, and for top rates. She wouldn't have to rely on her uncle for a roof over her head or food on her plate.

This truly couldn't have been a more convenient opportunity. Tessa would get the Marylebone Spiritualist Association to award her membership by the week's end if Mary proved to be a clever student—by month's end if not.

Still, as the Elizabethan ghost followed them into the dining room, Tessa couldn't help but wonder whether there was an easier way to legitimize herself to society. She did have the most terrible habit of doing things the hard way.

THREE

IN WHICH ONE ARRANGES

THE DINING ROOM WAS much like the rest of the house, well-loved and unchanged since she last dined here. Tessa squared her shoulders, noting the door at the other end leading to the kitchen and scullery. The large bay window centered on the right wall faced a private courtyard, while the left wall featured family portraits. It was a well-appointed room, and well-suited for a quick escape if needed. She turned her attention to Sir Hubert, who held the cane that allowed her to perform the feats to which Dame Hartwell alluded.

Tessa felt exposed without it. That cane had saved her from quite the attack last night, one she hadn't expected in such a grand home. She resolved to retrieve it once everyone disbanded for the day.

Sir Hubert, having already piled his plate with breakfast notions, plopped into a chair beside Hartwell, whose plate was empty and his coffee cup at risk of spilling over. "Did I read in the papers that you're to marry this lovely woman? I am all agog. We all thought dear Alex would never walk the aisle after his accident."

Mary's mouth sagged open. Tessa rolled her eyes.

"Good to see you, too, Sir Hubert," Hartwell said affably. "I suppose Tessa never told you my accident was nothing more than Florence tossing a teapot my way because I teased her too much in front of her new husband."

Sir Hubert blinked. "Certainly not. And how is Sir Kirkham?"

"As complacent as he ever was," Hartwell said. "Having died rather unexpectedly in his sleep last year."

"I'm sorry," Mary interrupted, clearly objecting to all this untoward familiarity from Sir Hubert. "But have we met?"

Sir Hubert chuckled. "We danced once upon a time during your Season, back when your father was trying to prevent you from attaching to another gentleman . . . Steele, I think it was? It's been years, and of course, I'm certain I was too old for you even then. I was sorry to hear of your father's passing."

It was Tessa's turn to be confused. "You know each other? You knew her father?" She bit her lip before asking anything further.

"When we were younger, we frequented the same clubs," Sir Hubert affirmed.

Tessa studied the glow around Mary, which grew brighter as they discussed Mary's father and she grew increasingly distressed. "He haunted you, didn't he?"

Both Mary and Hartwell caught their breath as one. "Miss Preston has a very strong Sense," Dame Hartwell explained. "And she amplifies those with their own Sense."

"We don't know that for certain, my lady," Tessa said. "There is something special that happens to individuals haunted by close family. It opens doors, sometimes doors that should have stayed shut. Did you know of his presence?"

"Almost constantly," Mary said, with a bemused smile. "For the first time in weeks, I almost wish for his spirit's incessant chattiness."

Hartwell took Mary's hand, squeezing it. Tessa averted her eyes, embarrassed.

"He's now at rest," Mary continued, "but I assure you, before all the excitement that led me here to London and with my dear Alex, my father's ghost was my constant companion, and rarely let anything go unremarked."

Tessa nodded. "It's clear that I need to stay. This house is too active with spirits. Pardon my directness, but you must be why. We must teach you how to control your Sense." She bit back a gasp when Dame Hartwell, unable to contain her delight, patted her hand until it ached from the attention.

"I haven't any Sense," Mary said, her tone brooking no arguments.

"Of course you do. You're the most sensible person I know," Hartwell teased.

"Oh, yes, you do," Tessa said, ignoring Hartwell. "And if we don't teach you how to control it, you will put yourself in great danger. You are an open honeypot to the fruit flies of Beyond. It simply won't do to hide your head beneath a pillow about this."

"Both an eloquent and disturbing metaphor, Tessa," Hartwell said.

"Well." Mary folded her napkin neatly on the table. "Is there anything you need to do to prepare the house, any . . . protections you need to put up?"

"I'm not a witch," Tessa said, more than a little affronted. "I'm a medium. It's not like I can say some magic words and put a bowl over the house to keep the flies out."

Sir Hubert made a small noise, holding out the cane.

Tessa blinked. "Right, well, I only know one magical phrase and it only seems to work with this cane and only when spirits are attacking someone. So no, I cannot put up 'protections' in the room."

Mary rubbed her temple, shaking her head.

"So Mater finally wore you down," Hartwell said to Tessa, "and she's hired you on."

"Don't be rude," Dame Hartwell said. "It's for Mary's benefit. Tessa's come home. You ought to be glad for her help."

Hartwell's expression turned mulish, but he said nothing as Mary squeezed his arm.

"I assume Miss Preston and I will share a room, Dame Hartwell, as I have with your other mediums?" Mary said.

Tessa cleared her throat. "We have yet to discuss the particulars of my employment. I hardly think I should live with the family when I'm only here to clear the house of lingering souls before the wedding."

"Don't be silly. You shared the room with dearest Florence when you were younger. Why wouldn't you share it with Mary now?" Dame Hartwell asked.

"Surely you see *some* impropriety," Hartwell said. "Mary is to be your daughter-in-law and my wife. Surely she doesn't need to share a room for your entertainment. No offense, Tessa."

Tessa's jaw tightened, and she gulped her tea.

"I insist Miss Preston stays with me," Mary said, saving Tessa from further embarrassment. "I believe she might actually know what she's talking about. It will be quite refreshing, and perhaps even a bit fun, to give these spirits a bit of their own back."

Dame Hartwell clapped her hands, delighted. "Oh, that's quite excellent, my dear! What a lovely attitude to have about it, finally."

Tessa caught how Mary's eyes narrowed, ever so slightly, in annoyance. She saved Mary from having to respond to the gentle jibe. "One cannot overstate how difficult it is to accept the constant presence of ghosts, my lady."

"I accept them just fine, I think," Dame Hartwell said, delicately slathering jam on her toast.

"Indeed, my lady, for you only have to hear them, and I think they must often sound like whispers to you."

Tessa poured a cup of coffee from the sideboard and held it with both hands. Her stomach, while no longer queasy from last night's exertions, recoiled at the sight of the breakfast spread. There were multiple meat options, with which Sir Hubert rewarded himself handsomely, with soft-boiled eggs, buttered toast, and a variety of jams. Tessa missed the lighter fare of the Mediterranean and ultimately settled on toast. She took her time selecting a slice, using the moment to assess the Sense in the room.

Dame Hartwell had a faint glow, as expected. Just enough to know paranormal activities happened around her, perhaps even hear or suffer physical effects by the stronger spirits, but certainly not strong enough to influence anything. In the morning light, Tessa could now see Hartwell had a similar glow, something she had never noticed before. Or perhaps it was his exposure to Mary Trentwood that had increased his Sense? For Mary glowed as brightly as Tessa herself, but the glow flickered as though a stiff wind worked to stifle a kerosene lamp. It could only be Mary herself attempting to control her access to spirits, or perhaps the spirits' access to her. Either way, it explained Mary's strained expression. It would take an immense amount of concentration to dampen a Sense that strong without practice.

Dame Hartwell frowned at Tessa, but thought better of whatever she intended to say. "It is most curious. My dear Alex and I only seem able to hear the spirits. Mary, though she will not admit it, I'm certain can both hear and see the spirits . . . like yourself."

Tessa glanced at Sir Hubert, unsure whether Dame Hartwell thought she was being subtle. Sir Hubert focused on his plate, as did Hartwell. "Yes, I both hear and see the spirits. My uncle does not."

"Fascinating," Dame Hartwell said. "And is that why he carries your mystical stick?"

Mary frowned. "Mystical stick? Do you have mystical artifacts hidden in your luggage, Miss Preston?"

Tessa appreciated Mary for having the ability to say such a sentence without sarcasm. "Hardly." She pretended to sip her coffee, taking a moment to breathe deeply and calm the pressure rising in her chest. "My uncle carries the cane because he indeed lacks Sense—of the paranormal kind, of course—and doesn't attract spirits the way I might. Or Miss Trentwood, for that matter."

"Thank you for the mention, m'dear," Sir Hubert said, raising his coffee with a chuckle. "We received the cane from a lovely Roma who insisted we take it for our protection, and for others'."

"You wielded it masterfully last night," Dame Hartwell said, having forgotten her breakfast entirely.

"What *did* happen last night?" Mary asked. "The drawing room was in shambles."

"We tried to pick up," Tessa said, staring at Sir Hubert, "but one can only do so much in a short amount of time and a single set of hands."

Sir Hubert dabbed the corners of his mouth with his napkin, unperturbed at the implication, however accurate, that he chose not to soil his hands with righting the drawing room.

"It was extraordinary," Dame Hartwell said. She leaned forward, startling Mary as she grabbed her hand. "Miss Preston here identified there were malevolent spirits—three, in fact!—in the house and banished them in quick succession. I've never seen such acrobatics in a bustle before."

"Acrobatics?" Hartwell said. "Were they circus ghosts?"

"Don't be patronizing," Tessa said, unable to stop herself. "I may have been your sister's playmate once upon a time, but I assure you, not only were there three spirits, but they came with a warning I've been puzzling over."

"A warning?" Mary said, gently extracting her hand from Dame Hartwell.

Dame Hartwell nodded. "Poor Madam Sylvia. I don't think the spirits have ever possessed her before. 'Tessa, they're coming for you,' the spirit said through her. It rather startled all of us."

Tessa held back her questions, her suspicion growing that Dame Hartwell had known all along Madam Sylvia lacked the Sense. Instead, she mused, "Madam Sylvia was a victim. Even if she were practiced with possessions, I've never seen what I saw last night. And I've only once before come to physical blows with a spirit."

"Madrid," Sir Hubert chimed in, as if that explained everything.

Mary's eyes grew wide. "Possession? Blows? Surely you tease us."

Hartwell cleared his throat. "However, we are not entirely unaccustomed to such talk." Mary glared at him, but when Tessa turned, curious, he continued, "I believe ever since Mary's father returned to . . . Beyond, was it? I think his departure opened a gate and now Mary can see and hear other ghosts."

Ah, so easy to confirm Miss Trentwood's secret. "Your father haunted you," Tessa said.

"And possessed me," Hartwell said, "but it was always to protect Mary. In fact, he used me to give a friend a right walloping for some untoward comments. That was rather enjoyable, actually."

Tessa studied Mary, who, after a moment's hesitation, met her gaze with a defiant expression, which made Tessa like her immensely. If there were ever a woman worth Alex Hartwell's salt, it was one who could meet the challenge of her father haunting and possessing people, and still keep her wits. "And you've seen ghosts ever since?"

Mary shook her head. "Only since sleeping under this roof have I had the misfortune of seeing spirits."

Dame Hartwell slapped the table in triumph. "I knew you could see the spirits, though I hardly know why you wouldn't admit it."

"Don't you, Mater?" Hartwell said. "She's meant to be my wife, not evening entertainment for your spiritualist friends. And don't give me that look, Mary. I promised I'd wait until morning, and now it's morning, so I *shall* address it with my mother."

Mary raised her hands, glancing at Tessa. "I asked to not make a scene."

"He can hardly make a scene in front of Tessa," Dame Hartwell said. "She's practically a second sister, aren't you, dearest? Though perhaps you're a bit more level-headed than my own dear daughter. You're unlikely to toss a teapot at anyone's head."

"No ma'am," Sir Hubert interjected. "You may depend on Tessa starting nothing, but she shall almost certainly always finish it."

Dame Hartwell smiled. "That is exactly why I hired her. Now that she is here, we can finally have your ball," she said to Mary, who jumped in her seat.

"What ball?"

Dame Hartwell laughed. "Well, we must have a ball in honor of your wedding. You are marrying my son. Let's not forget."

"Mother, we talked about this," Hartwell said. "Mary dislikes the attention."

"Then this will be just the thing to disable her of her fear."

Hartwell sat back, his jaw tightening. "She's not afraid."

Tessa watched Mary turn different colors, annoyed and frustrated. "Miss Trentwood, would you mind giving me a tour of the home? Since we are roommates, I would like to hear what's changed since I last lived here."

When Dame Hartwell made to join them, Tessa said, "Ma'am, if I'm to succeed in my purpose under your roof, I must spend some time with Miss Trentwood alone. How else will I build her Sense?"

"Oh, very well," Dame Hartwell said, sounding cross. "I expect to receive regular reports on your progress!"

"Depend upon it, my dear madam," Sir Hubert said as Tessa beckoned Mary out of the room, "Tessa will let you know precisely what she wants you to know."

FOUR

IN WHICH ONE SEEKS HELP

HAGGARD WAS TOO GENTLE a word for the exhaustion plaguing Jasper Steele. He reclined in his mother's morning room, an arm draped over his eyes against the perky sunlight. Didn't the sun know they were in London, of all places? Surely there was some dark cloud somewhere to wink that light out. He had slept in his clothes, mussing his nice brown suit. His blond hair, now a little long because his unfortunate circumstances made him miss his haircut, flopped over his forehead. His lip was itchy from remnants of breakfast flecking his mustache.

One would never know it, but Jasper usually took great care with his appearance. But who cared about appearances if one was determined to never enter society again? How could he show his face without others suspecting insanity?

His mother sat purse-lipped across the room, her needlepoint consuming her attention. She sighed, no doubt thinking he had wasted yet another opportunity. He had returned the other night with no news of a certain (or any) young woman having caught his eye. And he smelled like brandy.

What Mrs. Steele had no way of knowing was Jasper Steele had indeed succeeded in one unexpected thing: getting himself engaged . . . of a kind. To a ghost. Who, while fashionable in every sense of the word, was a bit of a light-skirt while alive.

Eloise Carterprice, said affianced and floating spirit, continued her abuse of Mrs. Steele's choice of decor.

"Doesn't she know antimacassars are no longer in style?" Eloise said. "No wonder you weren't catching the eye of anyone's mama until I latched on to you. We shall do wonders in this space, darling Jasper-poo."

Jasper swallowed a groan. *Latched* was the operative word. He'd had a foreboding feeling before entering the Carterprice home. This was what came of him trying to keep his mother happy . . . Forever shackled to an obstinate, judgmental martyr of a girl, whose vices seemed to have only gotten worse in death, and already had him wondering who he might hire to get rid of her.

The fact was, Jasper knew who he had to entreat to help. He didn't relish the idea. In fact, Jasper had walked over to Hartwell House three times in three days, only to back away in a cold sweat upon seeing Mary Trentwood entering and leaving, preparing for her wedding with Alexander Hartwell.

Mary rejecting him in favor of Hartwell wasn't the cause of his retreats, per se. That was all done and gone, no matter what his mother suspected. Jasper put all resentment aside once Hartwell hired him on, with a salary increase, as an assistant in his law office.

No, it was how Jasper's head ached with phantom pains from an altercation with Mary's now-deceased aunt. He had this bad habit of hearing voices since his head wound had healed. He was rather certain these voices were real. Now that he had this ghostly fiancée, he was all but convinced the voices humming in the back of his head were spirits. The voices got louder in Mary Trentwood's presence, something he had never mentioned to either her or Hartwell.

Now he would have to admit that much, and more.

He eyed Eloise and her statuesque frame, pale blonde locks pulled up into delicate chignons that trailed from her crown to her nape. She wore lavender, the dress they had buried her in.

Her skin was an unseemly white, but as she was a ghost and rather transparent, Jasper supposed that was to be expected.

Eloise turned to smile at him. He froze beneath her steady gaze. An opaque whiteness clouded her eyes, and she lacked any hint of a pupil. He would need to ask Mary if ghostliness had also afflicted her father with such a horrific attribute.

"My dear," his mother said, interrupting his spiraling thoughts. "Was there no one who stole your attention?"

Jasper wrenched his attention back to his mother, focusing on her presence as if she were a buoy at sea. She wore her salt-and-pepper hair pulled back in a simple, elegant style. Her nimble fingers flew, not needing to check where the needle would go next. Her dark eyes studied him from beneath frowning brows.

"No," Jasper said, "no one stole my attention." His gaze drifted back to the fireplace where Eloise floated, grimacing at a little shepherdess figurine his father had given his mother. The room was full of such romantic little gestures. They disgusted Eloise to no end.

"I beg to differ," Eloise said with a sniff. "I did exactly that, I daresay. To anchor myself to you, I grabbed you with all the strength I had to give you that kiss. Could you imagine how dull it would be if I'd anchored to my bluestocking sister?" She shuddered.

"Edith Carterprice is a good sort of girl," Jasper said. He clapped his hand over his mouth at the sight of his mother's delighted expression.

"Edith Carterprice *is* an excellent young lady," Mrs. Steele agreed, dropping her needlepoint and joining him on the sofa. She prodded his leg so he would give her more room. She kept her skirts slim and functional in the current style, but age had softened her middle and there was the bustle to think of. "Her nose is in a book more often than not. I wouldn't have thought she interested you. But perhaps you need something a little different after that Trentwood girl."

Jasper sighed at the sour note the name held on his mother's tongue. "Mary is a good friend, Mother."

"You don't need a friend—you need a wife," she snapped.

"Don't upset Mother, Jasper-poo," Eloise warned. "I want her in a good mood when we tell her about me."

Jasper's eyes widened, horrified at the thought. He jumped from his seat, startling his mother. Eloise hadn't mentioned introductions to his mother yet. She'd kept him awake all night with her incessant prattling on about how maligned she was in death, and how she wanted him to print defenses and retractions against all the rumors that had surfaced in the newspapers after her passing some months back.

"I need—"

"And don't you say *drink*," his mother said, "for you positively reek of brandy. Just what happened at the Carterprices', if it wasn't an attachment between you and Edith?"

Jasper almost let it slip that she'd named the wrong Carterprice twin, but clenched his jaw against turning his own mother against him. For she would think her only child had gone insane, out of jealousy or mourning or lack of love. He doubted she would send him away, but these days, one couldn't be too careful.

"I need to seek counsel with Hartwell on an important case. That's all, Mother. It's so troubling that I've lost all ability to sleep."

Eloise cracked a grin at this masterful falsehood.

Mrs. Steele rose with him, resigned but still concerned. "Well, seek his counsel and come home to rest. You need to be focusing on building your future family. I won't let you throw away your dreams just because of how that Trent—" She paused at Jasper's darkening expression. "I just want you to be happy."

He kissed her cheek, slapping his hat atop his head. "Don't stay up. I'll be home late or not at all. You know how these cases can get."

Eloise sailed from the room ahead of him, chortling all the way.

FIVE

IN WHICH LESSONS ARE DISRUPTED

TESSA'S LESSONS WITH MARY, if one dared describe them as such, were miserable, maddening affairs. Between Dame Hartwell's watchful eagerness and Sir Hubert's silent scribbling in his large diary, they siphoned all curiosity and willingness to learn or teach from the room. Though Dame Hartwell interrupted at every opportunity, given or not, it was the loud silences from Sir Hubert that were cracking Tessa's calm demeanor.

Clearly, he thought she was doing it *all wrong*. And since her uncle took his position as manager and mentor seriously, he also refused to say anything about it. He gave no notes besides the ones filling his diary of ghostly observations over the years.

Today they sat in the library, the drapes drawn open to help Mary distinguish ghostly shadows from those created by the sun. Mary sat on the chaise placed before the empty fireplace, and Dame Hartwell sat beside her, urging and encouraging. Mary squinted and sighed, doing her best not to look directly at the four spirits hovering by the fireplace making baby noises and wiggling their fingers at her.

Sir Hubert sat at a little table on the farthest wall from them, his plate empty from a midmorning snack and his tea having cooled. Though he had filled two pages, he had yet to say anything since they all adjourned there after breakfast.

Tessa sat on a wingback chair to the left of Mary, doing her special blink now and then to open her Sense and watch how Mary's aura flickered and flamed with every interruption from Dame Hartwell. Mary seemed mere moments away from hysterics, if her twitching eyebrow was any indication.

With a slow, deep inhale, Tessa glanced to the corner to find her uncle staring at her with a brow raised. He frowned and scribbled something else in his diary before muttering something about checking on a new pot of tea and dashing off to the kitchens, diary and all.

Maddening.

Tessa often felt, despite being the most seasoned with her Sight, that Dame Hartwell was her governess instead, while she merely played pretend with a dolly. Which, while an unflattering description of Mary, succinctly summarized her level of engagement in the lessons.

"Shall we try again?" Tessa said, relaxing her jaw.

Mary clasped her hands in her lap, hesitating before she nodded.

"Do try to *concentrate*, my dear," Dame Hartwell admonished. She patted Mary's hands and gave Tessa a knowing look that Tessa did not know how to interpret.

"Concentrate on what?" Mary demanded. "I still don't understand what I'm supposed to be doing in these lessons, other than blinking oddly and hoping I see something I shouldn't."

"This frustration is unbecoming," Dame Hartwell said. "You must open your Sense."

"Everyone experiences their Sense differently," Tessa said, as much to Dame Hartwell as to Mary, "but there are patterns."

"Such as?" Mary mumbled.

Tessa held up her fingers, counting them with each example. "Well, it appears you can see and hear the spirits, or so you said it happened with your father. Clearly Alex has some ability to hear the ghosts if they want to be heard, and the same with our dear Dame Hartwell."

Dame Hartwell perked up at hearing this, and Tessa fought against rolling her eyes.

"I can, of course, see and hear the spirits, and with certain tools, I can affect them as well. My cane, for instance, seems to push and pull. I once heard of a young woman who could touch the spirits with her bare hands, but she also has the bad habit of getting possessed frequently."

"Possessed," Mary breathed, staring at Dame Hartwell. "I did not volunteer for this. I just want my headaches to go away."

"It's hardly painful," Dame Hartwell scoffed. "How many times have you spoken in voices and not realized it until after?"

Tessa frowned. "I don't understand."

She caught a fleeting scowl of frustration breaking through Mary's mask of composure. "It seems, because of my lack of sleep, I have fallen asleep during visiting hours."

"My spiritualist ladies absolutely adore our dear Mary's talents," Dame Hartwell gushed, leaning forward. "Without fail, if she falls asleep, a spirit uses her to speak to us. We've spoken with my friends' husbands many times now."

"My dear lady," Tessa said, jumping in her seat, "you can't mean to say you've encouraged this?" She watched, horrified, as Mary's shoulders slumped while Dame Hartwell's straightened, ready to argue her case. Well. This was certainly a bit of news that changed the dynamic in the room, and Tessa decided she was ready to stop their exercises or ban Dame Hartwell from her own library until further notice. Perhaps both.

Mary rubbed her temples, and Tessa thought she saw tears forming. Time to try a different tactic, then. "When did your headaches start? Are they worse when you see or hear the ghosts?"

Mary pondered this. "See, I think. The headache grows behind my eyes, and I see spots the harder I fight it."

That made sense. Those "spots" certainly must be the ghosts Mary avoided, and the four standing in front of her were doing their best to arrest her attention. They had resorted to party tricks, one of them having pulled their head from their neck, with the other three tossing it about like a hot potato, giggling like children.

"You mustn't fight it," Dame Hartwell said.

"Oi, are you teaching the lady, or is she?" one ghost hissed at Tessa. "She's a lot of opinions for barely having the Sense herself, and she having the dimmest glow of the three of ya."

Tessa glowered at the ghost, an emaciated young woman who had no fingers and was covered in cotton fluff. No doubt a victim of an unfortunate accident at one of those monstrous factories. The other three were of various ages, all with missing fingers and covered in fluff, except for the one who seemed to have suffered a decapitation and now was making the best of it. Tessa rolled her eyes; she couldn't help it. *Have some decorum*, she wanted to say, but knew it would only tease Dame Hartwell into staying in the room longer.

"Don't you make faces at me," the ghost huffed, floating across the room. "The dame's the one always interrupting you."

Mary's lip twitched, revealing she had heard the ghost after all. Dame Hartwell remained ignorant. Interesting.

Tessa used it to her advantage. Not every medium heard every ghost. That much was true. She didn't understand why, but it hardly mattered. To help Mary, she needed to get Dame Hartwell out of the room, and quickly. "The spirits would prefer you not take part in the lessons, my lady."

The ghosts rounded on Tessa, abusing her for blaming them so shabbily. Mary's eyes widened, her lip twitching toward a grin.

Dame Hartwell had the good social graces to look only mildly affronted. "Of course, if my presence makes the spirits uncomfortable, despite my obvious sponsorship of their existence, then I shall leave this instant."

"They aren't uncomfortable," Tessa said. "We must concentrate, as you say, and they find you . . . distracting. I think my uncle went in search of sweets. Perhaps you might take him to a favorite little spot of yours, and he might share with you some of his research from our travels?"

As Tessa expected, Dame Hartwell brightened at the thought of hearing more about Beyond and what they had learned while in Europe. She stood, smoothing her skirts, and beamed with pleasure. "Well, that is an excellent idea. I shall take him right away. We shall chat about your progress at dinner, then."

Mary's posture relaxed as soon as Dame Hartwell sailed from the room. She smiled at Tessa, and the effect on her somber expression gave Tessa a peek into the woman Alex Hartwell fell in love with. "Well done," Mary chuckled. "You know, I never thought to scapegoat the ghosts."

"Spirits," one ghost corrected Mary.

She held up her hands in placation and murmured an apology. The ghosts, now realizing that Mary could see them, found her less fun and floated off to find someone else to play with.

Tessa grinned, settling back in her chair while inviting Mary to relax on the chaise. "It was rude of me, but I know from years past that only the spirits move Dame Hartwell. I do what I must to accomplish my goals."

Mary's expression turned wary. "And what is your goal with me?"

Tessa assessed Mary, whose suspicion surprised and impressed her. While they had a common bemused annoyance regarding Dame Hartwell, Tessa wasn't sure she could trust Mary just yet. "Teach you so that I'm not the only legitimate medium in London," she said lightly. "It's frightfully burdensome."

"I have to suppose that's an understatement, Miss Preston." Mary cleared her throat, picking at a flounce in her skirt. "You might as well call me Mary. We're sharing a bedroom and will clearly spend many hours together."

"Call me Tessa." She wondered how to proceed with the lessons if the only problem was that Mary refused to loosen the hold of her Sense whenever in the presence of Dame Hartwell. She meant to marry the woman's son, after all. Tessa wandered to the window and used a finger to pull back the curtain and see the street better.

The lunchtime traffic was picking up even in their residential part of town, but Tessa paid no mind to any of that. Her gaze settled on a peachy-white, mustachioed blond man staring at their house. It was difficult to tell, but Tessa could have sworn he had done the same thing the last three days. She had been so busy managing all the personalities in the room that she hadn't bothered with the ones outside the house.

"Has something caught your attention?" Mary asked, joining her.

"That man has been staring at the house for close to an hour," Tessa replied, gesturing to the tall, blond, rather handsome man across the street.

Mary studied the street, concentrating. After a moment, she murmured, "So you see him, too."

Oh, no. Tessa turned to Mary, her concentration broken. "Of course I see him." Her tone lifted ever so slightly at the end, a gentle question hovering in the air. "He's very much *alive*, Mary." Unlike the blonde woman adorned in a high-fashion lavender gown floating possessively beside him.

Mary smiled. "Yes, of course he is," she agreed, patting Tessa's arm. "A bit of misplaced ghost—that is, spirit—humor."

Tessa's brows rose.

"That's Jasper Steele," Mary continued, facing the street again, her cheeks taking on some color at the lack of Tessa's humor. "He works for Alex, but very much dislikes visiting with us after our adventure in the countryside earlier this summer."

Tessa's head tilted. She stared, feeling as she once had upon seeing her first ghost. With her stomach tightened and her hand gripping the windowsill, she struggled to breathe. Jasper Steele. Goodness. That was a name that brought back unpleasant memories. Mary said something about how Jasper looked drawn, but all Tessa saw was the man she thought she had put behind her years ago.

Despite his slumped posture and clear exhaustion and resignation, Jasper Steele still sparked a small flame of attraction in Tessa. That he had a tall, lithe blonde woman hanging off him—no, that wasn't right—*hovering* while gripping his arms did not help. Tessa was so very glad her uncle wasn't around.

"Jasper Steele?" she echoed, striving to sound casual. At Mary's nod, she said something about knowing him, but avoided further details. Tessa was hardly ready to examine her feelings on the matter of him popping back into her life. She heard herself ask why he was staring at the house rather than visiting, as any normal person might.

Again came Mary's smile. "We had a bit of . . . bother with my father's ghost back near Swindon, and he was a party to it."

Ah, that explained some of it, then. Once one had an experience with Beyond, it was only a matter of time before other spirits found the affinity and took advantage. Tessa crossed her hands over her abdomen, striving for her very best governess stance. "So you see the young lady hanging from his arm?"

Mary started and turned to stare at her friend. She blinked twice, rubbed her eyes, and a low groan escaped. "I've seen her before."

"You have? I thought you only heard the ghosts?"

"Once before. She warned me danger was coming, but I thought she was being dramatic. They often are, these newly departed." Tessa smiled in agreement. "But how did he acquire, of all persons, the ghost of—good God. I believe that's Eloise Carterprice." Mary sped for the door, Tessa close behind in a swirl of skirts.

They paused, unsure how to proceed once at the curb. One couldn't shout across the way, and indeed, even waving a hand would be unseemly. Yet Jasper Steele simply stared at them, unwilling to come forward and greet them.

Tessa studied this ghost of Miss Eloise Carterprice, intrigued. She noted her height-of-fashion lavender dress, the way her hand rested on Jasper's shoulder, and how her blue eyes, clouded over with the whiteness of death, glared back. Tessa avoided rolling her eyes at Eloise's glossy blonde curls cascading down her back in an intricate imitation of the famed Empress Sisi of Austria.

The transparent gray ribbons trailing from Eloise's back arrested Tessa's attention. Similar to the ghosts that had led to Tessa's employment at Hartwell House, Eloise's ribbons seemed to originate from the location of her mortal wound.

The ribbons were a fascinating detail. Tessa had learned that those gray ribbons, depending on placement, hinted at a violent end. And only as recently as the night before had learned that such gray ribbons could enable possession of a medium. Ever curious, Tessa determined to learn more about the opportunity Eloise afforded by standing before her.

"Do you think Jasper is well? Why won't he come forward?" Mary asked. "What shall we do?"

"Call Miss Carterprice," Tessa suggested.

"Whatever can that mean?" Mary said, aghast.

"I'm not entirely sure myself, but . . ." Tessa's voice trailed off. She was too excited at the possibility of an educational experiment, and yet unsure how to describe something that felt fairly innate and had her Sense yearning. She flicked her wrist, winking to open her Sense more fully, and called silently to the ribbons.

Miss Carterprice jerked toward Mary and Tessa with an unflattering squawk.

Tessa's unladylike grin was short-lived. Eloise maintained her clutch on Jasper's arm, and, given how firmly Tessa called to the gray ribbons, he too came stumbling across the street.

Jasper and Eloise dodged the midmorning traffic amongst shouts of dismay, disbelief, and derision. Tessa flinched at the near collisions, not knowing how to reduce Eloise's speed or stop it altogether. "Oh dear."

Mary grabbed Tessa's arm when Jasper dodged an irate chaise and four. "What is Jasper doing?" she hissed. "Is this your doing? Did you mean for that to happen?"

Before Tessa could answer, Jasper crashed into her, breathless and red-faced. His arms flew around her and they stumbled together to avoid falling, stuttering and exclaiming all the while. Tessa caught sight of a pair of bright, alarmed blue eyes behind tousled blond hair. His mustache perched atop a mouth spewing embarrassed apologies. She froze, arms clamped to her sides as she stared back at him. Jasper Steele. Her heart raced beneath her corset, loosely tied as it was. This was certainly not the reintroduction she might have encouraged.

"You must accept my sincerest apologies," Jasper said, peeling himself off her. "I wish I had an explanation that could—"

"Get your hands off my fiancé!" Eloise shrieked, hovering beside Mary. "How dare you sully him with your . . . your darkness?"

Jasper dropped his hold of Tessa, and said under his breath to Eloise, "Keep quiet!"

Tessa pressed her hand to her abdomen, suspecting Jasper had no notion she could hear Eloise. She schooled her expression into disinterested calm. The way Eloise hissed about her darkness could mean many things. The strength of her Sense, the complexion of her skin—the point was, even as a ghost, Eloise claimed her superiority. Tessa stepped back, tugging at the hem of her pointed bodice and smoothing her overskirt. She met Mary's curious gaze and shook her head slightly, hoping Mary received her message: *Do not let Eloise know we can see and hear her.*

"I'm telling you, Jasper, you need to stay away from her," Eloise said, grabbing his arm.

Jasper shook his arm as if to straighten his sleeve, but Tessa knew it was to shake off Eloise's grip.

"If you thought Mary Trentwood had enough Sense to do something about me, then you ought certainly watch out for this one."

At this, Mary could stay quiet no longer. "It seems you've been busy since we last met. Your fiancée, Jasper?"

He turned to her, his posture wilting with relief. "How excellent. You can see her, can't you? I knew you would help me."

"I can hear her." Mary folded her hands over her abdomen. "Help you with what, exactly?"

Jasper leaned near, his shoulder edging Tessa out of the conversation. "Might we take this indoors where we can speak in private? I'd hate to further confuse or disrupt your visit with your guest." He turned to Tessa. "Please excuse me once again. I had no intention of ruining your morning. I've had the most awful week and thought to . . . call upon my dear friends here at Hartwell House. My behavior has been unpardonable—"

Tessa raised her hand. "Please stop apologizing, Mr. Steele, you've nothing to apologize for. Your . . . unconventional arrival was entirely my fault."

"Your fault!"

Mary gestured to the door, which remained hanging open with her butler standing at the threshold. His austere posture and shock of white hair contrasted with the interested glint in his eyes. Mary flashed a small grin at him. Tessa wondered just how much this butler had seen of Mary's first haunting.

"Perhaps you are right," Mary said. "We should take this indoors."

Eloise hovered beside Jasper, suspicious. "She's up to something."

"I've asked you to keep quiet!" he said.

Mary looked at Tessa, eyes wide in a silent appeal.

"Please join us inside, Mr. Steele. We might get acquainted with the situation that caused you to seek Miss Trentwood." Tessa couldn't help but smile then. "Perhaps it's this Miss Carterprice who stands, I mean, hovers beside you?"

Jasper swiveled from Eloise to Mary and back again to Tessa. "My God, you can see her too, can't you?" he said before keeling forward, unconscious, into Tessa's alarmed arms.

Tessa staggered under his weight with an awkward grunt, eyes wide.

Mary cleared her throat. "Jasper and ghosts don't entirely mix." She turned to Pomeroy, who remained coolly observant. "Ah, Pomeroy, as convenient as ever. Would you be so kind as to relieve Miss Preston of her charge? I think the library, perhaps, would be suitable for his convalescence."

As Tessa sank under Jasper's weight, she gasped. "Are you certain you've not had much experience with ghosts, Miss Trentwood? You're handling this all remarkably well."

Mary grinned. "I said nothing of the sort."

"But Dame Hartwell—"

"Well, really, Miss Preston. And who am I to correct my future mother-in-law, and a member of the peerage, besides? Now Pomeroy, if you please."

Pomeroy lifted Jasper from Tessa as if he were nothing more than an overweight cloak draped in her arms. Tessa coughed her surprise, thinking a man with that white of hair should not be nearly so strong. She followed Mary and Pomeroy into the house, mystified.

SIX

IN WHICH RELATIONS COMPLICATE

TESSA SAT ACROSS THE library from the prone Jasper, worrying her fingernail with her teeth. Mary had left her alone to watch over him, having followed Pomeroy to issue orders to the kitchen staff for a cold compress and notify the Hartwells of their new guest.

Eloise had shimmered out of sight upon their entry to the home, evidently satisfied with the trouble she had caused.

And so Tessa sat alone with Jasper, aghast at her terrible luck. Of all the people to have collapsed in her arms! She was careful to stay a respectable distance from him, now curled on the chaise, looking rather peaceful. He sighed. How dare he look so . . . sweet!

Tessa crept forward, emboldened by his deep, rhythmic breathing. She noticed the dark shadows below his eyes and his wrinkled clothing, details that had gone unnoticed upon his arrival. She wondered how long Eloise had haunted him, and whether she was having her fun, preventing him from sleeping.

Jasper Steele was as handsome as ever. He maintained a pert mustache over a mouth clearly prone to smiling, if the gentle wrinkles forming at the corners of his lips were any indication. He kept his blond hair short on the sides; the top left long and swept up into a becoming pompadour wave, though at the moment it fell across his forehead, inviting Tessa to sweep it out of the way. His clothing, while modest, fit as though tailored to his athletic build. Tessa wondered if he still rowed, for she spied strength hidden within his sleeves, and there was the slightest pinch of fabric across his shoulders.

Tessa touched the back of her neck, which had grown warm during her study. Had Jasper purposely not remembered her, or was he as self-centered as ever? She leaned closer, eyes narrow. The last she had seen this face, it had been at an evening party, the final one she had attended in London. She worked hard to not recall that night, and yet, she couldn't help but remember how dashing he had looked in his evening coattails, chuckling with his friends over a joke that she later learned put her in the center—

Jasper turned, his arm flailing as he adjusted in his sleep.

Tessa dropped back to avoid being slapped. Her temper flared. Right. Well, enough reminiscing. She had a job to do as the medium-in-residence. Tessa shook his shoulder. "Mr. Steele," she said, "you must wake."

He mumbled something about shoving off and hang propriety and all that, and cuddled a pillow against his unshaven cheek.

Tessa huffed. He could disregard propriety all he liked, she assumed, what with his charming blond looks and broad shoulders. Ever the dandy, always getting his way with little care for those inconvenienced.

"Has he not woken yet?" Mary said, reentering the room. She met Tessa, joining her kneeled position on the floor beside the chaise. "He looks awful."

"I suppose Miss Carterprice has haunted him a few nights, at least." Tessa did her best to not think about what Jasper must seem like at home, in his own bedroom. *What a cat that Eloise Carterprice is*, she surprised herself by thinking.

"She was ever looking for a bit of fun when alive, I hear," Mary mused, "of the sort that eventually led to her death. I can't imagine she is an easy ghost to suffer."

"What shall we do? I hate to think what Dame Hartwell will do if she finds him sleeping here, and haunted," Tessa said.

Mary grimaced. "No, we mustn't allow that. I suppose we must wake him, then. Oh, if only Alex were home, but he went to the office for the morning." She shook Jasper's shoulder. "Jasper, do wake up. You look positively disheveled."

"If that's so, then why won't you let me sleep?" he grumbled. Jasper opened one eye, caught sight of Tessa, and exclaimed, sitting upright in an instant, "Mary, really!"

"I've asked Miss Preston to help you," Mary said.

"Miss Preston? What can Miss Preston do to help me?"

"She can see ghosts," Mary reminded him.

Tessa met Jasper's inscrutable gaze with what she hoped seemed like unwavering confidence. She held her breath, thinking back to that night all those years ago. Would he laugh Mary off and say they were funning him?

"Clearly," Jasper said, his tone acidic, "but what can that mean to my situation?"

Tessa considered Jasper's manic twitching and fiddling with his cuffs, collar, and hair. If he didn't get some help soon, this ghost was certain to drive him insane or even do a harm to himself. "I'm teaching Miss Trentwood to learn how to best her Sense," Tessa said. "If anyone's handling your situation, it is likely to be me."

"Is that so?" He eyed her, his frown growing. "You look like . . ."

Tessa held her breath, dreading what he might say. A repeat of those jibes she was likely never meant to hear?

"A governess," he said finally. "Not a medium."

The response was disappointing and annoying. Tessa knew Jasper had more imagination than that, and what was wrong with looking like a governess? Tessa dressed practically. What was wrong with that? "I assure you," she said, "my appearance has very little to do with my professional capacity to dispel unwanted, ghostly companions. And I think Miss Trentwood would be the first to tell you, she is no medium, and has no desire."

Jasper's brows rose. "And you desire it, being a medium?"

Tessa squared her shoulders. "I aspire for the Marylebone Spiritualist Association. I have many clients upon whom you may call to verify my claims."

Mary held up her hands. "Please, please, might we at least have some tea before we bicker?"

Tessa clamped her lips together, stung by Mary's gentle teasing.

Jasper, looking mulish, combed his hair back through trembling fingers.

Tessa relented, feeling for his apparent discomfort despite herself. "How long has Miss Carterprice been with you?"

Mary shook her head. "No, no, we shall wait to discuss this business until we've all had a spot of tea and some biscuits besides. Jasper, you may borrow Alex's kit, I'm sure. You shall feel much better once you've had a moment to refresh." She patted his arm in a sisterly fashion. "He won't be back for a moment, and we've all agreed you ought to avoid Dame Hartwell until he returns."

"Yes," Jasper said, nodding, "thank you, Mary, you are right as always." He stood, a little unsteady on his feet. "No, no, don't get up, ladies. I'm only a bit overtired from Miss Carterprice's exertions. I shall return shortly. I beg your pardon." And with that, he sped from the room.

Mary assessed Tessa, who had returned to worrying her fingernail. "I think we could do with some refreshment. Did you know you could do that to Eloise? Calling her like that?"

Tessa shook her head. "My curiosity got the better of me. I only recently saw such ribbons, and their effect on a medium hired by Dame Hartwell. I should not have been so indiscreet. My uncle will be much annoyed."

"Well," Mary said, pulling herself to standing with the help of the chaise arm, "what are our elders here for, but for us to annoy them with our youthful indiscretions?"

Tessa smiled, accepting Mary's proffered hand. "We are neither of us young or indiscreet, Miss Trentwood."

"Speak for yourself, Miss Preston," Mary chuckled.

Their silence was amiable as they waited for the tea.

"Pomeroy is new to the house," Tessa said to fill the silence when it lingered.

"Yes," Mary said. "He is my father's butler, not Dame Hartwell's. Well, my butler, I suppose, but I shall always think of him as my father's valet."

Tessa nodded, encouraging Mary to continue.

"He is here until we are married and in our own home. Dame Hartwell's butler retired shortly after I arrived and . . . strange happenings occurred. Pomeroy has been happy to help."

"He looks like he could win a fight with a hand tied behind his back."

"I believe he has, many times."

Mary's smile was rueful as they sat. "You may have noticed, my relationship with Alex's mother leaves much to be desired."

Tessa nodded. "I have, and it puzzles me. You seem the exact sort of daughter-in-law one could wish for." Certainly higher on the spectrum than herself, she did not say.

"She remains convinced I could be a masterful medium, the toast of the Marylebone Spiritualist Association, if only I would simply be open to it."

Tessa stiffened. Dame Hartwell had never spoken such words to her, despite having hired her on as the resident medium. She leaned forward, her voice sounding sharper than she intended it to. "Has it occurred to you that your headaches are likely because you're fighting your abilities? You are far more imbued with the Sense than you give yourself credit."

"I never intended to have any portion of the Sense," Mary said. "I did not ask my father to haunt me, or to see and hear persons who cannot be there. It is exceedingly distressing. I have not one moment to myself, and it's only gotten worse since your arrival. Your powers of amplification are a nuisance."

Tessa brushed her skirts for crumbs that weren't there before she stood. "Mr. Steele has asked for our help, Mary. While I understand you have a history together, I do not believe you wish him harm, whereas the spirit following him does. I believe we can help him, but only if we do it together."

Mary grimaced and fluffed the pillow next to her with more vigor than required. "I suppose so. Alright then, what must I do?"

Tessa smiled. This was turning into a neat little applied lesson, indeed.

SEVEN

IN WHICH ONE AMBUSHES

WHEN JASPER HAD AWAKENED to a pair of beautiful dark brown eyes frowning at him, framed by a golden-brown complexion, shapely black eyebrows, a kissable wide nose, and a tower of curls and braids, he thought perhaps Eloise had sneaked into his dreams again to tease him. Bored with her ghostly existence, Eloise had been quick to learn she could drag to the fore memories he'd thought long since tucked away. And unfortunately, she had realized with disgusting glee that the memories that pained him most involved the quiet, curvy presence of one Miss Tessa Preston, from almost a decade ago.

So it was natural that he thought he was still asleep when he opened his eyes to find exactly Miss Preston, leaning over him, concerned and annoyed. Miss Preston, telling him to wake up in a very snide tone. Miss Preston returned.

By Jove, what a disaster. If Jasper didn't know any better, he would have thought Eloise had somehow planned this entire reunion just to torment him further.

Now hiding safely out of sight in the hallway awaiting Hartwell's luncheon break, Jasper allowed his thunderous heart to explore the myriad of emotions triggered by Tessa's presence. She was as lovely and serious as ever. She had never been overly large or soft, but it was clear the years had honed her into a rather strong, curvaceous build. Before fainting—collapsing because of exhaustion and strained nerves, thank you—Jasper had noticed how Tessa had caught his weight, and held it. She smelled of heady spices tempered by a lovely undercurrent of vanilla. It made him think of a delightful bakery in which to while the hours away, dreamily holding the hand of a lady smiling at him as they shared tea and secrets.

Jasper tried to remember the last time he had spoken with Tessa, and knew it must have been years and years ago, when he was young and bold and infinitely more stupid regarding women. Thus, he hovered in the comfortable foyer, content to mope under Pomeroy's knowing gazes as he went about his work, rather than dare reenter the library and face Mary and Tessa together. Jasper shivered at the thought. Having wronged both women in some form or another, it was embarrassing how quick they were to take care of him and consider his situation seriously.

It took another ten minutes for Hartwell to come whistling through the door for lunch, and Jasper pounced. "You didn't tell me Tessa Preston had returned to London!"

Hartwell paused, hat in hand. "I hadn't the faintest idea myself until this morning."

"Well, she's in your library!"

"Certainly better than that parlor Mother uses for her séances."

Jasper grabbed Hartwell's arm. "You're not listening, man. Tessa Preston is in your house. And she sees ghosts."

Hartwell nodded. "I'm afraid Mater wants Miss Preston to teach Mary to become a proper medium. It's the worst idea." He waved Jasper to follow him. "Let's hide in my father's study. You look as if you could use a sip of brandy."

"It's barely noon," Jasper said, scandalized even while following Hartwell down the hall. Brandy actually did sound rather delightful. To soothe the nerves, of course.

"And you look as if you've a story to tell me, so why not calm your nerves? I hardly think the tea that Mary likely called for you will help."

Before Jasper knew it, he had brandy in hand and a couple sips burning down his throat besides.

"There you are!" came Eloise's disembodied voice.

Jasper and Hartwell jumped, their brandy sloshing.

"Who is there?" Hartwell asked.

Jasper eyed him. "Does everyone in this house have an affinity for ghosts? I knew there was a reason I avoided the place."

"Only since Compton Beauchamp," Hartwell muttered. "I sometimes can hear them, if they want to be heard."

"Well, Eloise wants everyone to hear her, all the time," Jasper said.

"I beg your pardon!" Eloise said, still refusing to show herself. "How dare you speak of the dead in such a manner?"

"Naturally, this is all my mother's fault," Jasper said, ignoring Eloise.

Hartwell spluttered. "What could your mother have possibly done to make a ghost attach herself to you?"

Jasper rolled his eyes. "Not directly, my good man, but had she not goaded me into attending Mrs. Carterprice's silly séance, I wouldn't have her daughter haunting me, now would I?"

"I hadn't heard," Hartwell said, his voice hushed. "Do you mean to say poor Edith passed away as well?"

"No indeed," Jasper said. "This is Eloise."

Hartwell's eyes widened. "Eloise? *The* Eloise Carterprice?"

"Incomparable who eloped some months back but died before tying the knot? The same. Ow!" Jasper rubbed the back of his head.

Hartwell blinked at the vase lying on the floor behind Jasper's chair, having just watched it fly across the room of its own accord.

"Show some respect," came Eloise's voice. "You shouldn't *speak so of the dead*."

Hartwell stood, motioning to Jasper to follow suit. "No indeed, Miss Carterprice, we meant no disrespect."

Jasper scoffed, then cringed in anticipation of some other item flying across the room at him. Nothing happened, and he relaxed. "Could you at least show yourself, Miss Carterprice, so that your lovely presence may grace us?"

"Laying it on rather thick," Hartwell muttered.

Jasper shrugged. There was a shimmer in the air, and there stood Eloise by the fireplace. She looked much as she had earlier, with her blonde hair artfully arranged, her blue eyes lacking luster as if whitewashed, and her lavender dress expertly tailored to her slim curves.

"That's much better, thank you," Jasper said. He waved his hand at the fireplace. "Now tell me, can you see her?"

Hartwell squinted, rubbing his forehead. "I can't see her, no, but I can hear her. I now have the unfortunate pleasure of hearing about the ghosts my mother always insisted were there. And just like with Mary's father, it comes with a rotten headache."

"I'm sure Dame Hartwell taught her son better manners than this," Eloise said, inspecting her fingernails and sounding bored. "I'm standing right here. You needn't speak about me as if I'm not. And to imply I'm causing a headache! How rude."

Jasper advanced on Eloise. "It's *rude* to kiss someone when they had no intention of being kissed. It's *rude* to announce one's engagement to a man when he had no intention of being engaged. It's *rude* to eavesdrop on the gentleman when he was trying to enjoy a quiet moment with his friend."

Hartwell took another sip of brandy. "Well now, Jasper, I hadn't any idea you thought of us as friends. Wasn't it just earlier today you were complaining about the hours I ask you to keep at the office?"

Eloise stared at Jasper, horrified. "Don't tell me you're in trade!"

"A barrister's assistant," he admitted, pointing at Hartwell. "His, actually."

"A lawyer," Eloise breathed. "This is worse and worse."

"Lawyer's assistant," Hartwell corrected. "And I gave him the job after seeing he needed the distraction."

"May I remind you I didn't want any of this?" Jasper said between clenched teeth. "You needn't disparage me further."

Hartwell sat, rubbing his forehead. "Indeed, why would Eloise Carterprice be a ghost, and haunt you, of all people? Shouldn't she haunt the family of the gent who tossed her?"

"Tossed me, indeed! That's not what happened," Eloise snapped.

"What happened, then?"

"It's hardly important anymore." Eloise waved away the question.

"If it's the clue to send you to your earthly resting place, then I assure you, I find it important," Jasper said.

"You will lead me to my rest," Eloise insisted.

Jasper sent a beleaguered look to Hartwell, who said, "If you don't mind, Miss Carterprice, I've a private matter to discuss with Jasper here—and I promise, it has nothing to do with you."

"If it has anything to do with Miss Trentwood, you've nothing to hide from me. We all know about Mary Trentwood. She sent her own father back to his grave on good terms. You think we don't hear about such things?" Eloise gave both men a stern look. "I'll know if you try to exorcise me, so don't try it. I shall be back soon, my dearest. We have much to plan."

When she shimmered away, Hartwell and Jasper stared at one another.

"I must admit, Jasper, this is not how I expected discussing your future bride."

Jasper ran a hand over his eyes and downed the last of his brandy. "I suppose Mary won't be able to help me after all, and I'll need to apologize to Miss Preston?"

Hartwell rolled his eyes. "Apologize? Already? Jasper, what have you done?"

"Nothing," Jasper mumbled. He smoothed trembling fingers across his mustache. "Not recently, that is."

Dame Hartwell and a tan, bald man Jasper vaguely recognized descended upon them, saving him from responding to Hartwell's raised brows and impending onslaught of questions.

"My dear, I think we have a new guest among us!" Dame Hartwell said, her cool blue eyes bright with excitement.

Hartwell waved his hand at Jasper. "Steele has arrived. Steele, you must remember Sir Hubert Preston, Tessa's uncle?"

Jasper's mouth sagged open, and he sat bolt upright, knowing his face was likely turning multiple shades of red. Worse and worse and worse.

The dame waved her purse at Hartwell. "No, no, not him." She assessed Jasper and his wrinkled suit, unshaven cheeks, and many other hygienic faux pas. "Though hello dear, it's been too long since you last visited. Did my séance really frighten you *that* much? It must not have. I thought I heard your mother say the other day that she sent you to the Carterprice séance. Now what she thinks she has over my séances, I do not know."

Hartwell's mother rounded on him. He only quirked an eyebrow. "You're distracting me," she snapped. "I think we have another spirit among us. A young lady."

Jasper frowned. "Alex . . ."

Hartwell sighed. "It really has been too long, Jasper. My mother's latest theory is that we all came back from our Compton

Beauchamp adventure touched with a bit more of what she calls the Sense. She can hear them now, too."

"Too?" Dame Hartwell scoffed. "I've always been able to hear the spirits. It's you who chose not to believe me." Though she sounded cross, she patted her son's shoulder fondly. "It's a wonder you didn't send me to an asylum, and perhaps you might have upon your return from that little manor house, had you not had your own encounter. But again, let's not be distracted! Jasper, have you any details about this spirit? Have you heard her yet?"

Tessa's uncle watched them all with a far more studious expression than Jasper would have expected. But then, if he had come back from Europe knowing his niece could speak with ghosts, then perhaps this was just his everyday conversation. Jasper closed his eyes with a light shudder, hoping this wasn't about to become *his* everyday conversation.

Jasper reached for another glass of brandy, feeling more haggard than ever. "I suppose we ought to return to the ladies before they come searching. We can discuss this all together."

"You don't mind delaying our brief trip?" Dame Hartwell said to Sir Hubert, not waiting for a response as she skipped from the room.

"Not at all," Sir Hubert said, letting his narrowed gaze linger on Jasper.

Blast and damn, Jasper thought with horror. Even if Tessa didn't remember him, it was clear her uncle did.

Eight

In Which One Examines

Tessa straightened her posture upon Jasper and Hartwell's return to the parlor. Mary seemed unsurprised to find them together, but Tessa's heart skipped, just once. She frowned inwardly at the tiny betrayal. Alex Hartwell looked as hale as ever, perhaps more so, as he cast an admiring glance at Mary upon entering.

The nasty scar that cut through Hartwell's left brow marred his natural beauty, pulling taut the skin around his left eye. He kept his dark brown hair a little long, allowing it to flop artfully over the left half of his face to reduce alarm. He dressed both soberly and smartly, as becoming of a barrister catering to lower aristocrats like his mother.

Tessa's stomach positively dropped at the sight of Dame Hartwell and her uncle following close behind. "I thought you were in search of some Italian ices, or some such thing?"

"Tessa, my dear!" Dame Hartwell exclaimed. "I was about to leave with your uncle when we heard the news. I demand you must pause at once, for we are all quite curious about Mr. Steele's unfortunate situation."

Sir Hubert settled himself into the back corner again, happy to witness the spectacle but not take part. Tessa was certain he was trying to commit everything to memory, so he might catalog it later in his diary. What she would give to see the contents of it one day.

Tessa exchanged a wry glance with Mary. "And what, exactly, is his situation, my lady?"

"Why, he has a ghost aiming to be his fiancée! Surely you heard and saw her."

The room descended into heightened chatter as everyone attempted to apprise everyone else of what they knew of the situation. Tessa studied the irate young woman fuming in the doorway. No one marked her presence, and no wonder, for she was quite dead, and remained silent for the moment.

Eloise Carterprice wore the most expensive gown Tessa had seen in years. The layers of flounces and lace complemented her lithe form, and her white skin was almost translucent even without the effects of her being a ghost. Whomever had dressed her for the funeral had spent hours on her hair, making every twist just so. The translucent gray ribbons attached at the back of her neck floated artfully behind her, the ends disappearing out of sight.

Disconcerting and suspicious.

"Mary," Tessa said, hoping to sneak in another lesson despite all the hubbub, "do you mark a presence?"

Mary frowned at Tessa, refusing to look at the doorway and thus confirming she also saw Eloise.

Jasper looked from one woman to the other, and then behind him. He slumped into the nearest chair. "Hello, Eloise."

Dame Hartwell perked right up. "Oh, is she here? Have her say something. I can't tell where she is if she remains silent."

Eloise hardly needed the introduction, but she took the opportunity anyway. "You lot of gossiping nothings and nobodies. How dare you speak of my affairs like yesterday's news rag?"

Hartwell grabbed the morning's paper from a side table. "Miss Carterprice, you *are* yesterday's news rag. The newspapers are still talking about your elopement and the crash. Your poor mother and sister. What's this about you aiming to be Jasper's fiancée?"

"I am not *aiming* to be anyone's fiancée," Eloise said as she sailed across the room to place her hands on Jasper's slouched shoulders. "I *am* his fiancée, and shall be his wife, until death do us part."

Tessa stepped forward. "Fascinating," she muttered. "She seems so . . . *vibrant*." She shared a concerned look with her uncle and began circling Eloise.

Eloise looked down her nose at Tessa, taking in her black braids sculpted high above her head, her mixed complexion, her yellow dress a season out of date. With a small shrug, Eloise tossed her head with a sniff, taking Tessa's observation as a compliment. "I'd never say it myself, but my friends always said I was the most vivacious of the group."

"Vivacious or not, you should not be here," Tessa said. "This is hardly a safe house for you if you intend to continue haunting anyone."

"Believe me," Eloise replied coolly, her gaze measuring Tessa again, "I know."

Jasper's gaze swung from Eloise to Tessa, his eyes a little crazed with relief. "I'm so glad you all see her. The driver thought for certain I lost my mind, but ask anyone at the séance, they all saw her, too."

"Séance?" Sir Hubert piped from the corner. "Do tell."

"My mother," Jasper huffed, "is bent on finding a match for me, and she's resorted to sending me to places where other gents might not be looking."

"Clever," Sir Hubert said, not bothering to hide his amusement.

"Yes, well, I don't think she intended to have me come home with a ghost fiancée," Jasper muttered. "But honestly, these days, I think she's growing more and more desperate."

"Unlikely," Sir Hubert agreed. He sat back in his chair, happy to resume observing as he stretched his legs and settled his hands over his stomach.

Hartwell and Mary shared a sheepish expression, only to look away, embarrassed. Tessa wondered about the oh-so-many things behind that look.

Jasper turned to Tessa, startling her as he strode forward to grab her hands. "Can you get rid of her?"

"Rid of me!" Eloise said, sailing right through Dame Hartwell to shove herself between Jasper and Tessa.

Tessa jumped back, yanking her hands from Jasper to increase their distance and avoid touching Eloise. She wasn't about to take any chances with possession this early in the day.

Eloise shrieked, "I'm your fiancée! How can you get rid of me?"

Mary and Hartwell looked at one another. "How quickly events progress when love is involved," he said, grinning. Mary chuckled and pushed his arm a little, her cheeks blooming with a flattering pink.

"Stop teasing me, old boy, and help me out!" Jasper snapped. "You said Mary was haunted by spirits, and she isn't anymore. So I've come here because now *I'm* haunted, and I don't want to be."

"How on earth am I to help you?" Mary said. "I can't even help myself. That's why Dame Hartwell asked Miss Preston—Tessa. I assure you, I'm very haunted these days, and by ghosts strange to me! It's obnoxious."

At Jasper's obvious hesitation, Tessa raised her chin. "I'd be more than happy to help you, Mr. Steele."

"For a fee," Sir Hubert chimed from the corner.

"Indeed," Tessa said.

"Don't you dare exorcise me," said Eloise. "I'm the daughter of a lord, after all."

"You're also dead," Tessa pointed out, "so I should hardly think rank matters anymore."

"The gall! Are you going to let her speak to me so?" Eloise demanded.

"If Miss Preston talking to you with any sort of attitude will send you to where you ought, then she may say whatever she likes," said Jasper. "If only she'd be quicker about it."

"Beyond," Tessa said. "I would need to send her Beyond."

"Beyond, About, Through, I don't really care, just please do it." Jasper turned to Sir Hubert, who had pulled out a small ledger from his breast pocket. Always prepared for a bit of business, her uncle. "Take my last two pay slips. Alex will handle it, won't you?"

Tessa advanced slowly, blinking in her special way to heighten her Sense. There they were, those gray ribbons again, but now that she looked more closely, she realized they dangled from Eloise's hands and shoulders, much like a marionette. "Who sent you?"

Eloise frowned. "Sent me? No one sent me. I sent myself. I'm determined to be married, and Jasper-poo is just the man for me."

"Or so you're led to think," Tessa said under her breath. She had seen those ribbons only recently, and in this house. It couldn't be a mere coincidence that Eloise appeared with the same transparent gray ribbons. Just what, or who, had a vendetta against Hartwell House *and Jasper?*

Tessa huffed quietly. Dame Hartwell was right. She seemed to be the only one available to sort this mess out. And she was determined to do it, too, if only to prove to the Marylebone Spiritualist Association just why she deserved a spot amongst their ranks.

Well. She would solve this mystery, but she would have her fun, too. Jasper might not remember her, but she remembered him.

While everyone conferred, Jasper couldn't help but glance at Tessa to find her studying him. Her serious, dark gaze made him stand taller, and he smoothed back his hair. He wondered what her hair felt like, and whether the curls were as soft as they seemed. One of those curls had the nerve to spring free from a twist. It looked about the perfect size to wrap around his smallest finger. Tessa's hair was an impressive sculpture, too dark to understand unless close enough to witness how the curves of the tiny curls flirted with the light.

Today's hairstyle was both piled high atop her crown and allowed to drape down to her nape, accentuating the elegant grace of Tessa's neck. Jasper felt the back of his own neck grow hot, thinking about many other things not fit to mention in polite company.

The truth remained that Tessa Preston was a beautiful, intriguing woman. All the more so now that Jasper knew ghosts were her constant companions, such that she thought them mundane. It wouldn't be the first, or last, time Jasper would wonder just what might have happened all those years ago, if her parents hadn't died and her uncle hadn't whisked her away to the Continent.

And said uncle was now glaring at him from the corner of the room, his ledger book ready to wring every pence from his pocket, no doubt. Yes, the man most definitely remembered him. How unfortunate.

Jasper sighed as Eloise wrapped her arms around one of his, pressing as much of her body as she could against him without actually falling into him. The sensation was like an unpleasant prickle, the sort one felt if sitting in one spot too long and then suddenly remembering to move.

"You really ought to get some sleep," Tessa was saying to him. "You look awful."

Jasper froze at the undercurrent of—what was that tone? Was she *gleeful* at the sight of his exhaustion?

"I suppose Miss Carterprice isn't giving you an inch," she continued.

Jasper shook his head.

"No, I thought not. Well, if you happen upon some amethyst, place it by your pillow tonight to relieve your headache and prevent the night terrors." She spoke stiffly, with great formality, as one would any client, he supposed. Except, of course, the rather intimate nature of discussing his pillow on his bed. Thoughts not fit for polite company, indeed.

"And where might one find some amethyst?" Jasper murmured, for it looked as though Mary and Hartwell were returning from their tête-à-tête.

"Oh, I have some you can borrow." Tessa blinked at him, having surprised herself by sharing that detail, which immediately made Jasper suspect she was offering her private gem collection. She seemed more than a little mortified, and fell silent, perhaps hoping it portrayed a semblance of professionalism.

His eyes widened. To sleep with something that Miss Tessa Preston owned? Scandalous. Delightful. "Thank you, Miss Preston," he said, striving to sound solemn and grateful when inwardly he was rather gleeful himself. "That would be most welcome."

He must have sounded a little too enthusiastic despite his efforts, if her narrowed eyes and warm cheeks were any indication. Before she could retract her offer, Mary returned, announcing they must all break for tea, and have a proper discussion about what was to be done about Jasper's problem.

Dame Hartwell at this moment realized they were dreadfully late for their own dining appointment and dragged Sir Hubert from the room touting all the best meals and how she wanted to hear *everything* about their trip across the Continent.

Hartwell smiled at Jasper. "Tea, forever and always, is my dear Mary's cure."

Jasper shared the grin, unable to think about anything but amethyst, curls, and the beauty of a smart, suspicious lady. "Tea it is, then."

NINE

IN WHICH A MIDNIGHT LESSON OCCURS

THAT NIGHT, TESSA WOKE with a start. She froze, her hands tucked beneath her pillow and her knees against her chest. Her plain cotton shift had a line of lace around her neckline, and the silk bonnet she wore to protect her braids slipped forward, obscuring a clear view of the room. She shoved the silk aside. Mary stared at her from across the room, also frozen in bed.

Between them floated Eloise Carterprice, providing just enough light for them all to see one another's wary expressions. She regarded them down the length of her nose, her hands on her hips. "You are beneath me," she said. Her voice had a hollow sound to it, as if she spoke through a tube.

"Hmm." Tessa sat up, tucking her coverlet around her lap. She had wondered whether Eloise would find someone else to bother if Jasper's use of the amethyst repelled her. "And it's rude of you to float above us so. Come down here like a civilized woman and speak to us directly."

Mary had a hand pressed to her forehead as she sat up, a surprised smile forming.

"You shall address me only when spoken to, girl, and when you do, you will call me Miss Eloise," she said icily, dropping the hollow treatment to her voice, even as she descended so her pale lavender skirts touched the floor.

Mary whimpered, sounding pained.

"Are you well, Mary?" Tessa asked, ignoring Eloise. It was one thing for a ghost to be rude, it was another thing entirely to put on airs. Tessa simply had no patience for it.

"Do not ignore me!" Eloise advanced on Tessa, who held up a hand.

"A moment, if you please, I'm seeing to my student." To Mary, Tessa said, "If I know anything about Dame Hartwell, I'd guess she's been hosting séances and exposing you to as many mediums as she can?"

Mary nodded, rubbing her forehead. "You're my fourth roommate in as many weeks. When I agreed to marry Alex, I hardly thought I was agreeing to such . . . attention."

Tessa kicked away her bedsheets. She yanked her arms through an old dressing gown and pulled off her silk bonnet. "Right, well, I suppose now is as good a time as any for another lesson."

Mary's eyes narrowed. Tessa wasn't sure whether it was from the pain or suspicion. "I don't *want* to be a medium, Tessa."

"Honestly, neither do I!" she said, throwing her legs over the side of her bed and shoving her feet into her threadbare slippers. "But I had to learn how to control my Sense. It's the only way to avoid the headaches you're now struggling with, and worse. There's a certain amount of control you have to exert, even if it's only to dampen the sensations."

Eloise stepped between Tessa and Mary, her face an unbecoming shade of purple. "I'm warning you, you will not ignore me, and you will leave me and my Jasper alone."

"Which is it?" Tessa said. "Am I to ignore you, or am I to leave you alone with Mr. Steele?"

Eloise pinched the bridge of her nose. "You're just like my sister. You know exactly what I meant."

Mary stopped rubbing her temples to say, "Does Edith know you're here? Why aren't you haunting her?"

That stopped Eloise for a moment, and she looked moderately chagrined. "Why on earth would I worry Edith, when I could have fun flustering Jasper instead?"

Yes, why was Eloise Carterprice haunting a man with fairly loose connections to her family? Questions flitted through Tessa's mind as she sat beside Mary. "Pinch the spot of your nose between your eyes, and focus on that feeling. Have you been to Bath?"

The question distracted Mary. "I have not."

"Well, it's not important that you've been to Bath. Have you been to any Roman baths?" Tessa pressed. "You are in the middle of a large bath, where instead of persons exiting and entering, making idle conversation, there are spirits. If you don't take care, you will end up in the deeper end, up to your neck in the still waters. Opportunistic spirits will drag you under. You must wade into shallower waters."

Mary stared at her. "You make it sound awfully dangerous."

Tessa sat back, knowing her silence would likely convince more than any words.

While Mary pondered this metaphor, Eloise held her arms open, as if welcoming friends. And so she was, for more spirits descended upon the bedroom. They slithered in through the windowsill and from under the door threshold. These were old spirits, unable to hold human form. Just shadows, and menacing ones, that ate light and moaned for more. Tessa snapped at Eloise to stop this nonsense, but she would have none of that. She merely smiled as the room grew darker with otherworldly shapes. Mary trembled, her eyes squeezed shut.

When the shadows surrounding them became oppressive even for Tessa, she stumbled across the room, pulling the cane out from under her bed skirt. That got their attention. All movement stopped. Even Eloise held her ethereal breath.

"You don't know what you're playing with," Eloise warned.

Tessa rolled her eyes, much to Eloise's annoyance. "You really must come up with a more original line, Miss Carterprice. Please realize I've been in this business for years, and *everyone* thinks they are a danger to me." Her tone said clearly that they were not.

The transparent gray ribbons hanging from Eloise's back tugged sharply, yanking her away from Tessa. She bent at the waist, hurt by the action. When she righted, her voice was not her own. Deep and menacing, she said, "Tessa Baby."

Tessa stared at Eloise. No, no, no. Not again.

"Tessa Baby," the voice taunted, "they're coming for you."

Tessa pointed the cane at Eloise, her hand shaking. This wasn't Eloise's doing. This was the same voice that had taken over Madam Sylvia, leading to Tessa's employment at Hartwell House. "Show yourself."

Whomever held Eloise's ribbons dropped them as if they were a child bored with their marionette. Eloise had a hand at her throat, looking as mystified and nonplussed as Mary and Tessa. She was the first to recover, hiding her fear behind a haughty expression. "Put that thing down, I was only funning you." She shooed away the spirits who hadn't fled at the sight of Tessa's mystical weapon. "See? They've left, you sourpuss."

"What was that, Miss Carterprice?" Mary asked.

"Who was that?" Tessa corrected. "They spoke through you, didn't they?" She grabbed a shawl from the small vanity she shared with Mary and hugged it close around her. She was careful to keep the cane within arm's reach.

Eloise frowned, looking from one to the other. "What are you talking about?"

Tessa stepped closer, inspecting Eloise. There, a hint of confusion behind those cloudy white eyes, and an involuntary twitch when her ribbons shifted. Tessa sighed. "I don't think she knows what happened," she said to Mary. "Let's all get some rest, and we will practice controlling our Sense in the morning. I trust we won't have any more visits tonight?"

When no one spoke, Tessa turned to find Eloise vanished.

An hour later, Mary finally fell into a fitful sleep, which was better than Tessa staring at the ceiling, frustrated and confused.

Her first complaint centered on the painted cupids staring at her from the corners of the room. It was one thing to see them on the parlor ceiling during a brawl with a malevolent ghost, and another entirely to be watched during one's morning and evening ablutions.

The week's events bothered Tessa further still, and she turned them over and over in her mind, seeking the thread tying everything together and coming up short. It was odd enough that she had to banish spirits who meant harm from this fashionable little home. Odder still that Dame Hartwell seemed bent on converting her future daughter-in-law into the medium Tessa had inadvertently become, despite her best efforts.

While in Europe, Tessa and her uncle had encountered many spirits and learned about her Sense, but none had ever attacked her. It rather frightened Tessa that someone had a strong enough Sense to control Madam Sylvia and Eloise Carterprice from an undeterminable distance. She hadn't known that could happen. Did she have that power?

"Tessa Baby," the ghost had said with Madam Sylvia's voice, matching the familiar, lyrical rhythms of Tessa's mother, "they're coming for you." And again, using Eloise just now.

Tessa buried her face in her pillow. Lest anyone should forget, Jasper Steele had also collapsed in her arms. His ambivalent reactions to her made her wonder whether he even remembered they had a past, however short. Her confused feelings about the man were far more worrisome than her ghost problem. Ghosts, Tessa knew how to manage. Men, especially men with ready smiles that reached their sparkling blue eyes, were a terrifying enigma. What had compelled her to offer her amethyst to him for a good night's sleep? Tessa knew, and suspected he also knew, that it wasn't mere professionalism. Despite their years apart, and her sour last impression of Jasper, she still wanted to prove her worth. To him, to the Marylebone Spiritualist Association, to Dame Hartwell . . . even to her uncle.

She wondered whether the amethyst helped Jasper sleep better, knowing it held Eloise at bay. And where in the house was he sleeping, since Sir Hubert was sharing a room with Hartwell, and he certainly couldn't sleep with the dame or the servants. Perhaps he shared a room with Pomeroy? Though that seemed improper, too. Despite him being her client, Tessa hoped his sleep was as fitful as hers. She hoped he had a lumpy bed with a thin pillow, and the amethyst poked his cheek as he rolled over.

Though, the thought of Jasper rolling over in his sleep brought to mind mussed hair, and flushed cheeks, and the little tremble his lip made while unconscious. Jasper was rather sweet and vulnerable while sleeping. Tessa bit her lip. How to reconcile that sweet moment with the real man she knew hid behind those deceptive smiles. Tessa focused instead on returning her heart to its normal cadence. A traitorous organ, thundering in her chest. Well, Tessa resolved she could consider him handsome yet foul. He could be both. She fell asleep convincing herself she could be coolly civil, for he was nothing more than a client. A handsome, man-from-her-past, client.

Ten

In Which One Lurks

Unbeknownst to Tessa, Jasper was, in fact, tossing on the sofa in the drawing room downstairs, hugging her amethyst close. Upon her return, Dame Hartwell had insisted that he spend the night in the house, but only after Tessa and Mary had excused themselves for bed. It was likely for the best. He had noticed Tessa's tone had grown more acerbic as the night wore on until it was clear she remembered him, and had indeed somehow found out whatever stupid thing he had said that had made his friends laugh so hard.

Jasper rued his past self for ever trying to seem clever while scaring off his competition. He couldn't even remember the names of the gents. Just childish.

And while clearly annoyed with him, Jasper could tell the mystery of why Eloise persisted in haunting him, of all people, sparked Tessa and her uncle's curiosity and professionalism just enough to overcome whatever unspoken thoughts lingered. It seemed Tessa wanted to put him in his place, but also help him as her client. Jasper ran his fingertips along his mustache as he pondered this. Tessa Preston had always been a serious girl, and now that he knew she could see ghosts, that must explain it.

How could one laugh and flirt if one saw ghosts in every corner?

After waiting an hour or more for the amethyst to stop working, and for Eloise to descend upon him with her taunts and remembrances of the past, Jasper instead fell asleep with a soft smile on his face. Whatever Tessa Preston thought of his former self, he would show her just how much he had matured.

How much more he was worthy of her attentions, and perhaps one day, even her affections? For whatever Jasper's feelings had been for Mary Trentwood, they had been three-fold for the quiet and stunning Miss Preston.

When he woke the next morning, Jasper felt enormously improved. He'd slept the night through without nightmares or Eloise. He stared at the amethyst still clutched in his hand, wary and a little impressed. It had to be something to do with Tessa's supernatural affinity than the stone itself, surely. His thoughts returned to how Tessa must have kept the stone close to her for it to absorb some awareness and repelling attributes to those of the ghostly inclination. Did she tuck it in her pocket, or close to her heart?

Jasper combed his hair back, content to lounge on the sofa until he heard the rest of the house wake. He could smell the delicious acidic warmth of a pot of coffee brewing, and some sort of meat—sausage, perhaps. His stomach growled, and he moved to sit up just in time to see the doorknob to the room turn. He fell back down out of sight, frantically tugging his clothing into place and rubbing the worst wrinkles out.

He peeked over the back of the sofa to see Tessa tiptoe into the room, as quietly as one might with the layers of skirts and bustle. She wore a somber gray dress with white lace at the neck and cuffs. It was serviceable, ornamented with flounces and a draped overskirt beneath the point of her bodice. She didn't wear a chatelaine, and that made sense, given she was unlikely to want to draw ghostly attention to herself. Her hair was a celebration of braids and twists and curls piled high atop her head and knotted down the length of her neck. A whimsical little white ribbon threaded through the entire construction, and Jasper wondered whether it was decorative, or if one might, with a strategic tug, topple her hair.

Tessa's expression was a mixture of exasperation, frustration, and curiosity. Jasper slunk lower to avoid being seen. He peeked through the ornamental opening between the two pieces of wood that topped the back of the sofa. Tessa winked one eye, the other dilating as she turned slowly on her heel, surveying the room with a sight Jasper knew he could never mimic.

This must be how Tessa focused on her supernatural Sense to see ghosts. Though it seemed she could see the ghosts with little effort, he hadn't seen Tessa wink yesterday when Eloise had thrown him at her. Perhaps this let her see miasmas or some other such thing he didn't actually care to know existed. She stepped forward, a hand outstretched as if she were blind and feeling for her next physical landmark.

What was it Hartwell had told him? That Dame Hartwell had hired Tessa to be the medium-in-residence to rid the house of its persistent hauntings? Not that it mattered at this exact moment. Jasper still clutched the amethyst, and Tessa had insisted it would repel any wandering spirits. She wouldn't find anything, but hang it if she didn't look adorable trying.

Tessa huffed her annoyance and squeezed both eyes shut as she brushed her hands along her overskirt. "Nothing special in here," he heard her mutter.

Jasper grinned. That was his cue. "I beg to differ," he said, standing up as if it were entirely natural to be lurking on a sofa in a home that wasn't his own.

Mary, it seemed, was an early riser, for her bed had been empty and cold by the time Tessa padded across the room. All the better. Tessa had been in no mood for pleasantries and even shooed away the servant who popped in, offering to help with her morning toilette.

After sculpting her braids up into the fashion of the day with ribbons and bobby pins, Tessa rolled her shoulders and ventured to the drawing room. She wanted to investigate when the light was in her favor, and alone, while everyone ate in the dining room downstairs. It was clear from their merry chatter, audible even from here, that when Tessa finally entered the room for a cup of coffee, she would not enjoy it in silence. She had made for the drawing room instead, thinking this would be a good, quiet time to study the room where she first "met" the person who threatened her through the possessed Madam Sylvia.

Tessa peeked into the parlor, confirming it was empty. She swept into the room, spinning around to guide the door shut so the click was nearly silent. Not that she needed to be so very secret; it was just her habit. The less noise, the less attention she called to herself, the more likely she could accomplish her task uninterrupted.

Dame Hartwell's whimsy revealed itself via the intricate tile floor and cupids on the ceiling. Tessa shook her head at them, not wanting to know what all they had seen over the years with the dame's many séance attempts. The heavy velvet drapes, which had stifled the room with the gathered séance crowd and candlelight, were now drawn open to reveal the private courtyard below. Weak sunlight streamed through the windows, doing little to illuminate the many shadows from the side tables, chairs, and chaises strewn about.

With an annoyed little huff, she winked to focus her Sense. She spun slowly in place, scanning the room. There were no spirits or transparent gray ribbons. There were no lingering ripples that could point her toward a spirit or person who could command from afar. She was alone, which both relieved and annoyed her.

"Nothing special in here," Tessa muttered to herself, turning slowly, letting her Sense stretch to the corners of the room.

"I beg to differ," came a voice from behind the chaise.

Tessa froze. That was the rub with having the Sense. She could tell when there were ghosts in the vicinity, but heaven help her if she came upon a living person. She blinked thrice to release the concentration of her Sense and focus instead on that voice, that melodious voice that sent a small thrill down her neck.

Jasper popped his head over the back of the chaise, combing fingers through his tousled hair. "Good morning. Have you discovered how to rid me of my ghost?"

Tessa jumped, all senses screaming. She froze, half-crouched with her palms splayed open to ward away a spirit, eyes locked on Jasper's. He seemed both startled and rather impressed by her quick reflexes. She cleared her throat and corrected her posture, smoothing her overskirt. "Have you been there all this time?" She took in his rumpled clothing. "Did you *sleep* in here?"

Jasper shrugged, his expression rueful as he draped his arm over the chaise back. "Well, I arrived unannounced. I could hardly expect to have a room prepared for me. I tried to go home, but the dame simply wouldn't hear of it. And then your uncle said it would be best for me to remain close, and I could hardly argue against that." He chuckled. "It's much easier not having to pretend Eloise exists while here. It's been a struggle, keeping this from my mother. She's already worried about me."

Tessa dipped her head, not knowing what to say.

"So, have you exorcised her?" Jasper craned his neck, both to stretch it and to look for his ghostly companion. "I fell asleep soundly, I'm glad to say."

"She didn't disturb your dreams?"

Jasper shook his head, hiding a yawn and holding her amethyst in his other hand. "This must have worked."

"Of course it did. Didn't I say it would?"

"It did wonders."

"It certainly did. Your fiancée visited us instead, giving Miss Trentwood a nasty headache and me a fright besides."

Jasper's brows rose. "She's not my fiancée. And did she, now? Well, we knew Miss Carterprice for being a jealous one in her day." He tossed the amethyst in his hand. Tessa stiffened, fighting the urge to grab it from him in case he dropped it. "So should I keep this with me, and Eloise will go away? What should I pay you?"

"It's not for sale," Tessa said, stepping forward with her hand out.

"But it works," Jasper said, holding on to the gem.

"It's not for sale, and besides, it only works for a few days before the effects wear off. And then your ghostly friend will return, peeved beyond belief, so it would be best if you gave it back." Tessa held her hand out. She wasn't about to let Jasper Steele keep her mother's gem. She knew she shouldn't have given it to him.

His eyes narrowed, and he studied her warring expressions. She strove to seem annoyed yet uninterested, merely bored that he wanted to purchase something she had no interest in selling. "This means something to you." He looked at it, studying the chips in the corners of the raw stone. "This is ancient, isn't it? Your mother's?"

Tessa stepped back, blinking. He remembered her; he remembered everything; she was sure of it. And he was still playing his games. She watched warily as Jasper took her hand and placed the gem in her palm. The movement was gentle, as one might approach a skittish horse, and she refused to acknowledge the trill of delightful unease that ran down her back when his fingers brushed hers.

Her breath caught as he smiled down at her. She stood a little taller, straightening her shoulders and wiping her unclaimed hand down the peplum hem of her bodice. What nonsense. Tessa knew she was hardly an object of attraction, not for a flirt like Jasper. She wore her everyday gray, a sturdy thing of stiff fabric meant for traveling, but with the right tucks and flounces to disguise the room for the quick movements sometimes required when dealing with ghosts. No one in their right mind thought this dress was attractive.

"Your hair," Jasper said, shifting the topic and the ground beneath her. "I've not seen anything like it. It's . . . wonderfully sculptural."

Tessa choked. She had thought he was assessing her professional presence, not her personal. Had someone else said such a thing, she would have categorized them as ignorant and not worth her attention. But the gentle awe in Jasper's voice made Tessa's cheeks warm with unexpected pleasure. It was no small feat to do her hair. Its tiny curls disliked the summer heat and humidity, causing her to braid it tightly and then pull those braids high off her neck. She left a bit of fringe at her forehead, as was the fashion, but again, the curls hugged her temples and often stood upright in this weather.

"I assure you, my hair is not where I keep my secrets about ghosts," was all she could think to say.

"You have an interesting relationship with these Hartwells," Jasper said, changing the subject yet again. He brushed his clothing to smooth the wrinkles. "No one speaks to Dame Hartwell the way you do. You're the medium-in-residence?"

"As of this week, yes."

He nodded, as if this made sense. "And what are you looking for in here? It couldn't have been me."

Tessa frowned. "No . . . I'm seeking the reason Dame Hartwell hired me." Jasper waited, smiling. It was thoroughly disarming. Tessa threw up her hands in a minute semblance of defeat. "Alright then, Dame Hartwell lured me here with one of her silly séances, but it turned out not to be silly at all. I know Madam Sylvia to be a charlatan. Yet, a week ago, a very strong, rather malevolent spirit possessed her from afar." Her brows drew together as she turned to the chaise where everything had happened. "And then three spirits attacked me, and I heard my mother's voice. It was all a bit unsettling. Dame Hartwell hired me on the spot after I exorcised them."

"That sounds awful," Jasper said, his eyes wide. "How on earth did you exorcise them?"

"I have a special cane enabling me to do so, but it is very draining to use. It's for emergencies."

"Fascinating." Jasper touched the amethyst, which still lay in her palm. When he looked at her again, his expression had softened. "When did the spirits reveal themselves to you? Mary only began seeing ghosts after her father's ghost finally rested."

Tessa tilted her head. Interesting how he referred to her as Mary, rather than Miss Trentwood. And that he knew details about her ability to see the spirits. She swallowed the sudden sour note of jealousy sitting at the tip of her tongue. "I've always seen the spirits," she replied. "But it happens far more often with my parents' death. I believe they shielded me when they lived."

"Do they haunt you now?" Jasper looked around the room, waiting for someone to jump out of the corners.

"Does who haunt—my parents? No, what a rude thing to ask!"

Jasper blinked. "My apologies."

Tessa moved to the window, looking out to the calm court-yard below. The neighboring house shared the courtyard, but if she remembered correctly, the elderly woman living there only came out for a bit of sun a couple times a week.

"Does your uncle see the ghosts too?" Jasper said, trying again.

"No, I inherited this from my mother."

Jasper nodded. "She was rather exotic."

Tessa's jaw tightened. "Only as exotic as my father was in her home country."

Jasper raised his hands. "I meant no offense. She had a won-derful singing voice, if I remember."

Tessa turned from the window at that comment. "You knew my mother?"

At this, Jasper colored. "I believe my mother hired your mother for a couple of séances. And so, we come back to my original question. Do you know how to help me beyond a single night's sleep?"

It was now Tessa's turn to study Jasper, and while she looked him over, he also stood taller, puffing his chest ever so slightly, pulling his shoulders back. He was a rumpled mess, and she rather liked him for it. It was clear last night that Jasper wished to be seen as rather a dandy, so she enjoyed seeing him mussed up. She preferred this genuine openness and concern.

"Not yet," she admitted. "I haven't yet had my morning coffee."

Jasper smiled. "Well, by all means, let's get you some coffee."

ELEVEN

IN WHICH BRIDGES MEND

EYEBROWS ROSE AT THE sight of Tessa and Jasper entering the breakfast room together, but the room's occupants kept their comments to themselves.

Jasper poured Tessa a cup of coffee. When their fingers touched as he handed her the cup, she jumped but managed not to spill any of it. She gave him a rueful look, wondering what he was playing at as she sank into the empty seat beside Mary.

"And how are you this morning, Miss Preston?" Mary asked wearily. She had dark circles under her eyes and she slouched over her breakfast, paying no attention to the concerned looks Hartwell sent her.

Tessa felt for Mary. She couldn't keep resisting like this. Mary would explode in a storm of anxiety and call all the hungry spirits to possess her in a moment of true weakness if Tessa didn't figure out how to help her accept this new Sense of hers. "Worried and frustrated," Tessa said cheerfully.

Mary and Hartwell snapped to attention, while Sir Hubert and Dame Hartwell kept chewing their breakfast with thoughtful smiles. Jasper abandoned the breakfast buffet with a plate piled high with toast and jam, and a single egg. He sat opposite Tessa, and it was clear he was careful to keep his expression neutral.

"That hardly inspires confidence," Mary said. "Worried and frustrated about what?"

Tessa sipped her coffee, knowing she needed to be careful about what she would say next. She leaned forward, conscious of the exhaustion on Mary's face. "Last night wasn't the first time a spirit interrupted your sleep, I assume?"

Hartwell took Mary's hand, seated as he was on her other side. She clutched his hand and pressed her lips together.

Jasper winced. "Miss Preston mentioned Eloise paid a visit?"

Mary nodded as the woman herself materialized into view. Jasper moaned, slumping in his chair as Eloise came forth, all smiles.

"Exactly that," Tessa said, pointing to how Mary rubbed her temple as she gripped Hartwell's hand. "You're fighting your Sense. It's not nonsense, it's *another* sense, and one you must exercise if you ever want a good night's sleep, or to escape these headaches. I'm worried about you, Mary, and I'm frustrated that you don't want to take these lessons seriously."

Dame Hartwell and Sir Hubert exchanged glances, their expressions assessing and amused. Jasper bit into his toast, his gaze swerving from Mary to Tessa and back again.

Hartwell's eyebrows drew together. "Would it hurt very much to try?"

Mary's expression was mulish as she glanced at Eloise, who hovered by the buffet, appalled. "And have to deal with the likes of her every day?"

Eloise straightened at that. "I beg your pardon! Deal with what, exactly?"

"She has a point," Jasper said, pointing his toast at Eloise while speaking to Tessa. "It seems you were correct, my girl, about the amethyst only working for the night. Eloise is back—"

Dame Hartwell squealed and turned in her seat, frantically trying to locate Eloise.

Tessa focused on steadying her heartbeat at being called *my girl*.

"—and poor Mary here is clearly suffering a headache for it, and I'm still tethered to her. Does Mary really have to control her Sense for you to take care of my issue?"

Tessa stiffened at Jasper's imperious tone. She looked at him over the rim of her cup, taking a slow sip to measure her response. Of course Jasper cared only for his problem to be solved. No wonder he had been so gentlemanly, walking her to the dining room and pouring her coffee, helping her sit. These were things that a gentleman just did. It had no bearing on what he thought about her, or in fact, she about him. Tessa sighed, disappointed that once again, she was right about Jasper Steele, that he only showered attention on those who might be of use to him.

It was an excellent reminder, just as she was thawing toward Jasper, not to drop her guard. As soon as she relieved him of Eloise, he would leave, and Tessa would remain with the same unfortunate feelings that continued to plague her dreams of a life that might have been.

Jasper bit his lip, seemingly ashamed of his word choices. "Forgive me, that came out all wrong."

Hartwell and Mary blinked at Jasper, having never heard him apologize, ever.

"Your issue?" Eloise said, her voice rising. "Are you calling me an issue? I'm a gift, you fool. I'm here to protect you."

"From what?" Tessa spun in her seat, entirely focused on Eloise. "From whomever is tugging at your ribbons?"

Dame Hartwell looked to Sir Hubert, annoyed to be left out of the conversation. He shrugged, unable to be of any help, having lived years only hearing half a conversation and entertaining himself with what he heard.

Eloise scoffed, waving her hand at Tessa and her silly theories. "I'm not a dog on a leash, you insulting thing. I mean that as long as I'm engaged to Jasper, no one else could take advantage of him."

Jasper ran his hand through his hair with an irritated growl. "For the last time, we are not engaged."

Mary dropped Hartwell's hand to rub both her temples. Tessa placed a hand on Mary's shoulder, whispering something about breathing and not fighting the shivers. She kept whispering, coaching and cajoling, until Mary finally sat back, blinking in her chair, her hands dropped into her lap. She stared at Eloise directly, a small, triumphant smile lurking on her lips. "I'd forgotten what it felt like to not have a constant headache."

"There you are," Tessa murmured. She couldn't help a triumphant grin of her own, shared with her uncle. Take that, Marylebone Spiritualist Association.

"Stop that," Eloise said, hovering closer to Jasper. "You've an unnerving stare, Miss Trentwood. It's appalling."

"Well then," Mary said drily, lifting her teacup, "I suppose one ought not disturb another's slumber either. You are above us, after all."

Eloise drew back, hand to her chest as though she hadn't already suffered her mortal wound. Before she could round on Jasper, he held up a hand to silence her. "Yes, yes, I know. How dare I let her speak to you that way?" He dipped his toast into the soft-boiled egg, turning instead to Tessa. "You know, I think I'd like to join your lessons with Mary, if you don't mind. Perhaps the both of you could have a winning influence on my dearly departed fiancée."

Tessa looked at her uncle, unsure whether this was a good idea. His encouraging nod, coupled with Mary's sudden bright interest, Hartwell's relief, and Dame Hartwell's glinting satisfaction, led her to nod her acquiescence.

Eloise emitted a loud, "Ugh!" but was otherwise ignored for the rest of breakfast as everyone turned their attention to today's lessons and activities. After all, Eloise was but one ghost in the house. She couldn't monopolize all of their attention all the time.

They agreed Jasper should refresh at home and return for lessons. Tessa posited this would be an excellent way for Mary to practice her Sense, as Eloise was determined to stay, and Mary was determined to not acknowledge any other spirits in the room (there were five, today).

Sir Hubert agreed, pulling out his leather journal stuffed with his musings and learnings over the years. He had a theory that there were different medium categories, and perhaps Mary's hesitance wasn't because of her inability to focus, but perhaps instead her style or category of mediumship.

Tessa had a hard time not rolling her eyes whenever her uncle dove into this sort of philosophical theorizing. Jasper caught her rolling her eyes when he joined them in the library, and his amused grin made her cheeks warm. The days passed quickly in this manner, with Hartwell bounding off to work in the morning, and Jasper joining him at home for lunch to partake in Tessa and Mary's lessons.

An odd camaraderie formed between the four of them. Sir Hubert, in his reflective moments with Tessa, announced he couldn't have been more delighted for her. Too many years of running around chasing after spirits and settling old regrets for others had made Tessa too serious, too quiet, he said. He loved to see her crack smile after smile these days, or even roll her eyes at him as he pointed out a note in his journal. Their lessons had a surprising amount of laughter as they teased and ignored Eloise, whose furious silences only fueled their amusement.

It was all Tessa could do to not melt into the floor with embarrassment over her uncle's enthusiasm. She couldn't help her seriousness any more than she could help her amusement. And as time went on, Tessa found she forgot, more often than not, to be annoyed or shy around Jasper.

She noticed him noticing her, and how he was always ready to offer a hand if she was carrying her bag of gems, or to be the object of their lesson should she need a test subject to show for Mary. Her confidence grew all the while, for she knew what she was talking about, and they were seeing some progress with Mary's headaches as she acknowledged more and more spirits.

For Jasper, it was heaven to be part of a group of friends again. To see Tessa in her element, moving him around to test the strength and distance of Eloise's tethering, or Mary's awareness of the tether. Tessa's wry humor, which never seemed funny at the outset but was hilarious upon reflection, surprised him. His lunch hours at Hartwell House were the brightest moments of his days, and it was always a bit of a letdown returning to work. More often than not, though, Hartwell would cuff him about the neck, inviting him over for dinner, and Jasper could not refuse. Anything to see Tessa's dark brown eyes sparkle at him, surprised yet again that they both found the same thing amusing.

As he turned down the gas lamp by his reading chair, having slipped into the house after his mother retired for the night, Jasper mused over the dark depths of a fine pair of brown eyes. He had to confess that Tessa Preston intrigued him. And not in the manner his now-married (sometimes twice over) friends had once found her exotic during her youthful season. No, her calm practicality intrigued Jasper, and its odd, almost humorous juxtaposition to her uncanny talents with ghosts. She was unfailingly polite, and it was only by getting to know Tessa that he could now hear the teasing sarcasm lending levity to her manner. In short, he found Tessa charming and hilarious.

It occurred to Jasper that maybe Tessa wasn't funny at all. Maybe she picked up her humor from Shakespeare himself, if he was a ghost. Now Shakespeare, however unlikely, would be quite the ghostly companion. Definitely preferable to Eloise's moping presence.

Jasper crawled into his bed, not bothering to undress with Eloise perched atop his desk. She did her best to seem thoroughly bored, but her keen interest in his nighttime regimen was apparent in her tense posture and the way she watched his every move.

"Do ghosts not sleep?" he asked, glad he sounded as irritated as he felt.

"Why should a ghost need to sleep? What on earth would I dream about?"

"Passing to Beyond, as Miss Preston says? Don't you find it dreadfully dull hovering about me like some horsefly?"

Eloise drew to her full height and floated a couple of inches off the ground for extra effect. "I beg your pardon? A horsefly? I have never heard a more insulting thing in my life."

Jasper snorted, punching his pillow into a shape that suited him. "That, my dear girl, is only because you were never around to hear such comments. And rightly so, for we kept such jibes at prospective wives amongst the lads."

Eloise sniffed. "My Rupert never said such horrid things, I'm certain of it."

Jasper, about to pull the coverlet over his head so he wouldn't have to suffer the light glow emanating from Eloise's specter, froze. "You don't think the man who whisked you away for what was certainly *not* Gretna Green, in a madcap race that ended in both your deaths, had only pristine things to say about you?

Please tell me you're not that naive. You've had nearly a month of this . . . ghostly stage of being . . . to know better."

Eloise chewed her lip in an uncharacteristic show of uncertainty. "I'm told he haunts his family seat. He was to inherit, and now everything has gone to his cousin. It's such a shame, Rupert promised we'd hold such fun parties. A more boring person you've never known, his cousin. So serious and studious."

Jasper pulled the coverlet over his head. "He *would* haunt his cousin over something like that. Rupert was not someone to cross."

Whatever Eloise retorted sounded muffled, so Jasper poked his head out to demand what she said.

"Pleasant dreams about your Miss Preston." Her tone was snide and smug, and hit exactly as she intended.

Jasper muttered something about how she wasn't *his* Miss Preston, and hid beneath the blanket until he fell asleep to Eloise's persistent and unkind giggles.

TWELVE

IN WHICH ONE LOSES TIME

IT SHOULD SURPRISE NO one that Eloise filled the afterlife with the same activities that filled her living days: Annoying the daylights out of everyone around her. It was her chief entertainment, and to have found herself latched to the easily flustered Jasper Steele was perhaps the best way she could live out her afterlife. These lessons that Tessa Preston imparted to Mary Trentwood were, on the whole, rather dull. Eloise suspected Tessa could exorcise her at any moment, but chose not to. Why not was a puzzle to Eloise, along with the stark and recent realization that she had been losing time.

It was one thing to wake from one's everlasting slumber, startled by a deep voice commanding her to kiss Jasper Steele, of all people. It had amused Eloise, and horrified her mother, who had hosted the séance that called Eloise forth, and so she had done as the voice bade. But that voice was commenting on her activities more frequently these days. In fact, that deep, unsettling, hollow voice seemed to precede moments when Eloise couldn't have said just what had happened to the hours.

Eloise had never been one to worry overmuch when alive. Things worked out, until they didn't, and she'd landed face down in a wet ditch with a broken neck after being thrown from her elopement carriage beside her also deceased fiancé. Poor Rupert. She hoped the rumors weren't true that he now haunted his family home. If so, egads, what a *boring* place to haunt. And that staid younger cousin of his who'd come running after them and probably spooked their horse into the accident that ended their lives, well! If Eloise could ever convince Jasper to travel to that part of the countryside, she'd give that brat a taste or two of her displeasure.

And so it was with these dark thoughts that Eloise floated amid the carefully curated plants of the Hartwell's courtyard, annoyed that she was rather too depressed to annoy Jasper today.

"It's not like you to woolgather," came that unwelcome voice.

Eloise stopped to pick a petal off a flowering tree, striving to hide the way her edges shimmered in fear. It was an odd thing to be afraid as a ghost. She hadn't a heart anymore to beat loudly, or a breath to catch, or even any sweat to perspire. But she could feel her edges fan out, as if her ghostly presence would rather fade into nothing, than face the owner of that voice.

"You'll not ignore me, my girl, when I'm the one who brought you here."

"My sister brought me here," Eloise spat. "That stupid girl never knew how to stand up to our mother."

"Your sister was the mouthpiece, but I hold your strings, puppet."

Eloise felt a frisson of abject horror at the sound of the endearment. "I am not your puppet."

He chuckled. She would have sworn to Tessa that she felt his breath move the fine hairs on the back of her neck. She shuddered.

"What is it you want?" she asked, not daring to turn around.

"Nothing, my dear, nothing. You've been doing splendidly. I just like to check on my little project now and again, to make sure everything's progressing as it should."

"What on earth are you talking about?" Eloise worried her lip with her teeth, a habit her mother had cured her of as a child. Ruined one's chances for a nice, full lip.

A powerful tug on the gray ribbons at the back of her neck—which yes, she knew they were there despite saying otherwise to Tessa—made Eloise straighten. She could not turn around. She could not move. Indeed, she couldn't speak.

"You're going to continue to lose time, because I need your time. If I'm to complete my assignment, I can't stay around forever without . . . rejuvenating."

Eloise's eyes widened. So she hadn't been mistaken. He, whoever he was, was stealing time from her. For what? She glanced at the house to see Mary, Tessa, and Jasper walk past the window, chatting as they made their way to luncheon.

"Don't you worry about your friends," he whispered as she felt herself fade into a beam of sunlight. So this was how it went . . . she must fade because he was taking something from her. How many more times until she would fade to nothing? "I've plenty of fun lined up for them, yes I do."

Eloise tried to fight it, but the ribbons bade her fall away. She left her consciousness with the sad, sacred thought that she hadn't many moments left to sacrifice to this creature. And what did she intend to do with her remaining moments, if this ghost meant to harm these flustered fools of hers?

Thirteen

In which an outing distracts

It was a quiet morning that found Tessa and Mary enjoying a breakfast together. Both had noted, early in the meal, that breakfasts were entirely too active at Hartwell House, and ought to be milder and more unremarkable as the dinners that often occurred, likely because of everyone's exhaustion. With Hartwell at his office, Jasper resting at home after their latest experiments with Eloise, and Dame Hartwell suspiciously absent, it was a delightfully peaceful spread of toast and eggs and coffee for Tessa and Mary.

They indulged in larger and larger bites of their food, and loud slurps, until they couldn't help giggling at their childish behavior. Tessa felt some of the strain release from her neck and shoulders. It was nice to giggle for no reason. It was, of course, around this tiny epiphany that Dame Hartwell stormed into the room.

Tessa paused mid-chew, staring at Dame Hartwell's broad grin. It was an entirely unseemly thing to view first thing in the morning. "Dare I ask, my lady?"

"Oh, get dressed," Dame Hartwell said, flapping her hands at them. "We're late for our picnic!"

Mary ducked her head, focusing on cutting her tomato and swallowing a sigh of relief at not being included.

Tessa swallowed her toast with a light cough. "Is it just the two of us headed out? I'm sorry. I don't remember us making these plans."

"Nonsense." Dame Hartwell pulled on her gloves. "You can hardly remember plans that I only just made myself this morning." Her eyes twinkling, she looked down her nose at Tessa, who remained frozen in her seat. "We are bringing Mary, and Alex of course, and then there's your uncle, and I've already sent for Jasper."

"And so I've arrived, with Hartwell in tow, as requested," came Jasper's voice from the doorway.

Tessa swallowed a shriek, clutching the frayed neckline of her dressing gown closed. Not that she was indecent . . . her gown was as high-necked and frilled as Mary's modern, fashionable one, and left much to the imagination. Even Tessa, who hadn't an eye or a care for keeping up with trends, knew that the state of her dressing gown was five years past needing a replacement, despite its comfortably worn edges. She couldn't remember if it had always been gray. She had patched it several times . . . one rips clothing when leaping out of bed, startled by yet another uninvited spirit.

And for Jasper to see her in it! Tessa felt heat crawl up her neck. She caressed her fingers across her collar nervously, and couldn't help but notice Jasper's arrested attention at the motion. She dropped her hand to her lap.

"I don't suppose I'm to get any work done until we're married and Mater's satisfied you've controlled your Sense?" Hartwell asked, clearly annoyed and pushing past Jasper to kiss Mary's forehead.

"I suppose not," Mary said, smiling up at him. "But it is awfully nice to see you midday again."

They shared a sweet smile, and it gave Tessa heartburn. She didn't think she could ever say something so sweet to someone, even if she were so clearly in love with them the way Mary was with Hartwell. She glanced at Jasper, unnerved to find him still watching her.

"Well, I welcome the distraction," Sir Hubert said, entering the room wearing a flat top hat that Tessa had never seen before. "We've been all business, and this is my vacation at home, you know."

Tessa frowned. Sir Hubert's entire outfit, light fabrics and newly tailored, made her suspicious of where he had gotten the funds. Did the dame now assume she ought to clothe them? Her presumption knew no bounds.

"My dear uncle," Tessa said, rallying, "we are here as subject experts and instructors."

"And you're not doing either very well," Dame Hartwell retorted, waving her other glove at Tessa. "And so I've decided we all need a break so we can refocus on the true task at hand."

Tessa stole another glance at Jasper to find him grinning at her. Eloise floated beside him, her expression stormy. Tessa cleared her throat. "I suppose it would be nice to have an afternoon off."

"An afternoon off. As if you were a governess!" Dame Hartwell scoffed. "This is precisely your problem, Tessa. You are our guest, and here I have to make you come to a picnic with me! And don't give me any sour looks. I know this wasn't part of your agenda for today. Come along now, let's not waste our pleasant morning!"

With a bit of flurry and hubbub, Mary and Tessa dashed to get dressed and seated in Dame Hartwell's carriages for the ride to Hyde Park.

Despite her best efforts, Tessa found she sat between Jasper and her uncle. Despite her best efforts, she found she didn't mind it in the slightest. She rather welcomed Jasper's grins these days, especially if they appeared after one of Dame Hartwell's exclamations, and hadn't noticed when she had thought of them as *her* special grins, for *her* benefit. Jasper had always been a handsome man. Tessa just hadn't known he came with a delightful sense of humor.

Sir Hubert flanked Tessa's other side, and she did her best to ignore his waggling eyebrows every time she looked his way.

They were quick to set up their picnic blanket, and the servant who traveled along tossed large pillows on the ground for the ladies' comfort. Hartwell helped Mary settle on a pillow, as did Sir Hubert with Dame Hartwell. Tessa plopped onto the remaining pillow, resisting the urge to stretch her legs as her skirts fanned around her. Jasper swallowed a laugh and sat beside her. Eloise huffed and floated to a nearby branch to perch like an affronted bird denied its breakfast.

"I am most pleased with this little spot," Dame Hartwell declared, as they all watched the glinting water of the Serpentine.

Tessa pressed her lips together. The water was deeper than it looked, and, for whatever reason, had always seemed rather sinister to her. She never understood its popularity with courting couples and shook her head at the lazy rowboats floating down the length.

"Do you enjoy the water?"

Tessa jumped, turning to find Jasper leaning close. His mustache twitched over a small smile at her startlement.

"No," she said with a small sigh. She picked up a bowl of strawberries, offering it to him. "I love the look of water. It can be so peaceful. But I'm actually rather terrified of it. It can also be quite rough." She shivered. "I'm not a fan of crossing the Channel."

Jasper nodded, selecting a strawberry and popping it into his mouth. "Well, that may be because you've had poor stewards at the helm."

Her brows rose at his cocksure tone. "Are you saying you could handle a boat across the Channel better?"

His smile was sly. "No, but I could definitely row you across the Serpentine with no harm."

Hartwell, hearing this, leaned over. "Don't tempt him, Tessa. He rowed in his college days, and he's likely itching to show off his skills, for old times' sake."

"Me? Tempt him? Never," Tessa retorted, tossing a round of cheese at Hartwell. She felt Jasper stiffen beside her and ignored it. A shadow passed beneath the surface of the lake. She blinked, and it was gone. Another inconvenience of her Sense . . . It really was so difficult to not become completely paranoid about environments where one couldn't control the variables. There truly was nothing more volatile than a body of water when dealing with spirits.

"I should like to see Archibald 'show off his skills,' and why shouldn't he?" Dame Hartwell said before sipping her wine as everyone fell silent around her.

Eloise popped into view, towering over them. Mary and Tessa exchanged a glance and rolled their eyes.

"Archibald!" Eloise said, accusing Jasper. "Your name isn't Archibald."

Tessa swiveled to face Jasper, who colored.

"It is," Dame Hartwell said to air above Hartwell's head, even though Eloise was now sitting beside Jasper. "And it dismays his mother he goes by his middle name. Jasper, really. Archibald is a fine name!"

"But hardly dashing," Jasper said. He picked the leaves off another strawberry, petulant. "No one would think twice about Archibald Steele. But Jasper Steele, now that's a name you can't ignore."

"It's the name of a villain," Tessa observed. "All *s*'s, very snake-like. If you don't intend to be a villain, I much prefer Archibald."

Jasper frowned at her. "You're making fun of me."

Tessa inclined her head with a small grin. "Not at all."

"You couldn't prefer Archibald over Jasper," he exclaimed, laughing.

"Actually, I do." She took an arch tone, a laugh fighting to escape. "I am a complex woman, you see. I can both make fun and still prefer it . . . *Archie*."

Jasper's eyes took on a sudden heat as he muttered something about complexity being a delightful challenge. Tessa's neck felt like it burst into flames, and she cleared her suddenly dry throat.

Eloise, watching their repartee, took on a musing expression. "I believe you're flirting with my fiancé."

Tessa stopped breathing. Goodness, was she? "I'm doing no such thing!"

"Come, come," Jasper said. "Even if you were, I started it. I can't help admiring beautiful, clever women."

Tessa straightened her shoulders, striving to regain her professionalism. "I am *not* flirting. Miss Carterprice would do well to keep quiet for once. And you," she said, pointing at Jasper rudely, "are too comfortable handing out compliments you don't mean."

Sir Hubert took a healthy swig of wine, looking absolutely delighted. Tessa saw him exchange a look with Dame Hartwell and realized they were in league with one another. Her stomach turned at the sight of their self-congratulatory expressions, and she sat a little taller. When she met Jasper's gaze, she kept her expression neutral.

Jasper's blue eyes darkened. "Are you really that unused to admiration that a simple compliment makes you uncomfortable?"

Tessa didn't know what to say to that, and so said nothing.

"Jasper, stop teasing Tessa," Mary said, adjusting her hat so it shaded her face a little better.

"Why don't we all go for a row after all?" Hartwell said, standing and brushing his pants. "A quick little race across the water. See if you've really got what it takes."

"Miss Preston," Jasper said, ignoring them both, "you are deserving of praise. Just because you are, and not because of all the people you've saved."

Tessa was sure her heart had stopped. Just because she deserved praise? *What is he playing at?* She narrowed her eyes and studied his earnest expression. Unable to find evidence of Jasper mocking her, she decided to escape the conversation altogether. Tessa reached out a hand to her uncle, and after a moment of confusion, he leapt to his feet so that she might stand. "I think I need to stretch my legs, after all. It's been so long since I've had a walk."

Mary poked Hartwell, and he pulled her to standing. "I'm happy to join you."

Eloise chortled, grabbing Jasper's arm. "Good for you, Miss Preston. Even if my Jasper-poo *clearly* doesn't seem to remember good manners, you certainly have. One doesn't flatter the hired help, my dear."

Tessa's fingers twitched, aching to have the cane in hand, but it was too soon. She needed Eloise around to help teach Mary. She exhaled slowly, unsure what she wanted to do more . . . infuriate Eloise, or put Jasper in his place. He was perilously close to repeating his old mistakes, and she was not interested in waiting around for it to happen. Then again, at the sight of Eloise leaning in close to whisper something in his ear, causing him to turn a shade darker and even look embarrassed . . .

"Alright," Tessa said to Hartwell. "It's a race. You and Mary against *Archie* and I." She turned to Eloise. "So sorry, no spirits on the water, isn't that right?"

Eloise looked uneasy as she studied the Serpentine. "Well, I don't know that I would—"

"Is there something about bodies of water and spirits that I ought to know about?" Mary asked. "That seems like a useful bit of information to learn."

"Not entirely," Tessa said slowly, watching Eloise. Tessa blinked, really blinked to fully engage her Sense, and saw Eloise for a moment as she must have been at her death. Neck akimbo, hair wet and sticking to her face, clothing soaked and heavy. She blinked again to find Eloise staring at her, aghast. "Simply that ghosts with a . . . history of water, shall we say, really ought not to test their fate twice."

And with that, Tessa stalked off toward the boat rental stall, with a musing Mary and Hartwell following.

Eloise hissed at Jasper as he detached himself to catch up. "Don't you dare leave me behind with these two old—"

"Eloise, my dear," Dame Hartwell snapped, "I think Tessa was right, you ought not speak."

FOURTEEN

IN WHICH ONE SURVIVES THE SERPENTINE

Now that she stood at the dock, watching as Jasper and Hartwell climbed into their boats, laughing and testing their balance, shouting jibes at one another about falling in, Tessa realized her folly. Her throat tightened and her breathing grew shallow, her gaze clouding as she watched the water lap and splash the boats. "What on earth was I thinking?" she muttered.

Mary sidled close, pretending that she was looking for her glove in her fringed purse. "I really would enjoy a walk about the park with you, if you'd rather stretch your legs."

Tessa sighed, hearing Mary's unspoken way out of this mess. "You really are so kind." She rubbed her temple. "But I'm stubborn, and cannot ignore a challenge once raised. I might be afraid of water, but I'm not a coward."

Jasper heard this last bit, having now balanced in his boat, and grinned at her. "That's the spirit! Don't worry, Miss Preston. I'll keep you safe." He held out his hand for her. She took it before her mind caught up. He tightened his grip on her fingers, his smile warming as he gently tugged her closer to the dock edge.

With a nervous and quick lick of her lips, Tessa tried to focus on his confidence, but couldn't help staring at the shadows in the water. Certainly there was something in there. How many souls had breathed their last beneath the surface, fighting for air, knowing no one would hear their last call . . .

Water, especially beneath its surface, was dangerous for mediums. Too close to the edge of Beyond, one might say. A moment too long, and one could become a spirit. And though she dressed lightly in her comfortable corset and walking skirts, Tessa knew her layers of clothing would not help her if she fell in . . .

"Miss Preston."

Jasper's voice broke through Tessa's panicked haze, and she looked down to find him holding her hand as tightly as she held his. She exhaled. "Mr. Steele."

"Archie," he corrected.

She smiled at that, and let him pull her until she had to drop her foot down into the boat. The sun shone against his blond hair, highlighting reddish undertones. His blue eyes twinkled at her as he made sure she sat properly with the advice that she remain in the center of the boat, and then he got to work. Jasper grabbed the oars with a shout at Hartwell for taking advantage of such a head start and rowed.

Tessa clutched the sides of the rowboat, not in the least bit interested in looking regal, serene, or even graceful, the way Mary did. Jasper hid power beneath his suits. With little discernible effort, he caught up to Mary and Hartwell's boat. Tessa discovered it felt better breathing with Jasper, taking large, measured breaths with each pull of the oars as they sliced through the water.

"Have a care!" Hartwell said as Jasper dragged his oars, slowing his speed so the boats just bumped one another. "Are you trying to terrify the ladies?"

Jasper, now deigning to pant slightly, grinned at Tessa. "I had to take advantage of Miss Preston's trust, and show it was worth it. We are in the middle of the Serpentine, my dear lady. What do you think?"

Mary's eyes, bright with excitement, met Tessa's, and they burst into laughter.

Hartwell relaxed, and suggested perhaps they all ought to float about for a bit, to acclimate. Mary quickly agreed, and Tessa was alone with Jasper.

Leaning on his oars, Jasper's expression sobered. "You are alright, aren't you?"

She saw his gaze linger on her hands, which still clutched the sides of the boat. She chuckled lightly and carefully released her grip. "I trust your abilities, Mr."—at the sight of his narrowing eyes, she corrected—"Archie. I wouldn't have thought any one person could move so fast, and through water, no less. I'm impressed."

"That's gratifying to hear. I don't think you impress easily."

Tessa cleared her throat, looking away from his warmth to find Eloise floating near the Serpentine's edge, looking distressed. "Have you spoken with your family about Eloise?"

She could hear his frown when he admitted he had not and didn't intend to. "I love my mother dearly. It was her suggestion that sent me to the Carterprice séance, you know. She was hoping I might catch someone's eye."

"At a séance?"

"Speaks to her desperation for my future matrimonial bliss, doesn't it?" Jasper cringed, rowing at a leisurely pace. "Anyway, it's not as though I could admit that I *had* caught someone's attention, and that she had followed me home, and can't you see her, Mother? No? I'm off to an institution then, am I? Right then."

Tessa laughed. "Fair enough, but isn't she suspicious of where you run off to every day?"

He shook his head. "I think she's hoping I found someone, and that she'll hear about the lady soon enough."

"You really ought to tell her *something*, so she isn't disappointed."

Jasper kept rowing, glancing over his shoulder to ensure they weren't on a collision course with anything. "What's the harm?"

Tessa's stomach tightened. "What will she think when you suddenly stop leaving for hours at a time?"

"Who said I intend to stop?" He glanced at Tessa, his cheeks reddening, no doubt from the sun. "She's not entirely misled, thinking I've found someone."

Tessa's lips clamped shut. Before she could lecture him on his flirting, Hartwell and Mary sped past, crowing all the way. Mary splashed Tessa, cackling at the sight of her flabbergasted sputtering.

"What are you doing?" Tessa demanded, waving away Jasper's open grin and raised eyebrow. "Get them! Beat them! How dare they!"

Jasper saluted her and went to task. Mary and Tessa cheered on the men with delighted little screams as they wove between the other lazy boats, whose occupants shouted at them to slow it down. Thanks to their head start, Hartwell and Mary beat Jasper and Tessa . . . but only by a margin, and none of it mattered anyway, for they were all laughing too hard when they returned to the dock. As Jasper helped Tessa from their rowboat, Eloise popped into view beside him.

"You were gone so very long," Eloise hissed. "Don't you know how dangerous water is for a medium?"

Jasper paused, his expression curious and concerned as he looked from Eloise to Tessa.

"Why Eloise, I didn't think you cared," Tessa said. She wiped lingering water droplets from her sleeve and hat, chuckling.

"Is it so very dangerous?" Jasper asked, taking Tessa's elbow and guiding her from the dock's edge.

Tessa shook off his gentle grasp. "Only if one isn't vigilant, and believe me, I'm always careful around large bodies of water."

Eloise clucked her tongue in a very un-Eloise, very matronly sort of manner. "Your arrogance will do little to protect you, when the day comes."

Hartwell and Mary, having clambered out of their boat, heard only this last bit. "Was that a threat, Eloise?" Mary asked.

Wringing her fingers together, Eloise backed away from the dock. "I'm simply letting you know I'm the least of a medium's concerns when it comes to spirits."

"I'm well aware, I assure you," Tessa said. She tossed her gloves into her purse. "I've helped, and handled, many."

"Let's return to the house. I've had enough of these shenanigans for one day." Eloise shooed Jasper, her hands fluttering through his torso and causing him to shiver.

"You're behaving rather odd," Hartwell said, hearing the tension in Eloise's voice despite being unable to see her.

Misunderstanding, Jasper straightened his tie. "Well, Eloise did just shove her hands through my chest. It's not a pleasant experience!"

"No, no, I meant Miss Carterprice," Hartwell said. "What are you up to, our dear Miss Ghost?"

Eloise stomped her foot, though no sound came of it. "I'm not up to anything, you ungrateful children. I'm simply asking everyone to leave this terrible place so we can return to the house like civilized Britons!"

Tessa tilted her head, hearing genuine fear in Eloise's frustration. She caught Mary's puzzled gaze and shrugged. "I daresay the afternoon's done for me anyway. All this excitement—" She choked on her words as she felt a wet hand grab her ankle. Unable to speak, she whipped her gaze at Jasper, who turned to face her much too slowly. With a tight scream, Tessa dropped to her knees. She grabbed for the boards of the dock as the wet hand dragged her to the edge. She looked behind her, seeing only a huge, dark shadow beneath the serene surface of the Serpentine. "Oh—"

"I told you, I told you!" Eloise shrieked, floating over Tessa and flapping her hands in hysterics. "They don't like mediums, and they don't like me, and they really, really hate you, Tessa Preston!"

Tessa screamed for her uncle, who was already en route with the cane.

"What on earth!" Jasper scrambled after Tessa amid Mary's screams for help. Hartwell grabbed an oar, tossing it to Jasper. He caught it deftly, holding it above his head as if to smack whatever dragged Tessa from him, but as he couldn't actually see the spirit, wasted his moment.

Tessa locked eyes with Jasper. "I told you I hated water."

Another hand speared up and out of the water, lashed itself around Tessa's throat, and dragged her down with a loud splash.

Jasper dropped to his stomach, his hands flailing in the water, but he was unable to catch Tessa. He blinked. The water grew still, as if nothing had happened.

Mary whimpered, holding her head with her usual pains when spirits acted as they were wont to do.

Jasper's old head injury pounded as he calculated. With a growl, he threw the oar into the water and scrambled to a sitting position to remove his jacket and kick off his shoes.

"You can't go in there!" Eloise cried.

"Shut up, Eloise!" said the others.

Sir Hubert, red and panting, shoved the cane in Jasper's hand. "She'll know what to do. Just get it in her hands, my boy."

Jasper dove in the direction the spirit took Tessa. It felt like no water he'd ever experienced before, and he had rowed and swam through many a pond and river. Heavy and murky, as though he swam through pudding. He gripped the cane, letting it rest against his forearm. He struggled to keep his eyes open against the pressure.

There! He saw a brown hand move, slapping away a substance one might describe as sentient black tar. He jabbed the cane forward, and the tar swirling around Tessa's hand repelled. Jasper jabbed again, shoving the cane into Tessa's hand. Once in her grasp, the cane glowed. Jasper grabbed Tessa's waist as she kept jabbing, breaking the spirit into little oil slicks that couldn't combine quickly enough to attack again. Jasper swam up and away, dragging Tessa with him.

They broke the surface, both gulping air and water. They fell beneath again amid the shouts of their friends. His lungs burning, Jasper wrapped his arm around Tessa's back and over her chest, his other arm lashing through the water as he pulled as he had never pulled before. They broke the surface again, this time with Tessa shouting unintelligible words that caused the spirit-end of the cane to explode with such force, it blasted them through the water within reach of Hartwell and Sir Hubert's ready hands.

Jasper pushed a limp Tessa forward, not having the breath or words to instruct Hartwell to take her. Sir Hubert grabbed the cane before Tessa dropped it into the lake, while Jasper pushed himself up onto the deck. He crawled over to Tessa, whom Hartwell had dropped to her side. Jasper grabbed his jacket, wrapping it tightly around her. Her hair had come completely undone from its chignon, and strands of wet, bedraggled curls stuck to her face. Her dress seeped with lake water. She breathed, but lightly. Jasper touched her cheek.

Tessa's eyes popped open. She sat up and screamed, slapping her hands against him as if he were the spirit.

"Tessa, Tessa!" Jasper leaned away from her slaps, not wanting her to fall back into the Serpentine in her distress. "You did it, you're fine, you're out of the water."

She grabbed fistfuls of her hair, her breath heaving. Her dark eyes dilated, and she stared unseeing at him.

"Let me pass," came Dame Hartwell's imperious voice. "I should have known better, what with all the goings-on at the house. Of course they would find me here, find us here. The Marylebone Spiritualist Association has always been quite clear about the liminal state of mediums and spirits with water."

Jasper spun around, holding his arms out to block Dame Hartwell.

"I beg your pardon! She is my charge—after her uncle's," she was quick to amend. "How dare you! It is my fault she's in this state. Let me look after her!"

"Mother," Hartwell warned. He and Mary stood off to the side, keeping a careful watch on Eloise's movements as she flitted by the edge of the water, quietly wailing.

"Listen to me," Jasper said, grabbing Dame Hartwell by the shoulders. Her mouth fell open at being handled so rudely. "They don't want you, ma'am, they've never wanted you. They want her."

Tessa shuddered. She kept her arms wrapped about her ribs, looking as though fighting a frost within. Jasper fell to his knees beside her, rubbing his hands along her arms. It did not help. A frigid cold sped across her body so that even Jasper could hardly feel his fingers anymore. It felt as though the ghosts were making her one of them.

Tessa moaned, falling forward to rest her head in her wet skirts.

"Tessa," Jasper murmured.

She peeked up through her black, tangled curls.

"We're going home."

Fifteen

In Which Experience Falters

It took every ounce of Jasper's willpower not to throw his arm about Tessa's shoulders and bury his face in the glistening curls as they rode back to the house. She sat alone on her side of the carriage, unable to stop shivering. With her hair dripping all over her, she looked absolutely miserable.

Sir Hubert had timed a poke in the side with a large bump in the road causing Jasper to jump from his seat. Jasper gave Sir Hubert a sidelong questioning look, and at his insistence, joined Tessa on her side of the carriage. He threw another blanket around her shoulders, lifting her heavy hair out of the way.

There really weren't any scenarios in which Jasper could have ever expected finding himself with his hands buried in the sweet coconut-scented braids and curls atop Tessa's head.

Tessa's curls were both slick and soft, with errant fairy knots wrapping themselves around the braids half-collapsed from their coif. Jasper braced himself against the side of the carriage, quick to rejoin Sir Hubert opposite Tessa, who stared at him wild-eyed for taking such liberties in such a confined space.

Jasper bit back a retort at her confused, alarmed expression, thinking this was hardly the time to blame her uncle for his forwardness.

Pomeroy sprang into action at the sight of their sodden return. At Hartwell's insistence, servants took Dame Hartwell upstairs to her bedrooms to rest from the shock of the day, though Dame Hartwell made it quite clear she was none too pleased with his high-handed manner. Pomeroy instructed a fire to be drawn in the drawing room, while Sir Hubert worked to remove Tessa's bodice and skirt. She shivered uncontrollably, her teeth chattering despite the summer heat and fire.

Mary paced the room, her eyes wild. Tessa could guess at her thoughts: Ghosts didn't attack people—they were merely annoyances, pale reflections of those once passed, surely?

Mary began muttering to herself, quietly so Tessa could only hear snippets . . . About not taking the lessons seriously, and something about a dangerous medium lifestyle. That her aunt's passing was more about a bad jump than ghosts. But to be dragged underwater by what had clearly been an angry ghost . . .

Tessa froze, focusing on Mary's agitated movements. She grabbed the blanket Sir Hubert placed around her shoulders and batted him away. "Mary, stop it."

Hartwell and Jasper, who had been setting up the tea and working on the fire respectively, turned to find Mary holding her hands over her ears with her eyes screwed shut.

"Mary, you must not let them—!" Tessa scrambled to her feet, dropping the blanket and not having a care that she stood in her white underthings with three men in the room. It was happening. The spirits were taking advantage of her weakened state, and she could not help Mary in time. No, no, no!

A roaring noise slammed against the house with a terrible boom. Everyone stumbled, and somewhere in the house, a servant girl screamed. Spirits poured in through the windows, the hallway, down the chimney, streaming into the fireplace. They whipped around Mary, creating a cyclone and extinguishing the fire.

Though Sir Hubert, Hartwell, and Jasper couldn't see the spirits, they witnessed books lifting from the shelves to circle

Mary, the curtains whipping as though a gale blew through London. Their stomachs dropped intuitively at Mary's silent scream.

Tessa, still shouting at Mary to let go, to stop fighting her Sense, to not let the ghosts overtake her, braced herself. Mary's dark glow all but engulfed her. If Tessa didn't interfere . . . well, she didn't want to think about what might happen. She shivered, remembering her own moments of cutting it close. One foot planted behind her, Tessa launched forward. She bent her elbow to shield her face, her wet braids and curls lashing her cheeks. Her other hand gripped the cane, using it as an anchor to press forward. As Tessa hoped, the ghosts turned their attention to her, descending upon her in a frightful swarm.

Hartwell caught Mary as she abruptly fainted. Jasper and Sir Hubert watched Tessa with narrowed eyes, unsure what they ought to do.

Gasping for air, Tessa stumbled, clutching the cane as the ghosts battered her, trying to wrestle control. What bragging rights they would have if they possessed Tessa Preston, of all mediums! Well. They were all of a single mind today, what with trying to drown her and now smother her. Pressing her lips together, Tessa fell to her knees, hugging the cane close.

What a *horrid* day this was turning out to be.

Not knowing what else to do, Tessa threw open her arms, brandishing the cane so it spun in her hand, disrupting the cyclone. The spirits recovered quickly. They rushed at Tessa, single-minded, acting as though they melded together into a single spear intent on impaling her.

Tessa held the cane like a sword, both hands clutching the hilt. Teeth clenched, she let the ghost spear impale itself on the cane. She closed her eyes against the explosion of ghosts falling away from one another, some floating out of sight, some fading into

Beyond, some screaming terror while dragged down through the floor by an unseen hand.

The cane ricocheted back into Tessa's belly. She fell with a breathless grunt, her head cracking into a side table. It all happened so quickly, she barely had time to think . . . if only her braids hadn't fallen, her piled hair might have cushioned the blow.

Jasper was the first to move. He caught Tessa before she hit her head a second time on the tile floor, slamming his knees in the process as Tessa's full weight landed. Her curves, which he so admired, came with a soft, muscular weight that made him very aware that she was still soaked and only half-clothed.

"Is she breathing?" Sir Hubert asked, his voice cracking.

Hartwell guided a sagging Mary to the chaise. *Careful*, Hartwell seemed to say with his eyes.

Jasper held his breath as he leaned close to Tessa's face. A soft huff ruffled his own fallen wet hair, and he looked at her chest to find a soft rise and fall. Alright then, perhaps he looked a moment too long, and snapped his gaze back to Hartwell with a quick, mortified affirmation that Tessa was unconscious, but breathing.

Hartwell coughed out a small chuckle and turned his attention to his shaking fiancée.

"She breathes," Jasper affirmed, adjusting his hold so he could carry Tessa to the sofa opposite Mary's chaise.

"Excellent," Sir Hubert said brusquely. "I'll grab her amethyst kit . . . and some clothing." He sped from the room, but not before Jasper saw his eyes, bright with unshed tears.

"Well, isn't this a sight to be seen?" came Eloise's voice. She towered over Jasper and Tessa, flipping her large blonde ringlet over her shoulder, looking amused.

Jasper's terror and frustration and rage found a target. "Good God, Eloise, how could you possibly be here after all that? Will you be useful for once and—and tell the other ghosts we're closed for business!"

"I shall do no such thing. I've never been useful. And it serves you all right, playing with things you've no notion about." Eloise picked at a nonexistent thread on one of her lace cuffs. She continued, rather sulkily, "I told you not to go on the Serpentine, but would you listen? No, of course not, it's just silly, annoying Eloise—"

"Then tell us," Jasper hissed. "You loiter about, complaining that you're bored, yet when something interesting happens, you do nothing but fall into hysterics. Why didn't you help Mary? Why let all those ghosts descend upon this house?"

"And risk being caught up in Miss Preston's ability to send us all Beyond? I should think not! I've things to do yet, my dear Jasper."

Hartwell frowned at the spot where Jasper glared, using it to direct his commentary in Eloise's direction. "Really, Eloise, you are too much."

"I am, am I not?" she said, whisking away in a flurry of theatrical fog.

"She's having far too much fun being dead," Mary muttered, resting against Hartwell's shoulder. "At least his ghostly state annoyed my father."

Hartwell chuckled. "Lest we forget, he still used it to his advantage."

Mary hummed, a slight smile dancing across her lips. "Perhaps you ought to take Tessa to a quieter spot, Jasper. I daresay Dame Hartwell will return sooner rather than later. We will send her uncle. He will know what we can do to rouse her."

Jasper paused, clearly wrestling with propriety, then nodded. He shifted Tessa in his arms so he could stand without dropping her. He crouched, swinging her legs onto his other arm with ease, having the practice of lifting his own boats in and out of the water with his rowing club.

As they left the room, Hartwell angled a suspicious smirk down at Mary, who now seemed very recovered indeed. She sat up, taking care to rearrange her skirts and tuck wayward locks of hair back into place. "My dear, are you sure you know what you're doing?" he asked.

Mary smiled at him. "I never know what I'm doing, but things seem to work out as I intend. I daresay it's one of my best qualities."

Hartwell shook his head, chuckling, though the small frown puckering his eyebrows didn't entirely lift as he pondered the direction in which Jasper carried Tessa.

<h1 style="text-align:center">SIXTEEN</h1>

<h1 style="text-align:center">IN WHICH ONE FEELS TENDER CONCERN</h1>

TESSA WOKE TO A pair of concerned blue eyes frowning at her. With a shuddering gasp, she shrank back, her forearms raised as a shield even as Jasper stuttered in his attempts to tell her she was safe. She looked wildly about the room, not understanding where she was or why she was alone with him, or why, good heavens, she hadn't a bodice or skirt on anymore.

"Please," he was saying, "please be still. Your head. Your uncle is fetching your gems, Hartwell is tending to Mary in the drawing room, and Dame Hartwell hasn't returned from her room." He held her hands in his, his thumbs caressing her knuckles. "Please be still. We don't know the impact of your injury."

The concern in his voice calmed Tessa better than any placation. In fact, she absolutely adored the fact that Jasper immediately recited everyone's location to calm her. It seemed he had been watching her closer than she realized. Tessa suspected even her uncle didn't know her compulsion with counting who was alive, and who wasn't, in a room. She cleared her throat, allowing Jasper to help her sit up. With an embarrassed little smile, she accepted a half-sodden blanket from him, figuring it was better than nothing, for decency. Feeling the weight of her hair on her shoulders, Tessa tucked the fallen braids, twists, and curls back self-consciously. She knew by touch which sections had grown frizzy from her resting on them without her silk bonnet. She sighed. This had to be the most unattractive she had been in her life, ever.

The heat in Jasper's gaze as he studied her, watching for any sign of distress, made her hold the blanket tighter. Alright—perhaps not the *most* unattractive she'd ever been, then.

"Why are you tending to me, rather than my uncle?" Tessa asked, breaking the heavy silence.

Jasper leaned back on his heels, an unconscious mimicry of Hartwell's nervous tic. "He said he would be faster, knowing exactly where to look in your things." His expression lightened as he watched her finger-comb and twist her hair back into a sturdy chignon. "You aren't in much pain then, I hope?"

Tessa shook her head gingerly, heat crawling up her neck. He was her client, for heaven's sake. A smile was hardly anything special. But an *Archie* smile . . . It did tingly things to her, as it always had, she admitted to herself. And why shouldn't she? After all, he dove into a lake to save her, and was ready with her cane besides. She could, she decided, in this moment of weakness and frailty, decide her hero was handsome, and charming, and funny, and witty, and . . . she had hit her head very hard.

"I'm glad of that," Jasper sighed. He had, while she lay unconscious, changed into a dry pair of clothes borrowed from Hartwell. Tessa struggled to not let her thoughts wander too far in that direction. "I know what it's like to have a nasty head injury. I daresay it's why I can interact with these spirits of yours."

"They're not my spirits," she corrected.

"Of course," he murmured. He reached his fingers forward, pausing just short of touching her hair. "May I?"

Tessa held her breath. Allow him to touch her hair? His many compliments seemed genuine. And if he had experience with head injuries, it was probably prudent, in the most professional sense, to let him examine the spot currently pulsing with a dull ache just at her nape. She dipped her chin to give him access.

Jasper's touch was light—reverent, even. The most tender of movements, Tessa couldn't avoid a light shiver as he felt along her nape. He stopped when a low hiss escaped her upon his finding the bump. He pulled back, studying his hand.

"No blood, that's good." He heaved a sigh, his frown returning. "Why did you take on that maelstrom by yourself? What if they had injured you?"

"And therefore unable to help you with Eloise, you mean?" Tessa winced at the strained sound of her own voice. She didn't know why she was being so snippy. Even if he was being selfish and careful about his own needs, he was her client. He had a right to ensure she was fit to see their agreement through.

"No," he said, elongating the word. "I'm asking you to have a care for your safety. After our . . . adventure in the lake, taking on that storm of spirits felt alarmingly dangerous."

She rolled her eyes, leaning back against the sofa. His eyes glanced across her prone posture and her cheeks grew hot. "It comes with the job, Archie," she said. Her cheeks warmed further upon hearing a slightly flirtatious tone in her own voice. Goodness. Maybe she *had* hit her head harder than she thought.

His brows rose, and he grinned. "With you, I suppose it does. Well," he said, rising from his knees and slapping his hands against his thighs, "I'm certain Hartwell is glad you absorbed . . . whatever it was you did on Miss Trentwood's behalf. Not that I have any say in the matter—"

"You don't."

"—but please refrain from harming yourself just to protect others."

Tessa froze at the tender admonition.

"But then, who am I to ask you to change who you are? It's why this family cares for you. Just . . ." Jasper took her hand in both of his, encouraging her to look up at him as she bolted upright. "You were unconscious for hours, Tessa. I don't know if that's normal, but your uncle was very concerned."

She stared at their entwined hands. "My uncle."

"And me, of course."

She found it difficult to breathe. "Of course."

As if on cue, Sir Hubert burst into the room, arms laden with gauzes and bags of gems. He stumbled to a halt, exclaiming his relief. Tessa ripped her hand away from Jasper before her uncle could notice or comment and clenched it in her lap. Whether it was to hide her embarrassment or hold on to the warmth Jasper had imparted, Tessa could not discern. Soon Mary and Hartwell descended upon them, and Eloise made her appearance, as always, interested in a commotion. Tessa avoided looking directly at Jasper, despite sensing that his eyes rarely left her as they all discussed the dangers of Mary continuing to practice controlling her Sense, and how magnificent Tessa was at saving Mary from the maelstrom.

Dame Hartwell, still miffed at Jasper, remained in her room for the rest of the day, to everyone's relief. Through silent agreement, they all realized they'd had enough of her clever schemes for the moment.

Seventeen

In Which One Insists

With all the excitement, one would have thought Dame Hartwell would be in a better mood. Instead, she sulked from room to room, unwilling to engage in conversation unless it was for her audience to hear how the spirits continued to ignore her. How dare they spend far too much of their energies on the young ladies who wanted nothing with them at all?

Dame Hartwell soon lost all interest from everyone but Sir Hubert, who scribbled thoughts in his leather diary, nodding as she poured out her frustrations. She answered his questions on her intermittent ability to hear the spirits, or feel one lifting a ribbon from her white lace cap. That sort of thing. She preened under his attention, thinking finally, someone was taking her seriously.

Sir Hubert delighted in finally having a subject interested in unraveling just what she thought was happening. Tessa, efficient as she was, never wanted to indulge in such speculations. She wanted to move on to the next thing.

"When did you realize you could hear the spirits?" Sir Hubert asked, interrupting Dame Hartwell's latest raving. "And why have you pushed for Miss Trentwood's Sense, when you thought this house to be a danger?"

Dame Hartwell froze mid-sentence, blinking. She dropped her hands to her lap with a frown.

"When you hired Tessa, you said she was to help your son and his fiancée so they might have a safe wedding in this house," Sir Hubert reminded her. "Yet everything we've done, per your theory that Tessa's presence amplifies the Sense of those around her, has only seemed to make the danger worse."

Dame Hartwell's sagging mouth snapped shut. "Are you insinuating that I brought this danger to my house for my entertainment?"

Sir Hubert shook his head, tucking his pen into its well. "Certainly not, my dear madam. You know I ask for scientific purposes only."

"And just what are you always scribbling in that diary?" She gestured at him, sitting across the small tea table from her, her tone low with suspicion. "What do you intend to do with this information?"

"I thought I might publish one day," he admitted. "One needn't go through the Marylebone Spiritualist Association to establish one's credibility, but you and Tessa seem determined to think otherwise."

Dame Hartwell leaned close. "Am I to be in this publication of yours?" Her ice-blue eyes twinkled, and Sir Hubert's entire head turned a delicate shade of pink.

"I would, of course, obscure names for privacy," he stammered.

"Oh," she exclaimed, throwing her hands in the air, "and what good would that do me? Of course, you must use our names, Mary's especially, so that we might showcase Tessa's talents and raise her up as a prominent medium!"

The sound of a throat clearing in the parlor doorway made them jump. They turned to find a stormy Hartwell standing there, hat in hand, having just returned to check on Mary during his lunch hour. He stepped into the room, his mouth working as he struggled to find the words he wanted to say. Dame Hartwell and Sir Hubert exchanged uneasy glances, unsure just how much he had heard of their conversation, but certainly it had been enough.

"Alex, my boy," Sir Hubert began, closing his diary, "you'd needn't worry—"

"Pardon my frankness," Hartwell interrupted.

"Darling," Dame Hartwell said with a tremulous smile, "I have been your mother all these years. I'm quite used to it."

"Then let me be unapologetically frank and remind you that Mary is to be my wife, and my wife first . . . Not your daughter-in-law. Not your test subject. Not your ticket to publication." He drew himself up, heaving a heavy breath. "You're determined to destroy her mind with your silly séances. No, don't deny it! All because you want so much to be seen. Mater, in your quest, you've made Mary your puppet, and Tessa has almost drowned!"

Dame Hartwell stared at Hartwell, mouth agape. "Why I—"

"If I hear of another séance, or triggered 'episode,' I will remove Mary from this house."

"Where would you put her without damaging her reputation?" Dame Hartwell protested, jumping from her seat to rush forward and poke her son in the chest. He stumbled back, furious. "We are trying to help souls, Alexander! This is more important work than your impending marriage!"

"Father is not a ghost!" Hartwell exploded.

Dame Hartwell stopped breathing. Sir Hubert stood, tucking his diary in his rucksack with a thoughtful frown.

"You think I don't know when or why we started having séances in this house? Why you joined the Marylebone Spiritualist Association, and began inviting like-minded friends over, people you'd never deigned associate with before?" Hartwell ran his hand through his hair and down the side of his face with his old scar. He softened his tone, looking away from his mother as he said, "Father's not coming back, and you're only hurting those of us who are still alive around you, hunting for a medium who will make him speak to you."

Dame Hartwell lifted her chin. "What would you have me do?"

"Get to know Mary for herself," Hartwell countered, "or re-move yourself from our wedding preparations until I can remove her from this house into my home."

Mother and son stared at one another, neither backing down, neither willing to admit their shattered emotions. Sir Hubert slid his hand to Dame Hartwell's elbow, gently pulling her away as he asked about that restaurant she had mentioned, the one with the ices. Wouldn't that be a lovely way to spend the afternoon?

Dame Hartwell allowed herself to be moved, her eyes never leaving her son. "I will never stop looking," she promised.

Eighteen

In which one relents, a little

With Dame Hartwell and Sir Hubert spending less and less time interrupting her investigations and lessons, and having seen Jasper sacrifice his own safety for hers, Tessa found herself . . . relaxing. Only a little, mind, and only the appropriate amount for someone who now saw the same five—six, if one included Eloise—people almost every day. It was unnerving to feel *comfortable* around people.

On one particular morning, Hartwell had taken Mary out for a treat, and so Tessa found herself alone, or as alone as one might be in a house full of servants and the very capable Pomeroy, with Eloise and Jasper in the library again. It seemed to happen more and more, and she minded it less and less. Tessa let her thoughts wander as she studied Eloise's transparent gray ribbons. Perhaps her uncle and the others were comfortable leaving her with Jasper knowing that Eloise wasn't far away, and could very well act as a chaperone, or at minimum a deterrent for anything untoward.

Tessa straightened from her crouched position, her cheeks aflame. She glanced at Jasper, who watched with interest but gave no sign he had any idea where her thoughts led. Tessa pressed her lips together, now making a show of studying Eloise, who was now bobbing up and down lightly out of boredom.

Just what untoward actions did Tessa think Jasper might take with her? And why, for heaven's sake, did the thought cause a flustered fluttering in her chest?

"You're different from other ladies," Jasper said, lounging on the chaise as Tessa circled Eloise, who floated rather rigidly beside him.

"Oh, do tell," Tessa muttered, squinting at Eloise's transparent gray ribbon, forcing her attention to the task at hand. If only to avoid wasting too much time noticing how brightly blue Jasper's eyes were today. Surely it was a trick of the sunlight. Or perhaps her dunking in the Serpentine had done more damage to her mind than they thought.

Tessa cleared her throat, refusing to meet his steady gaze, dropping instead to his hand as it rested lightly on his thigh. All thighs aside, somehow Tessa hadn't noticed until this moment that the ribbons now seemed to attach to Jasper's ring finger, as though doing their best to claim him as Eloise's husband after all. Tessa straightened, doing her best not to roll her eyes at Jasper's smirk.

"You must admit it," Jasper said, his voice dropping almost intimately. "You have a distinct air about you, and it's only gotten more pronounced since our adventure."

Tessa rolled her eyes. "You say that to all the ladies."

"I mean what I say," he protested. "You have an incorrect view of me, Miss Preston. I'm not nearly the flirt you think I am."

Tessa rested her hands on her hips. Jasper's eyes followed, and he snapped his attention back up to her raised eyebrows, flushing slightly. "Very well, and what makes me different, then? Leaving the ghosts out of it, of course."

"You're moody and cross," he said without hesitation.

That wasn't entirely what Tessa expected.

Eloise cackled, unabashedly listening to their conversation as she floated, bored out of her mind, near the tea service. "He has you there. You've such a sour manner."

Tessa's lips pursed together in a displeased moue. She had never really thought of herself as moody and cross. She certainly smiled more often than not these days, but why wouldn't she, having found a stable roof, employment, and an attractive client to spend time with? Her eyes narrowed.

"You're moody, and you're cross, and it's delightfully refreshing," Jasper said, sitting upright and running a hand through his hair. "One tires of simpering young ladies."

"I'm hardly young," Tessa ground out, "and I never simper."

"Exactly so," Jasper grinned. "Because you're cross. I suspect it must be because of the lack of sleep. I only have one ghost and hardly ever sleep . . . I don't know how you manage with these spirits always flitting about, trying to get your attention."

Tessa stared out the window for a moment.

"Well," she muttered under her breath with a deflated little huff. She let her thoughts wander, thinking about when she had come out only to realize society merely considered her exotic, rather than marriage material. How her mother had vented to her father about the backward minds surrounding them, how everyone ends up in the same place, so why not allow unconventional love to take root? To be cross and moody on top of having an unconventional beauty . . .

"I suppose that could explain why no one offered, in the end."

Jasper's voice lowered to a murmur, and she almost didn't hear him ask, "Do you wish anyone had offered?"

"Anyone?" Tessa glanced from him to Eloise, who now gave her full attention to this bit of gossip. She could read the thoughts flitting through Eloise's eager expressions as easily as if she were back in the ballrooms hearing the indiscreet whispers floating around her. Had the cold-hearted Tessa Preston actually desired a warm home, a provider, a love match, of all things? Tessa returned her attention to the ribbons floating between Eloise and Jasper. She wondered if . . . had she other talents, could she have seen ribbons attaching Mary to Hartwell and he to her? Perhaps the ribbons weren't just restricted to ghostly connections.

Tessa shifted her weight and schooled her expression. "No. Not anyone. But someone. Perhaps a . . . someone who sees my crossness and understands the number of things I cannot control, and partners with me despite my failings."

"Partners?" Eloise spun in the air lazily, bored again. "One doesn't marry to partner with their husband, my dear idiotic Tessa."

"And what does one marry for, then?" Jasper asked. He kept his tone light, but Tessa heard an undercurrent of annoyance that differed from the routine frustration of having to speak with Eloise.

"For status, wealth, or security, of course. I don't know what on earth I'd partner with my husband on, other than raising children, and even that would have been the nanny's task."

"You are the absolute worst," Jasper said under his breath.

"I am," Eloise said, so satisfied with herself. "But I'm also not incorrect. Marriage is a contract, to be sure. So I suppose if Miss Preston wants to make it a business, she might as well. Partner, indeed!"

"I am a medium," Tessa said. "Should this *someone* and I ever choose to marry, we would have to navigate that. Would I have liked children? Yes, I believe so. My parents were happy. And I was happy with them. I think the right person would welcome a world in which I maintain this consulting employment. What I do makes everyone a little safer, a little happier. Or if not happier, perhaps a little more peaceful. Who wouldn't want that?"

"A good many men," Eloise said. "You sound as if you're speaking of a love match where you are equal with your husband." She shuddered delicately. "Dreadful."

"Why are you still talking, Eloise?" Jasper said, waving his hand. "You died racing or eloping or something stupid like that. What makes you think you have anything to contribute?"

"One can do stupid things and still have wisdom," she sniffed.

"The point I'm trying to make," Tessa interrupted, though why she wanted to ensure they heard her about this uncomfortable topic evaded her, "is that I haven't married precisely because no one offered. Because there wasn't anyone who saw and understood me and my life. If such a person existed, I'm certain they would be worth waiting for."

Jasper blinked at Tessa with an odd little smile. "Well, well. Who would have thought the pragmatic Miss Tessa Preston a romantic?"

She grinned then, catching both Jasper and Eloise by surprise. "Come now, don't misname me. I'm the moody and cross Miss Tessa Preston, thank you. We wouldn't want a line of suitors banging down the door, would we? Certainly not, when we have more important tasks at hand." She waved in Eloise's direction, delighted to see her looking rather put out.

Jasper mirrored Tessa's grin. Unbeknownst to her, he suddenly knew, without a doubt, that he dearly wanted to be at the head of that line of suitors.

Tessa's hands clenched into fists and her grin dropped. "And yet, some things never change," she said, not bothering to conceal the snarl in her tone.

Jasper froze. "What do you mean?"

"You were always staring at me back then, too," she snapped. Jasper stared at her, aghast. "Why am I so offensive? And if you dislike my looks so much, why don't you just look elsewhere?"

Jasper stepped forward, a hand out to touch her arm. He dropped it upon seeing her flinch and frowned. "My dear girl, I didn't stare at you because you are offensive. Quite the contrary."

"Quite the contrary," she echoed. "You're telling me—you have the *gall* to say to my face—that you find me attractive?"

There was no mistaking the heat in his eyes or the embarrassed flush creeping up his neck. "Well, yes."

Tessa glowered at him, unable to contain her fury. "No. I don't accept that. You mocked me and made certain no suitor would consider me worth introducing to their mothers. A woman doesn't forget how it feels to have an attractive man cut her down."

He stepped closer, reminding Tessa that while she was tall, he was taller. She lifted her chin, defiant.

"So you think I'm attractive too?"

Tessa suspected that if she frowned any harder, her eyebrows would forever touch together. "That's not what I said."

"I know. But I think we both know what you meant." Jasper grinned. "Surely this is something you must have noticed." His heated gaze never wavered. "You continue to act as though we're old enemies, but you have always had my admiration."

Eloise scoffed. "He's just saying that to sweeten you up so you'll send me Beyond faster."

Tessa rolled her eyes. "Oh, do shut up, Eloise. No one was talking to you."

Eloise sniffed and faded from view.

Jasper stepped back and pretended as if he didn't hear Tessa's tiny sigh of relief at the increased space between them. He rubbed the back of his hand against his mustache, pensive for a moment. "I am sorry for the things I said back then. They're not worth repeating. You must know I was a stupid boy who said stupid things to reduce the competition. I never meant you to hear them."

Competition. *Competition?* Tessa went slack-jawed. "I thought you pursued Mary. Aren't you heartbroken over Mary choosing Alex?"

Jasper shrugged. "Mary liked me very much, and you disappeared from the country, for heaven's sake." His neck was now an uncomfortable shade of red. "I'm not getting younger, and I want a family, and you've come back."

Tessa fell back as though thoroughly slapped. Jasper wanted a family and thought he had chased away the competition? He thought he was a stupid boy and with no idea how stupid? Dear lord, he thought he was getting a second chance with her, and all this time, she thought he was her enemy. She shook her head, curls tickling her neck. This was shattering all her perceptions. She felt absolutely ill.

"Did the ghosts never tell you? I thought they were always gossiping and bothering mediums."

Tessa's eyes squeezed shut. She swallowed a very unwelcome little sob. After inhaling deeply, she opened her eyes to find Jasper standing very close, seeming very concerned. Concerned on her behalf. Heaven help her, he clearly thought he was telling the truth, that he had been a childish idiot with no idea what he'd done. "I didn't become a medium until that night. I hadn't been close enough to death yet."

She watched the realization bloom in utter mortification across Jasper's face. "Your parents," he whispered.

Tessa's lips corkscrewed. She would not cry. She could not open her emotions after all these years of balling them up and hiding them away. The ghosts had a tendency to take advantage of emotional outbursts, and she wanted nothing more than to stay present in this ridiculous, revealing conversation.

Jasper saved her from having to say anything. She heard him mumble something about pardoning his behavior as he pulled her into his arms. Her chin tucked into his neck, her forehead beside his cheek. The rough bristles of his mustache brushed against her ear. She held her breath. She couldn't remember the last time she had allowed anyone to get so close. He kept his embrace loose—she knew she could break away whenever she wanted to—but curse it, she very much needed this attention. She let her hand cup his elbow, and felt a small thrill as his hands settled in the small of her back, resting above her modest bustle.

"Miss Preston . . . Tessa . . ." Jasper murmured, "you're always helping everyone. Saving everyone. How can I help you?"

That did it. Tessa heard the genuine care in his words, leaned into him, all resolve lost, and cried.

Nineteen

In which one realizes

Tessa wasn't sure who was more appalled that she cried: Eloise, Jasper, or herself. Wrapped in Jasper's solid strength, she decided perhaps she didn't care. So many years of running around Europe with her uncle, solving everyone's ghostly problems, always waking the next day determined to try again with the Marylebone Spiritualist Association . . . Tessa was tired, and worn out, and honestly, rather defeated. She wasn't any closer to solving Eloise's mystery. And deep down, she feared that once she solved the mystery about why Eloise haunted Jasper, he'd no longer need her.

It was a humbling thought to realize that she dawdled at solving the haunting because it kept Jasper close. His eau de cologne enveloped Tessa, and she inhaled deeply, relying on the light and refreshing scent to soothe her overwrought nerves. His surprising insightfulness made her admit she took too much on, and perhaps this haunting was, in fact, beyond her abilities. How was she to instruct Mary, impress the Marylebone Spiritualist Association, and rid Jasper of Eloise? She had thought to use each problem against the others to accomplish all three at once.

Yet here Tessa cried in the arms of the man she had always sworn would never see her cry, never see how he affected her well-being. She accepted his gentle murmurs, his gentle caresses as he wiped her tears with his handkerchief. It was as though his admitting his mistakes, and her realization that he had always meant to pursue her if given the chance, had shattered the deadbolt holding back her feelings.

"You know I don't count as a chaperone," Eloise said, sounding very bored indeed. "And I've half a mind to chase someone in here to find you in this scandalous position."

Tessa froze, her impropriety slapping her in the face. She tried to back away from Jasper, but he kept his embrace firm around her.

"Eloise," Jasper said, his tone as cold as his namesake, "if you don't disappear this instant, you will regret it."

She snorted. "What can you do?"

"I will spend every day with my mother in her déclassé parlor, and make you listen to her complain about how I haven't a wife, and you will never see an ounce of anything entertaining ever again."

Tessa bit her lip to stifle a chuckle.

"Well, if you're going to be that way," Eloise huffed, "then I suppose I could find Dame Hartwell and tease her for a moment or two." She raised her eyebrows. "I advise you, Miss Preston, to mark my words. Gentlemen say many things and mean very few of them." She gestured to her spectral figure. "I wouldn't be in this state had I not followed my emotions and the promises of a handsome man." Eloise hovered closer. "You should know, it doesn't end with death, either."

Tessa frowned, glancing at Jasper to confirm his mutual bemusement. "What can you mean?"

Eloise flitted away, disappearing through the wall with a flirty flick of her wrist. "There are eyes and opportunities everywhere, my dear. You've no idea what you're involved in, and this won't help matters."

Tessa stared at the empty wall, her mouth hanging open. She snapped it shut upon feeling Jasper's fingertip below her chin and looked at him with alarm. His gaze remained tender and concerned for her. He kept his finger beneath her chin, with the barest hint of pressure. Her gaze dropped to his mustache, right as she noticed his gaze dropping to her lips. It had been a very long time since she had kissed anyone; long enough ago that the lad hadn't even a shadow of a mustache.

Scandalous was too tame a word for the heated emotions churning through Tessa's body. Despite Jasper's gentle patience, she felt her embarrassment keenly. He might have spent years pining over her, thinking that he had lost her forever. He might have even tried to convince himself he had loved Mary Trentwood, who couldn't be more different from Tessa . . . but this was all too new.

Tessa had spent years regretting not giving Jasper a piece of her mind when she had the chance. Years of plotting all the ways she could show him his careless words meant nothing to her as she rose amongst the ranks of reputable mediums.

"Thank you for comforting me," she said, carefully extracting herself from his gentle grasp, "but Eloise is right, we shouldn't. We wouldn't want to be discovered and—"

"And what?" Jasper said, his voice low and intense. His blue eyes took on a heated smokiness that made Tessa's heart flip. "And marry? Do you think I wouldn't march right up to your uncle's room and offer for your hand if I didn't think it would scare you off?"

Tessa blinked. "What?"

Jasper ran a hand through his hair with a frustrated little grunt. "I've been doing my best to show you the sort of man I can be, the sort of companion I could be for you. Eloise was the perfect excuse to be near you, Tessa."

She blushed at hearing her name on his lips, but didn't correct him.

"Have you not seen my attempts?" he murmured. "Have I not been clear?"

Tessa bit her lip, reaching for a loose curl at her nape to play with. When she saw the heat flare in his eyes as she flicked the curl this way and that, she dropped it. Heavens, this was what Eloise meant by men making promises they didn't mean. She was still just the exotic little Tessa Preston, protected only by her distracted uncle.

"Don't," Jasper warned, somehow sensing the change in Tessa's posture and expression. "Don't listen to Eloise. She was silly and mean in life, and has used none of the time in her current state to improve herself."

"What did she say that anyone else wouldn't?" Tessa retorted, turning to fluff the pillows on the chaise as an excuse to not have to read every emotion in his clear blue eyes. "We are lucky my uncle didn't happen upon us. Then you would be—"

"Thrilling my mother," he finished for her with a smile.

"I daresay she'd be very unhappy to find her son saddled with someone like me."

"Someone like you," Jasper echoed. "And what are you?"

Tessa flailed her hands. "I hardly need to say it! My dowry is paltry, most of it earned by my own hands by ridding the European gentry of their ghosts. I speak to ghosts! Many nights I'm interrupted by terrible dreams. What husband wants that disruption?"

Jasper stepped closer. "What husband wouldn't want the privilege of comforting you?"

Tessa held up a hand, backing away and shaking her head. "You said it yourself. I'm moody, and cross, and that's not likely to change."

"It's a delightful complement to my sunny disposition, don't you think?"

Too much, this was too much. How could he be so cheerfully obtuse? Tessa inhaled sharply. "What has gotten into you? You're confused, I think. Eager to prove you're no longer that insensitive boy, and I see that. You've been very kind these last weeks—"

"Kind!"

"But I will not allow a ghost to force a man into marrying me!"

Jasper's posture stiffened. "And this is your opinion of my efforts? Selfishly absolving my guilt of chasing you out of London with a stupid comment?"

"That's not what I meant."

"Well, you've confirmed one thing. I'm a very selfish man, indeed," he continued, his bitter tone increasing. "I don't really care about the boy I was, or the girl you were." He took her hand in both of his, running a thumb along her knuckles. "You are an amazing woman, Miss Preston. Whether you ever believe that, I'm willing to wait. I'm willing to help you believe some part of that truth."

Tessa pressed her lips together, hurt that Jasper had reverted from using her given name. She closed her eyes against the earnestness in his tone and expression. It was much easier to find her resolve that way.

"My mother knows about you."

Tessa's eyes flew open. Jasper's small, pained smile cut her deeply.

"When I returned from the country still a bachelor and with a head injury besides, it nearly drove her to madness. She knows you are helping me with Eloise."

"You told her about Eloise? About me?"

"When I came home from our Serpentine debacle, it was difficult to explain away why I was sopping wet in the middle of a sunny day." Jasper huffed, and his self-consciousness was actually rather adorable. "She'd very much like to meet you."

Tessa mulled over the idea that a mother wanted to meet her. A novel experience. Jasper took her silence as permission to step closer again, and she closed her eyes, trying not to react to his warmth and cologne. She would forever associate that scent with safety now. Curse it.

"Am I really so disappointing?" Jasper said, shoving his hands into his pockets.

"Mr. Steele," Tessa said, a little exasperated, "you've just put together that I left London because of my Sense erupting after my parents' death, you've made me cry, and you've held me in your arms. And you've announced that you wouldn't mind being my husband, after denouncing me as moody and cross." She pulled the peplum hem of her bodice down, needing to do something with her hands. "Surely you can see how confusing this is. I've always seen you as an adversary, not someone to love."

He tilted his head. "Always?"

Tessa flushed and couldn't meet his eyes.

Jasper smiled, relaxing his hunched shoulders. "Thank you for that, at least. Well, I suppose you're right. I've thrown all of this at you with no time to recover. Why don't we settle on a date to meet my mother a week or two from now? I daresay she will disabuse you of any charlatan behavior on my part and share all my most embarrassing stories for your entertainment." He leaned forward, his customary twinkle and grin returning.

"Well, if you can guarantee embarrassing stories . . ." Tessa smiled, and allowed herself a moment to bask in the warmth of Jasper's gaze.

They might have continued smiling at one another for a disconcerting amount of time, had the sound of a crash and Mary's shriek not caused them both to rush from the room.

TWENTY

IN WHICH ONE POSSESSES

JUST AS JASPER AND Tessa entered the drawing room, Eloise took her advantage of Mary's stuttering and sputtering. She stood there, dripping with tea, Eloise clearly having tossed the teapot over her head in a desperate attempt to entertain herself.

Eloise smirked at her audience, raising a finger to her lips as she tiptoed closer to Mary, who was too busy wiping to notice.

Tessa raised her hand in warning, but it was too late. Eloise hugged Mary, disappearing into her with a giggle.

Mary froze mid-sputter. Her eyes widened and her body shuddered as she looked at Tessa for help.

"Eloise," Tessa snapped, "get out of Mary right this instant."

Closing her eyes, Mary rolled her head from side to side with a long sigh, as if having woken from a deep nap. "No, I think not," she said, sounding like Eloise. She opened her eyes with a grin. "Oh, this is too delicious. Let's have some fun, shall we?"

Eloise sped Mary from the room, leaving Tessa no choice but to follow her to the library, where Hartwell sat reading the morning paper. He stood at the sight of everyone's clamoring entrance, immediately wary.

"Good morning, dear," Eloise said, affecting Mary's manner of speaking.

Hartwell frowned, glancing from Mary to Tessa. "Is it a good morning?"

"I daresay it is now that I've seen you," Eloise said, flipping her hand as she sauntered into the room. "Tessa's training has me up at all odd hours. I hardly know what time it is anymore."

Hartwell rubbed his scar, squinting at Mary. "Are you feeling quite alright?"

Eloise spun Mary on her heel with an enigmatic smile. "I shall be in a moment."

As everyone puzzled over her statement, Eloise grabbed Jasper by his lapels and pulled him into a fervent kiss.

"Mary! What are you doing?" Hartwell cried.

Tessa stopped breathing. Unable to think, her stomach fell to the floor as Mary's fingers slid into Jasper's hair. Her throat closed at the sound of his startled squeak, alerting everyone to when Mary's tongue slid into his mouth.

The sound of Eloise's pleased little moan jolted Tessa and Hartwell into action.

Tessa grabbed Jasper by the waist, using all her body weight to yank him away from Eloise. "You spiteful little—" she muttered when Eloise wouldn't let go. "Release him at once, you . . . you light-skirt!"

Hartwell grabbed Mary's hands, prying them from Jasper's head. He wrapped his arms around Mary, spinning her away. The abrupt release caused Jasper to fall back, landing with Tessa on the floor.

"What on earth are you doing?" Hartwell gasped, pinning Mary's arms to her sides. Mary cackled with Eloise's laugh, and Hartwell froze.

Jasper and Tessa scrambled away from one another, or rather, he scrambled off Tessa as she kicked her skirts out of the way and rolled to sitting. She brushed her lap as if she fully intended to sit on the floor, and accepted Jasper's hand, calmly ignoring his red cheeks.

Eloise frowned with Mary's mouth. "Why didn't that work?"

Jasper touched his lips, his complexion so red it was painful to see. "Eloise, could you please desist from grabbing me in such a manner? It's distressing that I can't resist your strength."

"She is surprisingly strong for a ghost," Tessa mused.

Hartwell dropped his hands, leaping back from Mary's body. "Eloise? What are y— Are you *possessing* Mary?"

Tessa rubbed her forehead as Hartwell and Jasper turned to her for an explanation. "Eloise, were you trying to make your way to Beyond by kissing Mr. Steele?"

Eloise placed Mary's hands on her hips and popped a hip to the side. "Well, it stands to reason. I died while trying to get married. I thought perhaps if I kissed my *new* fiancé, then I could go back and be done with the lot of you ridiculous fools. You won't listen to me anyway, so why should I keep trying to protect you?" She winked at Jasper. "You'd be welcome to join me. It's quite a party, Beyond."

"I am not your fiancé," Jasper ground out.

Tessa blinked at the idea that Eloise thought she had been protecting them all this time. And from what? Clearly, this was another ploy to keep their attention, though Tessa couldn't decipher the purpose.

"Eloise," Tessa said, using the voice that, if ghosts had skin, would have made their skin crawl. "Enough is enough."

When even that did nothing to persuade Eloise, Tessa's temper snapped. She spun from the room, rushing upstairs to grab the walking cane from her uncle's room. She returned, as breathless as she was furious, pointing it at Mary's body. Tessa's hand shook as she struggled to control the rage sweeping over her.

Just because Tessa couldn't bring herself to kiss Jasper, didn't mean she wanted to see other women, especially other women formerly endorsed by his mother, doing it.

Mary's smile dropped as Eloise realized what Tessa was pointing with. "What are you doing? Don't overreact. I'm just being silly."

As Tessa began the short incantation to banish Eloise to Beyond for perpetuity, Mary rushed at her.

"You can't! You don't know what you're doing! He needs me. *You* need me!" Eloise shrieked, grabbing the cane.

Tessa shook her head, her voice barely above a whisper even as Eloise/Mary wrestled with the cane. Expertly flicking her wrist, Tessa knocked her off-balance. Tessa held the stick against Mary's throat. Eloise shrieked again, this time trying to escape from Mary's body.

Now that the spell had begun, Eloise was stuck. Tears sprung to Mary's eyes, and Tessa saw Eloise in them. "I'm sorry, truly I am!" Eloise wailed. "I was just having some fun. You don't understand what you're doing. You've no idea what you're exposing yourself to. I've been protecting you!"

Tessa spoke the last word of the spell. The effects, never consistent, took hold of Eloise and Mary. The spell threw Eloise across the room rather than sucking her down through the floor. Mary shuddered and gasped as though doused with ice water. Hartwell wrapped his arms around Mary, dragging her to the opposite corner from Eloise's noisy sobs.

Tessa advanced on Eloise, who was already fading in the weak sunlight streaming between the thick brocade curtains.

Eloise, shoulders slumped, locked eyes with Jasper. "We had fun, didn't we?"

"Did we?" he said.

"Well. My haunting was nothing compared to what's coming," Eloise said glumly. She waved at Tessa, her hand now almost completely transparent. "Do give *him* my best regards. I don't envy your next adventure."

"Who?" Tessa asked, her voice commanding Eloise to stay long enough to answer.

Eloise's mouth worked, and she stomped her foot when she could not get the words out. Finally, she muttered, "The one your mother warned you about."

And with that, Eloise turned, her chin lifted as she faded into the sunlight with all the grace and hauteur of someone treating eviction as a choice.

Faintly, as though coming from a great distance, Tessa heard a deep, sinister chuckle accompanied by a whisper. "Oh, that weren't a good idea, my pet . . ."

The voice was musical, lilting, and male. It spoke of grim promises that Tessa knew she never wanted fulfilled. She clutched the cane close, frozen in place as she wondered anew just what Eloise thought she protected them from.

If this ghost—likely a poltergeist—could control one as strong-willed as Eloise, what on earth was Tessa to do?

The room's occupants blinked at one another before settling on Tessa's still form. Jasper was the first to break the silence.

"Are you telling me you could have done that this entire time?" he exploded.

Tessa turned a cool, assessing gaze on him. Clearly neither he nor the others had heard the poltergeist's warning, and did not know they now faced a larger problem. "Well, yes."

Jasper rubbed both hands up and down his face. "Tessa, I could just—! After everything I admitted, and everything I've suffered with Eloise's attention . . . You're telling me you could have taken care of her *weeks* ago?"

"As you know," Tessa murmured, "Dame Hartwell hired me to train Mary as a medium. Eloise's spirit was strong and stubborn, without being harmful. It was a perfect opportunity."

"A perfect opportunity," Jasper barked, lurching forward, "at my expense. Have you been laughing at me all this time?"

Tessa tapped the walking cane on the floor. "Of course not."

The remaining spirits in the vicinity heard Tessa's temper in the tapping cane and fled the house, lest she also banish them against their wills.

"Certainly puts our conversation into a different light," he muttered.

Mary and Hartwell's heads swiveled between Jasper and Tessa. They shared a concerned look and agreed, in the silent manner of a concordant couple, to not interrupt this quarrel.

"What's done is done." Tessa frowned at the spot Eloise had so recently inhabited, in corporeal absentia. She sighed. "Did you not hear Eloise's warning? One should, I suppose, always remember that upon removing one obstacle, it paves a path for another, scarier hurdle to contend with."

Jasper wiped his hand across his eyes. "My dearest Miss Preston, I've laid myself bare to you, yet you continue to speak in riddles."

Mary's hand came to her mouth and Hartwell was quick to shush her.

Tessa reddened as she shifted her weight, holding the cane behind her skirts. "And I've told you I need time. I can't respond so quickly."

"Can't, or won't?"

"Eloise is gone. Now we shall see."

"See what?" Jasper ground out. "What evidence are you seeking? What would convince you of my feelings?"

Tessa hadn't an answer for that, and so remained silent.

Jasper's jaw worked, his gaze jumping to Mary and Hartwell's engrossed expressions. He stepped back from Tessa, his expression smoothing. "As you say," he said, adjusting his cufflinks, "Eloise is gone, and we've solved my problems. Thank you for your services. Your uncle may bill me at his earliest convenience."

Tessa blinked, stunned by Jasper's cold demeanor.

"Good day, Miss Preston. Hartwell, I'll see you in the office. Mary, you look awful, dear. I hope you'll get some rest if Miss Preston will allow it!" Jasper straightened his lapels, marching out of the drawing room.

"Oh, but you can't leave," Tessa said, following him.

Hartwell and Mary looked at one another with small, knowing smiles and followed.

"The hell I can't," Jasper retorted. He slammed his hat onto his head. His eyes were a stormy blue, and Tessa blinked, surprised at the stuttering effect it had on her heart. She found, much to her surprise, that she rather liked him when he was absolutely furious.

But then, when had there been a moment recently where she had *disliked* him?

"Well, I wouldn't advise it, at least," Tessa said, mildly, to belie her traitorous heart. "It seems Eloise thought she was protecting you from someone—some*thing*."

"What utter nonsense," Jasper said. "She said those things to stop you from sending her Beyond. Don't be so gullible."

"Gullible!" Tessa swallowed her next heated words, for she knew she would regret them.

"Alright, let's say she was telling the truth," Jasper hissed. "What is this about 'the one your mother warned you about'? Sounds an awful lot like an old paramour. Tsk-tsk, Miss Preston, you shouldn't mix business with pleasure."

Tessa decided she would say the words after all. "You're one to talk, Mr. Steele." At his shuttered expression, she knew retreating to his formal name stung as much as it had for her. Who knew when she would be content enough to call him Archie again? "I find it highly irregular that you spend so much time with a woman who rejected you. Of course, I mean no offense, Mary. I'm trying to make out Mr. Steele's changeable character."

"Oh, none taken," Mary assured Tessa, leaning heavily into Hartwell as they stood in the doorway. "It's honestly something I've wondered about myself. Jasper was the first to reject me, you know. But then he showed up at my house, and it wasn't until he realized my father haunted me that his feelings became of . . . a brotherly sort."

Hartwell grinned. "Now that Eloise has haunted him, perhaps Jasper visits because now he realizes how shallow he was, and wishes to redeem himself? Don't tell me you're planning to whisk Mary away from me."

Jasper's face turned the most appalling colors as everyone teased him. "Redeem myself—whisk her away—what a ridiculous notion!"

"The sight of you kissing my fiancée did put a damper on my trust, old boy," Hartwell said, his tone sardonic.

"I was kissed by your *possessed* fiancée, might I remind you!" Jasper snapped. "I would have thought Mary immune to such an event, were she actually practicing at her Sense?"

"The fact remains that Eloise has warned us," Tessa interrupted, having no time for this frivolity with her emotions still running high. She brushed her fingers against Jasper's arm and willed herself not to jump at the spark that flew between them. She cleared her throat. "I don't think you should leave our sight."

Jasper rounded on her and in his raging state, seemed much taller. She held her ground as Jasper towered over her. A small squeak escaped as he leaned in close.

"Our sight, or yours, *Miss Preston*? Now that I know you'll use me for your purposes, what other subterfuge can I expect?"

Tessa held her breath and bit the inside of her cheek, fighting the rising irritation at his insistence on using her formal name. She told herself to stop looking at his lips.

Mary stepped forward, placing a hand on his trembling arm. "She was only trying to help me."

"I don't see how that can be, if what Dame Hartwell says is true," Jasper said, shaking Mary's hand away. "The longer you're around Miss Preston, the more likely the ghosts will flock to you. Isn't that so? If *Miss Preston* is truly an amplifier, and you're as powerful as she says you are, how does being in her presence help you?"

"She's teaching me to redirect the surges," Mary murmured, though her expression showed a shadow of doubt.

"And how have you improved in your lessons?" Jasper retorted, retreating to the door. Tessa felt the loss of his infuriated heat keenly.

"I don't have headaches anymore," Mary countered. "And you're being ungrateful. You came to us to relieve you of Eloise, and so we have. You ought to thank Tessa!"

Jasper turned once more to Tessa, and she froze under the coolness of his gaze. "Well. Miss Trentwood has spoken, and who am I to correct her? No, I won't thank a favor that came late and with stipulations. I shall bid you a good day."

As he stalked out the door, Mary called out, "But we will see you at the wedding, won't we?"

"I said *good day!*"

Tessa frowned at Jasper's receding back, worrying the loose end of a fingernail. "I don't like this."

Hartwell chuckled. "He really is so serious sometimes. Never fear, Miss Preston, he'll be back before you know it."

"He did seem rather angry," Mary mused.

"Sleep deprivation," Hartwell said with a wave of his hand. "Eloise kept him up at all hours, you know, just absolutely talking his ear off. You wait a week—he'll be back and we'll all be jolly again."

TWENTY-ONE

IN WHICH ONE SULKS

JASPER WAS NOT BACK within the week.

Tessa did her best not to unravel with anxiety.

Her anxiety had nothing to do with the spirits. The ghosts had cleared from Hartwell House. She suspected they very much disliked how her temper seemed to be the trigger for exorcism, rather than anyone actually *deserving* such treatment.

No, Tessa's anxiety had to do with her own behavior and riotous emotions, and the lack of Jasper's steadying presence to ground her. Over the years, Tessa had noticed that her grief had all the markings of rage. She often felt an almost constant thrum of anger layered atop the deep, unbearable sadness she felt at the loss of her parents and previously uncomplicated life. Her life before the spirits realized she could see them. Before the spirits realized they could touch her, possess her, even.

Angry mourning, however, was not en vogue. The dear queen's quiet and unfailing sadness permeated everything in this Victorian era. And so Tessa strove to bury her irritability under a pleasant, emotionless facade.

The remaining weeks until Hartwell and Mary's wedding flew by without incident, despite Tessa's increasing sense of foreboding. Even when the spirits began milling about the house again, they seemed subdued by Eloise's departure.

The sidelong accusatory glances Tessa endured from the spirits, most especially from their erstwhile actor in Elizabethan clothing, made her want to rip something to pieces. It wasn't Tessa's fault she had the Sense, or that she could do what she did. One might as well blame a bee for having a stinger.

Tessa could admit to herself she had acted rashly, which was not like her. It took her still a few days more to admit the emotion causing her to behave as she had: jealousy.

While Mary and Hartwell had teased Jasper as friends, their friendship was based on both men once caring for Mary. How deeply remained a question for Tessa, but when she saw Mary and Jasper kissing, and so passionately . . .

Even weeks later, the back of Tessa's neck grew hot and she had trouble swallowing.

It didn't help that Jasper was true to his word and stayed away from Hartwell House. Tessa had not realized how she had looked forward to his smiles over the dinner table. Or how he rolled his eyes at her over something silly Eloise had said. Jasper was the only one to remark upon her hair. While it felt vain, it was rather nice for someone to notice, for her hair took some effort.

Tessa realized, with a bodily grimace, that she felt desired in Jasper's presence, clever even, and rather pretty besides. She was reminded of a Jane Austen quotation: "Give me an occupation or I shall run mad."

With no ghosts to occupy their time, Mary dragged Tessa to the modiste to comment on the shape of her sleeves, and the style of her sweeping overskirt, and the size of her bustle. No one spoke of Eloise's warning, or Eloise's terrified and bitter expression when she realized Tessa had spoken too much of the spell and she could not escape her banishment. No, everyone pointed their energies at the impending joyous wedding.

It was both heartening—and a little discouraging—to witness a rested and rather giggly Mary.

Suddenly there were *looks* across the room between Mary and Hartwell, and the added disgrace of Dame Hartwell and Sir

Hubert grinning at the community secret of lovers having the energy to flirt again.

Meanwhile, Tessa stuck her fingers with badly done embroidery, or pretended to lose herself in a book, anything to distract herself from the fact that she had no one with whom to share a knowing, amused look, and it was all her fault.

Well, not entirely her fault. How dare Jasper admit to having feelings for her, and in that way? Could they not have gone on as they had, with her assuming he was a cad slowly redeeming himself into a tenuous friendship? Why had he let loose these bottled emotions that churned within her, reminding Tessa time and again when an acquaintance of Hartwell's stopped by, that it wouldn't be Jasper to ease her discomfort?

Tessa felt Jasper's absence keenly, especially with Mary and Hartwell ensconcing themselves in the library for moments at a time, coming back flushed and bright-eyed. She reminded herself, multiple times daily, that she was a professional, intent on establishing herself as a preeminent medium in the neighborhood and with the Marylebone Spiritualist Association.

With her uncle making headway with his book, Tessa was certain they could do very well for themselves, if only the Marylebone Spiritualist Association could stop sneering down their skinny noses at her. She redoubled her efforts to write a stellar application, recounting details of Eloise's exorcism and Mary's continued improvements as evidence she ought to receive admission.

Despite Tessa thinking her disappointment and ennui were subtle, even the self-absorbed lovebirds could tell she missed Jasper. Tessa threw herself into helping her uncle's research, reading accounts of hauntings and mediums, providing notes to his manuscript based on her own experiences. She hardly smiled anymore and woke with unnerving dark circles under her eyes. It was a reversion to the Tessa who had entered Hartwell House months ago. The ghostly quiet was not soothing. She saw it as the calm before a storm of indeterminable size, and a gnawing sensation had grown in the pit of her stomach.

Sir Hubert was about ready to drag Jasper back if it would break a smile across his niece's proud face, and he said as much one morning at the breakfast table before Tessa joined them.

"Let me speak with her," Mary urged. "We have the wedding in a couple of weeks. She can't say no to me, I'm the bride."

Sir Hubert's brows rose at this, saying Tessa had never, in the history of him knowing her, had difficulty in saying no to anything. But he was at his wit's end, and willing for help of any sort, from any quarter.

What no one seemed to realize, partly because Tessa was allowing everyone to believe otherwise, was that with no ghosts, she was also anxious about her placement in the house. Despite the informality, Dame Hartwell had hired her, not invited her as a family friend. Without the chief aspect of her employment to keep her relevant, Tessa had to assume Dame Hartwell, or even Mary, as the soon-to-be mistress of the house, might send her off.

Who needed a medium underfoot when newlyweds were establishing their household?

And so Tessa sat in the little courtyard between their house and the one next door, reading the classifieds quietly when a shadow loomed over her. Tessa started, thinking perhaps this was finally the specter Eloise had warned about. When she found instead Mary smiling at her, she relaxed, but only just.

Mary's smile was suspect. She wanted something. "Will you walk with me?"

Tessa stood, tucking her newspaper while Mary looped their arms together. They passed an amiable, quiet time together, the short gravel path allowing them to circle the courtyard twice with little effort until Mary spoke again.

"I must admit to an ulterior motive, Tessa, in seeking you out here."

Tessa stiffened, but maintained a pace with Mary. This was it. After the impulsive dismissal of Eloise, and no ghosts bothering them besides, Mary intended to let her off gently. Tessa was not one to be dismissed, so she interrupted. "I understand you completely."

"You do?"

"Yes, I shall resign and vacate immediately. I wish you the best of luck. I doubt the ghosts will return, though I'm certain the Marylebone Spiritualist Association, or any other such organization, could easily suggest a replacement if that's the case."

"Replacement!" Mary stopped, grabbing Tessa's other arm and turning so they faced one another. "I'm asking you to stand with me at my wedding. Heavens, I'm not dismissing you."

Tessa frowned. "But I sent Eloise Beyond."

"Just as you promised," Mary said.

"And Arch—Mr. Steele hasn't set foot here since," Tessa said. "I've ruined your wedding by chasing off the man who was to stand with Hartwell."

"If that's all!" Mary said. "You're practically family with the Hartwells and have helped me so much with the dame, who adores you. I haven't any family of my own, save dearest Pomeroy, and as you know, I couldn't possibly ask him, being my butler and all."

"But will Archie stand with Hartwell if I'm there?"

Mary waved her hand. "Alex is working on that. You must admit, he has a way of getting others around to his thinking. Even Jasper."

Tessa's begrudging nod made Mary's eyes brighten. Tessa couldn't help but think whatever Hartwell's influence was over others, it paled to Mary's clever machinations.

"You will join me?"

"Yes." Tessa hoped they wouldn't all regret it.

Tessa practically chafed at the idea of seeing Jasper again, not knowing his reaction. Would he glower and make snide remarks? Refuse to acknowledge her presence? Or worse, had he taken these last weeks to forgive her? If he appeared at the wedding ready with a smile and a special sidelong glance for her, Tessa knew it would be her undoing.

Mary clapped her hands in a passable imitation of Dame Hartwell. "How very excellent. We shall commission a new dress for you for the occasion, as my thanks."

"You needn't," Tessa protested.

"Nonsense. The benefit of being a spinster is I can spend my inheritance as I so choose. And with that lovely law that's passed, it's mine even after marrying." Mary looped her arm around Tessa's waist to resume their little promenade. "Think of it as my sincere thanks, both for teaching me, standing with me, and ridding us of Eloise and those other ghosts."

Tessa swallowed her objections. "Thank you."

Mary chuckled. "Let's save your thanks for when we head to the modiste. Our tight timeline limits us to their premade stock."

"As long as I can swing my arms, I'm certain whatever they offer will be delightful."

None of the dresses had sleeves loose enough to please Tessa, and she was panicking.

"You look as lovely as a painting." Mary admired Tessa from her seat, clearly having fun clothing her friend in the latest styles.

Unfortunately, the latest styles meant constricting bodices with tight sleeves.

"How am I to brandish my cane like this?" Tessa showed how she couldn't lift her hands much further than her elbow.

"Why would you need your cane on my wedding day?" Mary countered, nodding at the modiste to loosen the sleeves.

Tessa heaved a sigh as the fabric released and she could lift her arms overhead, as any self-respecting medium ought to. "I certainly hope I won't need it, but—"

"One can never be too prepared," Mary finished for her. "Very well then. What do you suggest I learn in the meantime if something occurs?"

Tessa studied Mary in the mirror, her mind whirring. "I have wondered why the spirits—" She paused, seeing the raised eyebrows of her seamstress.

The seamstress sighed, muttering about ribbon as she left to give them privacy.

Tessa looked at Mary in the mirror. "I've wondered why our *friends* do not approach you the way they do me. Speak to you, yes, but rarely ever touch unless to possess outright."

"Is that a meaningful distinction? I thought it was their method of ensuring I always have a headache."

Tessa inclined her head. "I hadn't thought so, but my uncle has a theory about different types and uses of Sense."

The modiste returned. Tessa bit her lip. With the seamstress as their audience, it was uncomfortable speaking freely about ghosts, the Beyond, and her Sense. Tessa brainstormed how to explain her thoughts in a way to make it appear they discussed philosophy, rather than ghosts.

Better assumed a bluestocking than mad. Despite Spiritualism's popularity in London, many thought the entire thing American nonsense.

"Should we encounter our *friends* on your wedding day and they're not pleased, do what is instinctual. Stop thinking, stop fighting. Do what feels natural and I think we will learn a great deal."

Mary pondered this and accepted this instruction with a slow nod. "I doubt I shall be of a mind to do anything else. I'm already a walking knot of emotions thinking how my parents won't be there." The modiste left the room again. "Sometimes I think I should have waited a few more months before saying farewell to my father's ghost."

Tessa pressed her lips together, understanding all too well.

TWENTY-TWO

IN WHICH ONE MOPES, GALLANTLY

JASPER STARTLED AWAKE TO find the sun past midday, and after a moment of panic, fell back into his rumpled sheets, realizing it was the weekend and no one expected him anywhere.

It was a bitter pill to swallow, knowing no one expected him. Jasper draped his arm over his eyes and bit back a groan, embarrassed by his declarations and Tessa's cool reaction. He now realized, weeks later, the error of his excitement in thinking they had understood each other.

He rolled onto his stomach, hugging his pillow close. He couldn't fathom that Tessa had held him in contempt all these years. And here he had pined after what might have been. And all because of one errant comment!

Of course, he was kidding himself; he had seen his companions change when he had made that flippant remark all those years ago and had congratulated himself over it. He had cleared the playing field with hardly any effort. His timing couldn't have been worse. Jasper let his face sink into the pillow.

A timid knock at his door caused him to flip over. He grabbed his housecoat from the chair beside his bed as his mother entered with a tray of coffee and associated breakfast items.

"You needn't do that," he said, frowning.

"Do what? Take care of my son?" She settled the tray and handed him the steaming cup.

"No, do servants' work." He sighed, clutching the coffee cup. The sharp, hurt look that flitted across his mother's face caused him to drop his gaze. He sipped. "I took a job so you could afford the life you deserve. I don't like to see you worrying over me."

Mrs. Steele huffed, sitting back with an annoyed, "Well, I like that! You've stumbled around this house an exhausted shadow of yourself, and I'm not allowed to worry over you?"

Jasper hunched over his coffee. He froze when his mother leaned forward to pat his knee.

"Did she not take it well?"

"I don't know what you're talking about," he said archly. He gulped down more coffee and shoved buttered toast into his mouth to avoid having to say more.

"The one who's helping you with the ghost." Mrs. Steele squinted at him. "I assume you declared yourself?"

"Of course not," he sputtered.

"But you've been coming home for lunch every day, and dinner besides. I thought perhaps you'd had a spat?"

Jasper's neck grew warm. "She exorcised the ghost, finally."

Mrs. Steele raised a single eyebrow and took his hand with both of hers. "No wonder you've been sleeping so deeply. My darling, you've had sunken eyes and gaunt cheeks, and you've been so irritable! I was worried this was all the doing of another romance gone wrong. I'm so glad it was only that ghost, and you're now rid of her."

Jasper's smile was tight. "I am."

He accepted a kiss on the cheek and an admonishment not to waste the day. After his mother left, he put aside the coffee and crawled under his blankets, wanting only to mope, in as gallant a manner as one might, over his concerns that he had ruined his chances with Tessa forever.

Mrs. Steele, while very glad to have her son back, was also rather concerned. He didn't rush off anywhere with weak excuses, a bounce in his step, and an amused glint in his eye. No one called on him, either.

Another week passed with Jasper resuming his regular work hours, returning for lunch and dinner. They spent quiet evenings together reading. Sometimes she picked up her needlepoint and would catch him staring off at nothing.

By the third week of this nonsense, Mrs. Steele was ready to call on Alexander Hartwell and ask just what happened to her son. He anticipated her, however, and came home with Jasper for lunch one day.

While Jasper busied himself with his hat and gloves, his mother took Hartwell aside to mutter something about him being lovesick.

"Oh yes, madam, daresay he is," Hartwell agreed, not bothering to keep his voice *en sotto*. "I've a similar case on my end of the neighborhood, and she is equally annoying with her sighs and morose looks."

Jasper rounded on them, eyes narrow. "Are you making fun of me?"

"Making fun, I should think not," Mrs. Steele protested as she led them to the dining room. "I'm glad to hear Miss Preston is as miserable as you are. It wouldn't be very sporting if she were anything but."

Jasper glared at Hartwell, who very cheerfully accepted a generous helping of cold cuts and seasonal vegetables on his plate. "How can you eat at a time like this?" Jasper hissed. "You're embarrassing me."

"I've no reason to be embarrassed," Hartwell said, picking up a fork. "I'm about to be married, and the friend I asked to stand with me on the day is hiding away, nursing I don't know what, rather than helping me select a new suit—which we both know, I asked you to stand with me for that express reason! You're putting a damper on what's meant to be the happiest season of my life."

Mrs. Steele blinked at Hartwell after this speech and waited for her son to speak.

"You know very well what suits look best," Jasper grumbled, leaning over his plate and poking at an insipid strawberry.

"Now this I cannot tolerate!" his mother cried. "You always have an opinion over clothing. What *is* the matter with you?"

"Likely the same thing that's the matter with Miss Preston," Hartwell said. He became serious for a moment. "She is a terrible liar and thinks we all don't know how she would rather our party have at least one more present."

Jasper scoffed. "At least one more . . . Well, she had two regularly until she revealed her temper and banished Eloise like that. Were you aware she could have done that the first day, instead of dragging it out for almost three months?"

Hartwell smirked. "I thought you didn't mind how long it was taking."

Jasper colored under his mother's watchful gaze. "I didn't until I realized she was using Eloise to antagonize me."

Hartwell and Mrs. Steele cried foul at this, but Jasper would not be dissuaded.

"She said so herself. Tessa's only thought ill of me for years and had no idea I had any intentions toward her. She thought we were reluctant enemies working together to solve a problem." Jasper waved his fork at Hartwell, and his mother winced at his manners. "You saw how she studied Eloise, not for her status, but for those mysterious gray ribbons that she swore meant Eloise was connected to something. I hardly would have thought her jealous except for how she reacted when Eloise kissed me—"

"Pardon me," Mrs. Steele said faintly, "but I do believe I'm missing some key information. Who kissed you?"

"Miss Carterprice did," Jasper ground out, "when she possessed Miss Trentwood."

"Miss Carterprice possessed Miss Trentwood so she might kiss you, and Miss Preston witnessed this?"

"Unfortunately," Jasper said.

"And then she . . . sent Miss Carterprice . . . away?" Upon receiving confirmation, Mrs. Steele studied Hartwell. "And you've no hard feelings for your fiancée kissing my son, possessed or otherwise?"

Hartwell leaned forward, taking her hand. "Depend upon it, madam, I've no fears there. My dear Mary and I teased your son mercilessly about it, and he left in high dudgeon. It's why I've come to luncheon with you, to confirm you also see Jasper is wasting his time nursing unnecessary wounds when there's a woman who very much misses him and regrets her rash actions."

"Tessa Preston isn't one to regret anything. It was just like her to deal with Eloise so swiftly once she decided," Jasper snapped. "And while I can forgive her that, I can't forgive her total dismissal of my feelings on the matter."

"But does she regret refusing my son?" Mrs. Steele asked, ignoring her son's rant.

"Refuse . . . ?" Hartwell's voice faded as he looked at Jasper anew. "Did you offer to marry Miss Preston?"

"Not in so many words," Jasper said. A blush spread across his neck and cheeks. "Eloise was teasing Tessa as she studied something about some ribbons trailing off Eloise, and I might have taken advantage of Tessa's lighter mood, and probably stepped too close. She was nervous, saying someone might see us."

"You might have . . . and probably . . . ?" his mother echoed, encouraging. "And then?"

"And then I might have said I wouldn't mind speaking with her uncle."

Mrs. Steele dropped her fork with a clatter. "Jasper!"

Hartwell held back his laughter for the briefest moment. "And here I thought I was a terrible romantic. Nothing like the threat of ruination to bring marriage to a woman's mind."

Jasper leaned back in his chair and crossed his arms over his chest, saying over Hartwell's laughter, "I said I wanted her to meet my mother," as if that were some defense.

Mrs. Steele rubbed her temples, muttering about how she knew she was a better mother than this, and clearly she would never become a grandmother. Hartwell burst into laughter anew, wiping tears from his eyes as Jasper sank further into his seat.

"And what of her ominous warning?" Jasper hissed. "I don't see that anything has come of that, either. Was it another manipulation?"

This sobered Hartwell alarmingly well. "Must admit, Miss Preston has been a step away from hysterics since you left, owing to her concern and worry. Apparently—and I learned this from my dear Mary only yesterday—Miss Preston heard a voice we did not. Miss Preston's theory is this spirit controlled Eloise. With her banishment, there's nothing standing between us and this unknown threat."

Jasper straightened at this. "Well . . . I'm glad to hear she didn't make that up."

"Or, she's now working her manipulation through Mary and myself. You may never know." Hartwell sipped his drink.

"Regardless, you must know Tessa wants you back. We can all see it."

Jasper straightened further still, his frown indicating to his mother and Hartwell that a decision was made.

"This isn't the first time that *Miss Preston*,"—he was careful to emphasize his use of her proper name, and it backfired at the sight of their grins—"has been attacked after relaxing her guard. And I suppose I'm the one guilty of encouraging such relaxation."

Hartwell snickered. Mrs. Steele glared at him, even though she couldn't stop a small smile escaping.

"So then, you'll stop being a nincompoop and stand at my wedding?"

"I will, if only to prove to Miss Preston that she cannot scare *me* away." There was a glint in Jasper's eye, and he dug into his breakfast with an energy most appalling.

Hartwell faltered. "Err, that's the spirit?"

Mrs. Steele raised her eyes to the ceiling, musing how children do so test one's patience.

Twenty-Three

In Which a Wedding Occurs

Tessa paid little attention to the ceremony. Her duties as maid of honor kept her far too busy—Mary's happiness was a beacon and Tessa had her hands full, shielding Mary from the crowd of ghosts descending upon the house. That, and Tessa had a difficult time not staring at Jasper. He was a vision in his gray waistcoat and dark suit. She couldn't countenance the relief that washed over her when he stepped jauntily into the house, not a hair harmed on his body.

Indeed, his blond hair gleamed in the afternoon sunlight, and his mustache danced atop his lips as he joked with Hartwell. He caught Tessa looking at him several times and had the audacity to wink.

Really! No word for weeks, and Jasper had the nerve to wink at Tessa as if she hadn't lain awake wondering what awful spirit Eloise had tried to warn them about. Wondering why a spirit would be after Jasper, of all people. Wondering why he had been furious about Eloise's departure and having the sinking feeling chivalry hadn't pushed him to talk about speaking with her uncle, but true feelings of affection.

Ah—there was that wink again. Tessa dropped her gaze to the little posy of flowers in her hand, feeling the back of her neck grow hot.

Finally, Mary and Hartwell spoke their words of marriage and shared a polite, if enthusiastic, kiss. Tessa's embarrassment sent her looking for something else to study, and to her mortification, she found Jasper's blue eyes blazing at her.

The intensity of his expression chased Tessa from the room for air as soon as permissible.

Jasper found her hiding, rather ineffectively, in the ballroom. They had set everything up the night before, and so the room was empty for their awkward reunion. Tessa pretended to admire the flowers strewn in artful garlands, feeling the nearness of Jasper all the while.

"I wasn't sure you would attend," she said, breaking the silence.

Jasper thumbed a leaf of the garland just above Tessa's head. He looked down at her, his eyes bright with unspoken laughter. "He's an excellent barrister. Argued me right into my suit before I knew which way was up, smiling the entire time."

They smiled at one another, their camaraderie reestablished with a hint of shy hesitation.

"Why did you stay away?" Tessa turned to stare out into the courtyard as dusk fell, holding her arms close as she felt him venture near.

"Don't tell me you've missed me," Jasper said. His murmur tickled a curl behind her ear.

"With everyone focused on the wedding, there was hardly anyone to speak to, and my uncle has become annoying and taciturn since I sent Eloise away. He's very annoyed."

Tessa tried to keep her tone neutral, but she knew she sounded defensive and sharp. She could feel him standing so very close behind her. It was unsettling, in the most delicious manner. Not that she would be so crass as to admit all that, but neither did she pull away. Tessa swallowed, her mouth suddenly dry.

"I hardly knew what to think, so I stayed away."

"For weeks?"

"I suppose I'm a slow thinker."

"Yes, well. You've had us worried about Eloise's warning, thinking some spirit could have harmed you and I—we might not have had any idea."

"I'm sure my mother would have sent word to Hartwell, him being my employer and all."

Tessa stiffened. "How can you joke at a time like this?" She spun around right into his chest with a little yelp. Her hands flew to his lapels. She didn't dare look up at him.

"Gaiety at a wedding, whatever shall they think of next?"

She felt, more than heard, Jasper's rumbling laughter in his chest. Her irritation bloomed. She looked up at him, furious to find a gentle heat in his eyes as he gazed down at her.

"Why didn't you trust me?" she asked.

Jasper's smile faded. "My, we *are* prickly, aren't we? Well, tell me what I was supposed to think. After weeks of letting me suffer with Eloise, letting me think you did not know how to release the bond or send her away? Only to watch you send her Beyond without a thought?"

Tessa stepped back, dropping his lapels, not liking his thoughtful expression. She liked it even less when a grin spread across his handsome face.

"You did it in a fit of jealousy, didn't you?"

"That comment doesn't deserve an answer."

Jasper chuckled. "Tessa, come now, you can admit you might like me a little. I won't tell anyone." His brow quirked.

Crossing her arms, Tessa wished someone would enter the ballroom so she could quit this tête-à-tête. "You're being obnoxious."

"And you're being obstinate." He sighed, stepping back. "This was hardly how I wanted to meet you today."

"Yes, I know. You winked at me enough during the ceremony. Did you think no one was watching?"

"I hoped they all were, so they might know my feelings, or perhaps speak on my behalf, since you don't believe a word I say. Tessa, I love you."

Tessa huffed, eyeing Jasper with annoyance more than anything else, for to admit anything else was sure to make her burst into tears. "You are impossible."

"And you do the impossible," he countered. "Don't you think that makes for an interesting pairing, at least?"

Before Tessa could reply, the ballroom doors eased open. She leapt away from Jasper, slamming her back into the window.

"If you were trying to be circumspect," Sir Hubert said, looking from Jasper to Tessa and back again, swinging the cane from his wrist, "you're failing."

Tessa relaxed only slightly, her hands gripping the windowsill as she waited for her uncle to challenge Jasper. When he instead rushed toward them, she noticed he had a sheen of sweat glistening across his bald head, and a wild look in his eye. She met him halfway, Jasper close behind.

"What's happened?"

"Nothing the guests have noticed, but something isn't right. Hartwell keeps stumbling as though someone is pushing him, and Mary has been looking for you everywhere. She's certain it's that poltergeist you've been worrying about."

Tessa tried not to lean into her feelings of validation, knowing that wasn't the thing to do at the moment, but she indulged in a side-glance at Jasper.

His lips pressed into a thin line with a gentle eye roll, acknowledging her unspoken, "I told you so."

They heard Dame Hartwell declaring outside the ballroom to the gathering crowd that the bride and groom would enter alone for a private moment, and might everyone queue for the receiving line?

Tessa strode forward, grim and glad to have her uncle and yes, even Jasper, there with her. She did her special blink, opening her Sense wide as Mary helped Hartwell into the ballroom.

Hartwell had a hand to his heart, and his other wrapped tightly around Mary's waist. Mary, likewise, held to his waist, and as soon as the doors shut behind them, pulled her head from his shoulder, instead shifting her weight as his knees buckled beneath him.

Jasper dashed forward, throwing Hartwell's arm over his shoulder. "Still with us, old man?"

Hartwell grimaced. "This is much worse than when Mr. Trentwood possessed me."

Mary and Hartwell really had the most *unusual* romantic history.

Tessa blinked her Sight into view, indeed seeing the bright white light that came along with a malevolent spirit tying itself to a body. Gray ribbons hung loosely around Hartwell's arms and neck, and one struggled to wrap around his chest. That one seemed repelled by Mary's hand, which pressed into his sternum to stop him from pitching forward.

"Mary," Tessa murmured, her eyes wide, "move your hand to his neck."

Mary did as told, and the ribbon dissolved with a hiss. She winced and rubbed her fingers against her palm as though she had touched something frigid. Tessa instructed Mary to do it again, this time on Hartwell's arm opposite her. Mary motioned for Sir Hubert to take her place. With Hartwell's imbalanced weight secured, Mary placed her hand wherever Tessa instruct-ed, watching as Hartwell writhed and breathed easier.

"Can you see what you're doing?" Tessa whispered.

Mary took a deep, steadying breath with her eyes squeezed shut. In the last moment of the exhale, she opened her eyes wide. Her pupils dilated and her mouth fell open. A cold, determined expression settled as she touched Hartwell's arms, chest, neck with purpose, no longer needing Tessa's guidance.

The ribbons continued to wind around Hartwell, resisting Mary's every push, until she finally wrapped her arms around Hartwell's neck and kissed him, forcing the gray ribbons away by pressing her entire body against him.

"Well," Jasper said, tearing his eyes away. "I can see why he didn't like it when she kissed *me*. Is that how we looked? By Jove."

"When *Eloise* kissed you," Tessa corrected. "And I think I know what Mary's talent is, my dear uncle."

Sir Hubert nodded with great enthusiasm. "She's a shield; we've only ever heard of a shield talent! What are you seeing? No, no, don't tell me. We shall speak of this later, when we've time to go through every particular. Is Hartwell better, then?"

Hartwell threw his arms around Mary, who laughed breathlessly against his pursuing lips.

"Seems he's feeling much better," Jasper said, shoving his hands into his pockets.

Tessa nodded. "The ribbons are gone, and—" She stopped, tilting her head at the sound of a distant roaring. "I think someone's paying us a visit."

TWENTY-FOUR

IN WHICH ONE SUCCUMBS

THE INCENSED SPIRIT BURST through the window, slamming the windowpanes open in a shock of blinding light. Tessa blinked past her raised arm, struggling to make out details.

He had been a ghost for quite some time—decades, perhaps. He barely had a face, just some hollows for his eyes and a mouth sunken in paper-pale skin. A frenzied rage contorted these into horrifying, buzzing voids. His floppy, shaggy hair, threadbare clothes, and twitching hands seemed familiar, though Tessa hadn't any reason to know this *thing*.

He had his own faint ribbons looped around his neck and floating upward, a macabre sign to Tessa that he had died of a hanging. She stumbled back, repelled by the absolute stench of death clinging to him. Jasper moved to steady her, but she shook him off.

"Who are you?" she demanded.

"Now, now, where are our manners?" He smirked, insomuch as a gaping hole in a face might smirk, and stepped forward. "They're coming for you, Tessa Baby."

Tessa tasted bile. Somehow, the spirit had thrown its voice, so it sounded exactly like her mother. She realized, with increasing dread, that Jasper had been right that day on the dock. All of this, for reasons unknown, was about her. Not Mary, Hartwell, Jasper, or even Eloise.

This was the voice that had taunted her the night she exorcised three spirits for Dame Hartwell. This was the voice that she had turned over and over in her mind during sleepless nights, struggling to find the connection between Mary, Jasper, and Eloise.

The spirit advanced, licking his lips. "Ah, but your shock tastes sweet," he said in his own melodious tones.

Tessa held the cane close to her chest, unable to speak or move. She stared at him, willing her mind to go back and back, to a time when she might have known that voice, but she simply could not place it.

The spirit was close enough now that Mary broke away from Hartwell, plastering herself before him with her arms wide. "You will not touch him," she warned, panting and her face rather red.

"And what will you do about it, child?" the spirit mocked. "Think yourself a proper medium now?"

Mary faltered, once again unsure. She did her hard blink, allowing her pupils to dilate into her Sense again, gasping at the blinding sight of the spirit.

Sir Hubert looked from Tessa to Mary, looking more concerned by the minute. Jasper inched toward Tessa, and the movement caught the spirit's attention.

"Ah, ah, ah," the spirit sang, shaking its head.

Tessa couldn't breathe. What was it about this spirit that held such a terror for her?

The spirit licked its lips and dove for Hartwell. Tessa cried out, but Mary stood firm, crossing her forearms over her face and spreading her feet wide. She repelled the spirit despite his demeaning shouts she would fail, and then he would have her husband's strength and no one could stop him.

A glint in her eye, Mary murmured, "I think not," and broke her arms apart as though unsheathing two small swords. She punched the air before her, no doubt a move her pugilistic butler had taught her, and the spirit crashed into the wall.

Tessa stared, more than a little impressed.

Hartwell caught Mary by the shoulders, steadying her as she swayed.

In the corner of her eye, Tessa saw the spirit rebound. He became a blur of light as it spun around the ballroom.

There was no time to react. Tessa held up the cane, mimicking Mary by crossing her arms. Instinct guided her as the spirit slammed against her repeatedly. Tessa clenched her teeth. Her feet slipped as she fought the spirit's full strength. She jerked her head at Mary, trying to tell her to get the men out of harm's way.

Between gasps, Tessa spoke a word of the spell to banish the spirit.

It had an unexpected effect.

Their collision sent Tessa flying back. She tripped on her frilled skirts, her sleeve ripping at the shoulder as she rolled to her hands and knees. The spirit spun out of control in the opposite direction, diving into the unsuspecting Jasper.

The impact threw Jasper against the opposite wall with a sickening crack. He lay there. Unmoving, unseeing, barely breathing.

"Jasper?" Tessa whispered, inching forward. "Archie?"

Jasper opened his eyes, revealing the opaque white of possession. "Dearest Archie ain't receiving visitors," came the deep, echoing voice of the spirit.

TWENTY-FIVE

IN WHICH ONE FAILS

BEFORE ANYONE COULD DO or say anything, the possessed Jasper stood with alarming speed. He sprinted across the room, grinning at Tessa all the while, toward the unlocked window. With a jaunty wave, he jumped.

A small scream left Mary's lips. Tessa was at the window, not knowing how she got there, in time to see him slipping out the back entry of the courtyard.

Tessa slid, sitting on the floor in her billowed skirts, pressing her forehead against the wall. She blinked at the cane in her lap. It was supposed to protect her, yes. It was *also* supposed to help her protect others. Not deflect so strongly that the ghost bounced off her to land in someone else.

Frustration strangled Tessa's heart and stole her breath. A wind seemed to howl in her ears, though there wasn't even a light breeze in the stifling room.

Sir Hubert knelt beside her, a hand on her shoulder. She knew what he wanted to tell her. That she wasn't to blame for this. That she had done her best.

The longer Tessa sat there, feeling the quiet pity of the others, the heavier her chest felt, until she gasped for air. It wasn't just that she had failed to exorcise that ghost. She had failed to protect Jasper. And in failing to protect him, had failed to admit even while he had stood there vulnerable *for her*, of his importance in her life.

What had Tessa learned these last weeks, except that she missed those sidelong glances across the room, and the warmth she felt whenever he grinned in her direction? What had she learned, but that Jasper had trusted her explicitly and cared enough to return despite her retreat into professionalism and bitter remarks?

Tessa inhaled a deep sob and shook her head. She *was* to blame for this. It was her responsibility as the resident medium. She was supposed to know how strong these ghosts had become, and use the tools at her disposal.

Good heavens, even Mary had protected her husband, and she barely knew what she was doing. Tessa wiped the tears from her face with the back of her hand, not understanding why she hadn't let Jasper stay behind her. Why did she have to challenge the ghost?

No wonder the Marylebone Spiritualist Association refused her application repeatedly. Too cocky by half, and careless, besides. What was she to do now?

There was no stopping the tears. Tessa allowed her uncle to tuck her close and even pat her shoulder, albeit awkwardly. Mary and Hartwell hovered nearby, unsure.

"Lost him, did we?" Sir Hubert said. There was a light challenge in his tone, one that made Mary and Hartwell glance at one another in some surprise.

Tessa yanked away from her uncle, her eyes narrow. "I've not given up, if that's what you're implying."

"I should say not. That wouldn't be very sporting of you, being the medium-in-residence. Besides, he hasn't paid us for his first exorcism yet, and clearly he needs to be of sound mind to clear his account."

Tessa rubbed her tears away with the heel of her hand with a hoarse chuckle. Clearing her throat, she accepted her uncle's handkerchief with a rueful smile. She was an ugly crier, her wide nose turning an odd shade of pink and her eyes looking rather bloodshot.

She was, in a moment of vanity, glad Jasper wasn't here to see it. Though the last time he saw her cry, he had been lovely about it. The thought almost sent her into another round of sobs.

"You really must let me take care of you once in a while." Sir Hubert's admonishment was both mild and wistful. "While you are admirably and annoyingly independent, I encourage you to ask for help."

Hartwell handed Tessa a glass of spiked punch while Mary knelt to wipe Tessa's tears away.

Tessa blinked as if seeing them for the first time, most especially her uncle.

All these years of traveling, of seeking answers to her Sense, and she had never noticed his mourning. Her uncle had loved her father and mother dearly, and for longer than she knew them, and in ways she could never fathom because he had been their friend. And rather than grieving together with him, Tessa had shut down. She had focused on learning to use her Sense, thinking maybe her parents would reach out to her, and in the meantime, earn an income. She had never once considered that Sir Hubert's support was more than a financial obligation from a bachelor uncle.

She thanked Mary quietly, pushing her hand away. She downed the punch with three large gulps and used the burning warmth trickling down her throat to ask her uncle what she had never dared ask before.

"What were you doing before you retrieved me that night?"

Sir Hubert stood, rubbing a handkerchief over his head. He didn't need to ask which night she referred to. "Researching claims that a spirit was possessing other spirits. It all came to naught. The cases stopped the night your parents died."

"So you knew my mother was a medium even back then?"

"Of course. I was the research arm of your parents' operation."

"Operation?"

Sir Hubert chuckled, helping Tessa from the floor while Hartwell helped Mary. "You cannot think you're the only one in the family who sees financial stability in providing your Sense as a service?" He nodded at the open window through which the ghost had thrown Jasper. "There are possessions and hauntings aplenty, and those among the living desperate for a connection Beyond. The question is, how many mediums can do anything about it?"

Tessa wandered to the window, her expression grave as she studied the drop to the ground. "My parents wanted to create their own spiritualist association?"

"They were well on their way when the incident leading to their deaths occurred."

"Who else knew such a thing?" Mary whispered.

A gnawing feeling grew in Tessa's stomach. She pressed a hand to her abdomen, waiting to hear her uncle's answer.

"Only Martinvale, and Dame Hartwell, of course. She was to sponsor them financially. He was to lend credibility via the Marylebone Spiritualist Association."

Tessa's hands balled into fists. "Martinvale." She thought back to his insulting letter about her pedigree never being good enough for his association. She scraped her fist across her temple. "Well, I think he finally called a spirit back."

Hartwell started. "You can't think Theodosius Martinvale's hands are behind all this? My mother speaks with him regularly!"

"I can, and do." Tessa spun on her heel, resolved. "Let's eat some cake, and then I need to figure out where Archie might have gone."

"I'd imagine home," Sir Hubert said. When Tessa, Mary, and Hartwell gave him bewildered looks, he shrugged, a remnant of their time on the Continent. "Tessa's mother used to say that children come home to die, as if it were some proverb. If Jasper's still in there, he's seeking familiarity and comfort. You need to speak with his mother before that spirit does something."

Tessa wasn't one for screaming. Instead, if one looked closely, one would notice Tessa's nostrils flare, her lips thin to a grim line, and her breathing quicken. Her narrowed eyes, combined with all the above, made her look positively feline, and rather feral at that.

"Not before cake," Tessa said firmly. "I cannot have that conversation on an empty stomach."

"As you say," her uncle said, following her from the room with a chuckle. They left a bemused Mary and Hartwell to receive their wedding guests and explain away the commotion.

TWENTY-SIX

IN WHICH ONE WAKES

JASPER WOKE ON AN unforgiving surface and blinded by an unforgiving darkness. He bolted upright, arms flailing to protect
himself from the last thing he remembered seeing, which had
been a dark miasma skewering the air to reach Tessa. The action
made Jasper fall from what he learned was a short perch. His
knees hit the ground hard. He bit back an oath as he felt around
for something, anything, to suggest whether something trapped
him in an unlit room, or if it were something more sinister.

After searching for far too long along the floor to determine
there were no walls and therefore no windows, Jasper felt the
air above him to determine he could stand. There was no
discernible ceiling, and therefore no hope of lighting a chan-
delier. His eyes watered from the unrelenting pressure of the
impermeable dark surrounding him.

"Where the devil am I?" he shouted, frustrated and panicked.

"Somewhere safe from prying eyes," replied a male voice.

Jasper froze. In all his searching, he had determined nothing
other than he was alone in a space with no walls, windows,
doors, or lamps. He had even lost his bearings regarding the
perch upon which he had woken, for there was no furniture,
and no amount of backtracking had led him back to the spot.

"Where are you?" Jasper said.

"Well, isn't that the wrong question? You've no interest in *who*
I am?" The voice was both near and far all at once. The voice

had an amused, deep timbre, and would have easily commanded attention and echoed in a crowded room, but here it sounded stunted, as if heavy velvet drapes lined the area.

"Let's not be hasty, one thing at a time," Jasper said, unable to help his usual sarcasm.

The voice chuckled, making the hair on Jasper's nape stand on end. "Ah, I can see why she loves you."

Jasper whirled, balling his hands into fists. "You keep your distance." He paused. "Who loves me?"

The voice made a tut-tutting noise. "I suppose I shouldn't have said anything. Now you're going to get upset and fight for your body."

Rubbing his temple with his knuckle, Jasper shook his head. Too much was happening too quickly, and none of it made any sense.

First, he was fairly certain the voice was taunting him with the idea that Tessa loved him, which would be wonderful and a huge relief, if true. Second, Jasper now suffered a terrible, sinking feeling that the voice was, in fact, telling him the truth. He hadn't gone anywhere. Something had *joined* him.

Really, all this ghost business was getting entirely out of hand, and his irritation revealed itself in his tone as he demanded confirmation. "Tell me what's happening to me. Where am I?"

The voice sighed, inasmuch as a disembodied voice might sigh. "You've not gone anywhere," he said, his tone quietly calling Jasper an idiot. "You're exactly where you have always been, in your body."

Jasper squinted, studying the horizonless white space. "It's so empty."

The voice chortled at that. "It's bloody crowded in here. You've a mess of thoughts, boy. It's just you've no control over it anymore. You see what I want you to see." The voice paused, letting the horror of what he was saying reach full impact for Jasper.

"What nonsense," Jasper said, wanting to feel as calm and brave as he sounded.

"Ah, I can sense your fear, right? I can almost taste it! Delicious. This is so much better from the inside."

"*Inside?*"

"Your body, man. I've possessed your body. Honestly surprised you're still here. I always thought a body could only ever hold one soul. But then, I also never thought I'd be called back from Beyond to haunt anyone after me hanging, so there's that."

"You're the . . . miasma?" Jasper could think of no other word to describe the black tar he had seen Tessa fighting in the Serpentine.

"The what?" the voice said, outraged. "What'd you just call me? I'm a murdering bugger who got caught in the act, so I'd be careful with what words you sling at me, my friend."

Jasper licked his lips as a stiff wind spiked his hair and ruffled his clothes, harkening back to the gale that had destroyed the Hartwells' library. Time to calm down the spirit before things really got out of hand. "A miasma isn't an insult, per se."

"Oh? Then what is it?"

"An . . . unpleasant and oppressive vapor," Jasper said.

The voice laughed. "Oh well, if that's all, then yes, I guess I was a miasma when I came at your lady, but now that I've got you, this will be a right trip. Should be so much easier to do me bidding now."

Desperate to change the subject to something he could understand, Jasper asked, "Why can't I see anything?"

"Your body took a beating when I jumped out the window. I didn't think we were on the first floor. Once I got us to a safe spot, I put you to sleep."

"But I'm awake."

"You are, but you don't control your body anymore. Your eyes will open when I tell them to."

"No need to sound smug about it. No one's ever possessed me before."

"And I've possessed no one besides other ghosts, so you'll have to let me congratulate meself."

Jasper fell silent, rubbing his mustache as he thought. He thought of Eloise and her odd, erratic behavior at moments, now wondering whether it had actually been this ghoul possessing her. "This is awful."

"Not yet, it isn't, but it will be," the voice promised.

Jasper chewed his lip. Well, he chewed whatever represented his lip. Hell, but this was confusing. All he really knew was that the ghost had taken him away from Hartwell House, which, he reasoned, was probably for the best. He hardly wanted this *thing* anywhere near Tessa, and though he wasn't a medium, he figured keeping the spirit trapped in his body for a while might give her time to . . . for lack of a better word, save him.

Jasper closed his eyes, shoulders slumping. How on earth had he found himself in need of true saving from a ghostly encounter again? He had been so careful these last couple of weeks. He had bought amethyst to keep beneath his pillow, though all it had done was remind him of Tessa's amethyst, which had kept him aware that she was likely also in her bed. This, of course, led to many sleepless nights.

By Jove, but he had missed her. Even though their reunion had been awkward, and perhaps he had laid it on thick with all the winking and outright flirtation and declaration in the ballroom. The fact was, it had taken all his willpower to not take Tessa's face in his hands and kiss her soundly.

"We can make that happen," the voice said.

Jasper froze, his thoughts racing. "Make what happen?"

"Kiss the girl," the voice said, delighted. "Not like I haven't earned me a bit of fun waiting all these years. I deserve it, I do."

Years, the voice said. Jasper realized he would rather send his body to the bottom of the Thames than let this spirit be the method his lips touched Tessa Preston. He was quick to banish the thought, unless the spirit could somehow sense the direction of his mind. Whatever his failings, and Jasper knew he had many, it was rather overdue for him to truly stand up for what he wanted.

And what he wanted more than anything was to protect Tessa from this lout, by any means possible.

Twenty-Seven

In which one informs

Though Tessa wasted much of the morning arguing with her uncle that she ought to visit Mrs. Steele alone, and to admit her part in putting her son in danger, now that she stood on the front step staring at the door, Tessa wished she had followed her uncle's advice. She trembled, and couldn't tell whether it was lack of sleep for having tossed and turned all night, or true terror at what she was about to do.

This was an unfamiliar experience, breaking news to the family of their beloved's possession. Usually, the family had already determined as much themselves, and so called for her services. It allowed Tessa to be taciturn and precise, having no need to waste time with social niceties, thanks to everyone's eagerness for their return to normalcy.

The entire cab ride over, Tessa played with turns of phrase. Twisting her purse in her gloved hands, she cringed at some of the better options. Nonsense like, "Hello Mrs. Steele, I've grown rather fond of your son and I accidentally let an evil spirit possess him." Or even worse, "Hello Mrs. Steele, have you ever met a possessed man? No? Well, if your son returns, you will."

Absolutely terrible. This was exactly why her uncle handled the business side of things, such as negotiating fees and comforting distraught clients. Tessa was better suited for handling the dead.

"My dear, do you intend to warm my step all afternoon, or would you join me for some refreshment?"

Tessa stumbled, almost twisting her ankle on the step at the sound of a jolly woman's voice. She craned her neck to find a plump woman with expertly coifed salt-and-pepper hair and twinkling green eyes leaning out of the bay window, clutching the windowpane lock. "Mrs. Steele?"

"The same. I gather you must be here about my Archie, I think?"

Tessa swallowed, fighting the urge to stumble down the steps and run away. So his mother also called him Archie. No wonder he gave her such odd looks when she teased him. "Indeed, ma'am."

"Well then, come in, don't dawdle," Mrs. Steele said, pulling the window shut.

Tessa entered the home, gently refusing the housekeeper from taking her hat, gloves, and purse. This wasn't a social visit, and she didn't intend to stay long. Merely long enough to break the news. She entered the parlor, noting the casually luxurious comfort of the room. Yes, this would be the home in which Jasper grew up; stylish but comfortable, well-appointed but not showy.

Mrs. Steele busied herself with the tea, gesturing for Tessa to avail herself of the plate of biscuits.

Tessa's smile was tight as she shook her head. Now. She must say why she was here now, or else she would lose her courage and let Mrs. Steele discover the awful truth on her own.

Mrs. Steele stirred her tea, placing the spoon on the saucer and taking a sip.

Tessa fought the urge to fidget beneath the steady, scrutinizing gaze of Mrs. Steele. "Ma'am, I have the unfort—"

"You're Tessa Preston," Mrs. Steele interrupted.

Tessa nodded. She clenched her fingers together in her lap. Right, introductions first, possession announcements after.

Mrs. Steele relaxed in her seat, a satisfied smile spreading. "You're the medium whom my son holds in high regard? How delightful. I'm so glad you've come."

Tessa stared. "I would hardly know that, ma'am. I came here to tell you—"

Mrs. Steele waved her hand. "Whatever it is you have to tell me on his behalf—I swear the child has an unnatural fear of me—I assure you I have no objections. My son had a near-death experience because of a woman who didn't love him. You released him from a most undesirable ghostly companion, or so he says, at some risk to yourself. I must say, you're not what I expected or imagined for my son, but I'm glad you are in his life." She smiled after this unexpected declaration, her expression turning soft and musing. "I knew your mother, you know. I thought her quite beautiful, and she helped my mother once, after my father passed away. You look just like her."

As Mrs. Steele spoke, the pressure rose in Tessa's throat until she nearly burst from her seat in alarm.

"My dear madam, you mistake me," Tessa said stiffly. "I'm not here to beg your permission for your son's affections. Those are his to give and . . . are none of my business!"

"None of your business?" Mrs. Steele said, eyes wide and her tone sharp. "What an odd thing to say. You saved him from a possession, did you not?"

"Yes, but—"

"And he is alive and well because of your care, is that not so?"

A chill settled at the base of Tessa's spine. While this was certainly not the conversation she intended to have, it *was* illuminating. "Mrs. Steele, are you saying you approve of your son's affections for me because I saved him?"

"It would be silly of me to reject you because you saved him, my dear."

Tessa leaned forward. "And what if I didn't save him?"

Mrs. Steele sat back, puzzled. "Whatever can you mean? You saved him."

"But if I didn't save him," Tessa pressed, "would you approve? If I weren't a figure of protection in his life, would you think other than how you currently do about me?"

Mrs. Steele's smile was gentle and knowing. "My dear, do you wish to quarrel with me? Are you afraid that if you had not saved him, I would find you lacking or undesirable?"

Tessa clenched her purse in her lap. This was not going at all as planned. Clearly, Jasper hadn't been exaggerating when he said his mother was obsessed with finding him a wife. But to be singled out in this manner, and speaking on his behalf! Tessa couldn't fathom it. "Mrs. Steele, I'm trying to tell you the exorcism worked, but—"

"Why, of course it did—"

"And it also failed. Miserably."

"My dear girl, you're speaking in riddles. Come out with it at once. Our tea grows cold and I so dislike a cold tea."

"I freed your son from Miss Carterprice, but I didn't notice there was another spirit, and—!"

The man himself sauntered into the room, all ease and smiles. Despite the murderous glow emanating in sickening waves from him, Jasper looked as though nothing was amiss. It was a masterful possession, and Tessa could find no cracks in which to assert her own Sense and free him.

"Archie, dear, look who's come to visit." Mrs. Steele beamed at her son, not noticing how Tessa pressed her hand on her stomach against waves of nausea.

Tessa glowered, wanting nothing more than to choke the ghost out of Jasper. She averted her gaze to his cheek, unable to countenance the opaque whiteness of his eyes boring into her.

Jasper's grin was boyish, and might have made Tessa's heart flip were it not accompanied by that echoing undertone only she could hear. "To what do we owe this unexpected pleasure?"

"She's been very insistent on trying to tell me something," Mrs. Steele said with a chuckle, "and I must admit I haven't been very polite in giving her the space to have her say." A cunning expression flitted across her face. "You never told me how pretty Miss Preston was, though I likely should have guessed it myself, having seen her mother."

Jasper gave an assessing, if dismissive, glance over Tessa's person. "If you like that sort of thing."

Mrs. Steele gasped, leaping to her feet and grabbing her son's arm. "I think you are right, Miss Preston," she rushed. "My son is clearly not feeling well." She glared at him beneath her lashes.

Tessa and Jasper stared at one another, and the room fell into a studious silence. She looked for some sign of Jasper—of Archie—once again, feeling pressure build in her throat the longer she couldn't find any. The way he stood with his hip cocked, his self-sure smile, even the way he slicked his sun-kissed hair back with an obscene amount of macassar oil . . .

Narrowing her eyes, Tessa decided a test was in order. Something to tease the real Jasper out from behind the facade of his possessor, whoever the blighter was. She tilted her head to the side, mind racing. What to do? She thought back, remembering how very much Jasper had always wanted to see more of her silly side.

Throwing an apologetic glance at his mother, Tessa stuck her tongue out at him and rolled her eyes. "Who wants you, anyway? It's Archie I've come to see."

Mrs. Steele made a strangled noise.

Jasper jolted awake. A grin broke across his face, his eyes returning to their ocean blue. "Tessa!"

"There you are," she whispered.

He stepped forward with his hand out for hers, but even with that single step, he stumbled. When he righted himself, his eyes were clouded over again. While it was not visible to anyone without the Sense, Tessa watched and knew.

An intense chill barreled through her.

Tessa kept her balance, only just, and had to throw a hand to her mouth, fighting the urge to lose her breakfast right there on the coffee table.

Mrs. Steele wrung her hands, her attention swinging from her son to Tessa and back again.

The ghoul shook Jasper's head in amused admonishment and smoothed his lapels.

Tessa backed away, apologizing. This was not the time or place for their inevitable confrontation. "I'm afraid I'm late for another appointment."

"You've only just arrived," Mrs. Steele protested. "Surely you must stay for our luncheon. I should like to get to know you better."

"All the same," Tessa said, not taking her eyes from Jasper, whose frigid aura grew, reaching for her as she escaped. "I'm certain you shall be welcome at Dame Hartwell's residence for tea anytime. Please do visit while I'm a guest."

Mrs. Steele prodded her son, but he already followed Tessa's hasty retreat.

Tessa grabbed the door handle, turning it to escape. The ghoul slammed Jasper's palm against the door, holding it shut. Tessa spun around to find him looming. She shrank back, whipping her hands up to push his chest away. "You wouldn't dare do anything in this house and bring attention to yourself!" she hissed.

An eyebrow lifted. "Wouldn't I?" he breathed.

Tessa stopped breathing when he leaned down to whisper in her ear, "Do you think anyone would believe you, dearie, over me word? In this genteel house?"

He pulled back so she could see the hard cruelty in his smile. "His ma's a nice one, but she's so desperate for grandbabies I wager she wants him to marry anything."

Tessa winced, his word choices not lost on her. Anything, he called her. He had no qualms about hurting her or anyone else. He didn't even think of her as a person. She was a conquest. A tease. An exotic challenge. She froze, wanting to do something, say something. Call for help. Knee him where it counted. Show she wasn't afraid of him even though they both knew she really, really was.

Struggling to breathe through her rising panic, Tessa marveled that they remained alone in this little foyer, with no servants walking past. Hadn't they been standing there for hours, locked in this battle of wills?

And then he licked his lips, his eyes so lustful, his manner so very *unlike* the Jasper that Tessa knew . . . She blinked and came into her own.

"Archibald Jasper Steele," she hissed, "if you're *anywhere* in there, you tell him to back away *now*."

Jasper froze for a moment, a confused expression drifting across his face. The whitish glaze clouding his irises faded, and Tessa saw a sparkle of blue. His eyes widened and he whispered to her to run as he fell back a step, clearly fighting for control of his own body. It was this imbalance that allowed the ghoul to take the upper hand.

Though Tessa was concerned Jasper couldn't push the ghoul out, the point was, she thought with satisfaction, he was still in there. And she had drawn him out, *twice*. The ghoul was quick to crowd her against the door again. She lifted her chin.

"Don't you worry, pet," the ghoul said, rubbing Jasper's knuckles along her jawline, "I won't do anything yet. I've got my agreements with Martinvale, same as you. We'll have this out with him as a witness, and then we'll know who's strongest."

"Strongest?" Tessa snapped. "Is this all a game to you?"

He frowned. "Of course it is."

"And what could Martinvale have to do with any of this?"

Jasper's hand patted her cheek. "Eloise tried to warn you, didn't she, though?"

Tessa inhaled sharply. "I want you to say it. What does Martinvale have to do with this?" she asked again.

He unlocked the door behind her. "Let's not get ahead of ourselves, pet. All in good time." He all but pushed her out of the house, leaving Tessa staring blankly at the street, wondering how, in all that was good in the world, she was going to prove the head of the Marylebone Spiritualist Association was collaborating with that monster.

TWENTY-EIGHT

IN WHICH ONE FIGHTS

JASPER STOOD IN THE white expanse, alone and annoyed. He felt as though a haze covered his eyes, and no matter how often or hard he rubbed them, the haze wouldn't clear. He heard words being spoken and knew it was his voice, his body. Yet, he had no control. He flexed his hands and felt nothing. He kicked his own shin with his heel. Nothing.

In the far distance, a window appeared.

Jasper crept forward, foreboding slowing his movements. As he neared, he realized it wasn't just a window; he was looking through his own eyes. He couldn't stop the words the spirit spewed from his corporeal mouth. A quick study confirmed his body had returned home.

The spirit turned Jasper's head, revealing his mother and Tessa. Well, that was just excellent. Of all the people. Here were the two people on earth Jasper would do anything to keep safe, and they spoke with the freak controlling his body, not realizing what was happening.

But there . . . A moment of doubt stealing across Tessa's face? It flitted by; Jasper couldn't be sure. Her expression turned musing. Jasper, knowing deep within that it was all futile, still couldn't help shouting at her to not fall for the spirit's deception. He rubbed his eyes, trying to remove the haze, but it changed nothing.

And then, his darling girl stuck out her tongue at him, and said "Who wants you, anyway? It's Archie I've come to see."

Jasper's heart leapt into action. She knew. Tessa knew he was still in his body, and was baiting the ghoul to give him control again. He leaned against the windowpane, laughing aloud, delighting in how the silly action transformed her face. Her daring seemed to light her from within.

The windowpane shifted open under Jasper's sudden physical weight, and when he blinked, it was as though he were actually in the room with his mother and love.

"Tessa!" he said, grinning.

"There you are," she whispered.

Jasper swallowed, unable to find the words he wanted to say. His relief that she had followed him home, her clear intent to warn his mother of the danger she housed under her roof. It was her protective streak he loved, and worried about. Jasper wondered whether Tessa had what she needed to free him from this cage. This ghoul was strong. So strong that a single step toward Tessa threw Jasper back again, and he felt the windowpane slam shut and lock before his eyes, once again covered in a haze.

"Testing your boundaries, are we?" the ghoul said, sending shivers through Jasper's soul. "Try that again and just see what I'll do to your ladies."

Jasper stumbled to his knees, panting. "I won't let you hurt them."

The ghoul chuckled as he moved Jasper's body to follow Tessa to the front door. "And what'll you do about it, my boy? You're no medium."

Jasper pressed his fists against whatever substance made the ground upon which he kneeled. The ghoul was right. He wasn't a medium. He didn't understand what was happening, or how he had broken through for that brief, delicious moment.

The windowpane floated toward Jasper. The ghoul *wanted* him to watch what happened next.

Bile rose as Jasper watched the ghoul close in on Tessa, forcing the door shut and making her turn to face him. Jasper saw the defiance in Tessa's lifted chin and stern lips, and winced at the fear shadowing her dark eyes. Her nostrils flared as the spirit ran his knuckles against her cheek.

Jasper slammed his fists against the windowpane, snarling at the ghoul to leave her alone.

The ghoul made him lick his lips as they both stared down at Tessa.

A cold fury billowed through Jasper's body. He slammed his shoulder against the windowpane.

"What do you reckon she tastes like?" the ghoul said to Jasper. "Shall we find out?"

"Archibald Jasper Steele," Tessa hissed, "if you're *anywhere* in there, you tell him to back away *now*."

Jasper wound his arm back, smashing through the windowpane to unlock it with a bloody hand. He blinked, having gained control again.

With a sharp inhale, Jasper yanked his hand from Tessa's face. He stepped back, whispering at her to run.

By his second step, Jasper was on his incorporeal back, the wind knocked out of him. When he propped up on his elbows, he saw bars lining the windowpane, imprisoning him for good. "Why are you doing this? What have we ever done to you?"

"It isn't what you did, it's what her ma did. It was supposed to be a simple job. Scare the horse, throw them from the carriage. But that damned woman saw me. Martinvale never warned she was a medium. When she realized whose ribbons held me, she trapped me with her dying breath."

"Trapped you?"

"I'm stuck here, same as you," the ghoul said. "The longer I'm here, the less of me I am. I'll be a shade, a mindless shadow, before you know it. Then the hands will pull me down."

Jasper thought he heard a quiver of fear in the ghoul's voice, and realized that if he were to get rid of the ghoul, he needed to figure out how to call those hands forward. "Why would the head of the Marylebone Spiritualist Association ever call someone like you?"

Wind whipped Jasper's hair, lashing his face.

"He wants the Preston line gone."

TWENTY-NINE

IN WHICH ONE REALIZES

TESSA PRESSED A HAND to her abdomen, bile again rising at the thought of Not-Jasper leaning in for a lecherous kiss. She felt hot and cold all over, confused by how she actually wanted to kiss Jasper, while also wanting to punch that ghoul out of him. And that revelation about Martinvale! She shook her head, trying to clear her thoughts.

Tessa descended the steps, deciding she would not hire a hackney back to Hartwell House. She needed the time to reflect. It was startling how many times Martinvale's name had suddenly become relevant.

She still carried Martinvale's latest rejection. It had been most insulting, almost cruel. He had taken extra effort in no uncertain terms that he and his board would *never* admit her to their ranks.

As she wandered down the pavement, Tessa pulled the letter from her purse. She unfolded the letter, the careworn edges threatening to rip apart. As mentioned by Martinvale in his elegant hand, the rejection within was hardly her first, yet this was the one she kept. The self-righteous prejudice both enraged and scared her. She was powerful, perhaps the most powerful medium living in England.

This bitter old man delighted in cutting her down.

She couldn't quite believe his disdain was so strong that he sent a murdering ghost after her. She turned the theory over in her mind, seeking evidence, shifting her perspective.

Perhaps Martinvale was more than annoyed and peeved by her continued appeals. Perhaps he felt a personal affront by her applications. Maybe he had concluded she no longer needed to live.

If so, he was a coward. And a fool. And a cowardly fool. And most importantly, an idiot. What was he going to do if he killed her and she haunted him?

Tessa crumpled the letter in a tight fist. Too many close calls. Too many coincidental mishaps.

Everything had begun the night Martinvale handed her the rejection letter personally, an unkind glint in his eye. That was the night she and her uncle visited Dame Hartwell's séance and banished three malevolent spirits. Where she exorcised a spirit from Madam Sylvia.

And weeks later, Jasper arrived on their doorstep, the ghost bride in tow, upping the stakes.

Despite the warm afternoon, Tessa shivered. She ran her hands along her arms, thinking of her dear Roma mentor who bade her return to England and reestablish the balance.

Tessa had assumed it was Mary's uncontrolled beacon coaxing spirits. It was far more likely to do with those pompous councilmen, oh-so-determined to keep women from prancing down their hallowed halls. Had they an open-door policy, perhaps Mary could have received training and built control.

Dame Hartwell had taken steps in her own meandering way. And while Tessa and Mary had thought her silly, Tessa now realized that Dame Hartwell had known exactly what should be done.

This imbalance fell to Tessa's shoulders. She rolled them, readying for battle. She would show the Marylebone Spiritualist Association just who they had rejected.

The smile that crept to Tessa's face was not unlike the one she last saw on Martinvale: eager, unkind, and resolute. She turned her direction toward the association's headquarters, her heels clipping against the pavement with all her determination and anger.

She would demand Martinvale account for the ghoul possessing Jasper. Tessa's mind churned, thinking of ways to trick him into exposing his deeds as the worst medium she had ever met.

But how to arrest the board's attention? Tessa knew she had to trick Martinvale into a confession, so the board might hear and depose him as their leader.

As she moved ever closer to the grand home housing the Marylebone Spiritualist Association, her pace slowed. Tessa couldn't shake the feeling of that *thing* inside Jasper, leaning forward with a lascivious grin, trapping her against that door. Her stomach turned, thinking of those white eyes focusing on her lips.

Tessa realized the ghoul probably knew her next steps, too. His knowing look as he shooed her out, as though he already knew her every move, daring her to follow through.

When his hand had snapped back as if burned, and she saw Jasper's clear and horrified expression, she had almost taken him in her arms. It had taken all her willpower not to push back the hair falling across his forehead.

Tessa ached seeing Jasper in so much pain.

The feeling of a possession was, as one might imagine, intolerable. Each spirit shoved aside the rightful soul with their own flair. Tessa imagined this one delighted in cornering Jasper and taunting him with his impotent position.

Would Jasper ever forgive her failure to protect him? He had already been livid with how she handled Eloise.

And yet.

Jasper had said he loved her.

How could he say he loved her even while so frustrated?

Tessa could never. She couldn't even tell her uncle how much she adored him, despite his unfailing support all these years.

As Tessa rounded the corner, her eyes lit upon the association's building. She came to a sudden stop, causing the annoyed mutterings of those streaming around her, hurrying about with their midday activities. She steeled her spine.

She might have to admit she loved him too.

Or she might scream it in battle against the ghoul. Her love might have to blast the damned thing from his body. These spirits were so unpredictable.

Thirty

In which one confronts

The Marylebone Spiritualist Association suitably outfitted the front room to impress and instill awe. The fireplace, unlit in the summer heat, was an ornate classical masterpiece of intricately carved marble, sitting atop another marble slab for the hearth, and surrounded by a herringbone pattern of marble tiles on the floor.

Tessa glared at all of it. Every piece of marble was like an irrationally personal affront. She worried a thread from the hem of her gloves, having decided she wouldn't remove them as this was likely a brief visit ending with the door slamming in her face.

"Miss Preston," a deep voice, heavy with tired annoyance, said from the doorway, "why are you here?"

Tessa faced the chair of the association, tucking a small snarl into the corner of her mouth.

Theodosius Martinvale was a squat man of both height and personality. He wore suits on his moderate build well, spending neither too much nor too little, as befitted his station. The inevitable weight he had gained with age settled about his chin, giving him a soft, jovial appearance. His severely short beard came to a point to stress what remained of his chin.

More than once, Tessa had wondered how Martinvale came to be the chair, having no charisma, no genuine talent for mediumship, and seeming afraid of ghosts besides. His thick dark hair was thinning, and he carried spectacles he didn't need for theatrical effect. His complexion was rather ashen, far more than what was popular amongst the London crowd. Lack of sunlight—he looked ghastly.

Tessa stepped forward with a squint. With no strain, she saw the ribbons hanging from his fingers fading into the ether. How had she missed this?

"I'm here to test a theory," she said.

"A theory?" His chuckle lacked amusement. "And what would a woman like you even have a theory about?"

She took another step forward. "My uncle tells me you were fond of my parents."

Martinvale's eyes narrowed, and his hands clenched at his sides. "Hubert Preston doesn't know what he's talking about." He gestured to the door. "My decision stands. You are not welcome and I must ask you to leave."

"Did you know?" she persisted. "They were planning to open their own society." She watched his face lose all expression as he became eerily still. His fingers flexed, and she thought she saw the ribbons twitch. She took another step forward, determined not to cower. "They were returning from a meeting with Dame Hartwell when something spooked their horse and their carriage overturned."

"The hell they were," he said through clenched teeth. "We had just gotten some notable clients and sponsors for our association. Who were they to start a competitive group?"

"There are many societies and associations," Tessa pointed out. "Were you never upset at the founding of the British National Association of Spiritualists, or the Society of Psychical Research?"

"What do you want, child?" he demanded.

"I want to know if you killed my mother."

"No," came another voice, a dear voice, from the hallway behind Martinvale. "That was me."

Tessa closed her eyes, opening them to find Jasper lounging against the door frame.

"Hello, Tessa Baby," said the ghoul.

Martinvale flinched. "I'm handling this."

"What rot. You couldn't handle a parked bicycle." Jasper sauntered into the room. "Quite a risk you're taking, Tessa Baby, coming here in all this state. And to do what? Accuse this poor cuss of murder? No, no, I'll not let him take my credit. I killed the Prestons, and with great pleasure."

Tessa touched her throat. She stumbled back, bumping into the fireplace mantle corner. "Why?"

"Because I could. Because this idiot didn't know how to put me back after calling me from Beyond. When I realized I could possess people *and* ghosts, your mother trapped me. So I stopped her, and her lapdog husband."

Jasper smirked at Martinvale in a manner Tessa had never seen before. It was a revolting sort of self-satisfied.

"Martinvale would never do a thing to harm Fimienye Suoton Preston. Damn fool loved her too much."

Tessa recoiled. This man, loving her determined, smart, courageous mother? This man dared to think he might compete with her sweet and loyal father? It was not to be borne.

Tessa couldn't imagine him ever daring to court her mother. Fimienye Preston was the opposite of everything he deemed genteel. She had been strong-willed, unafraid to claim her place. Martinvale simply could never.

"If you loved her so much, why didn't you allow her into your society? Why not allow me?" Tessa snapped.

Martinvale's involuntary flinch revealed all.

"You were embarrassed," Tessa said.

Martinvale scoffed half-heartedly, his eyes shifting to the ghoul, who grinned at their conversation with Jasper's mouth. "Nonsense. Embarrassed by what, child?"

"Your feelings. The intensity of them." Though she spoke at Martinvale, Tessa studied Jasper, wondering if he could hear her beyond the spirit's shackles. "You never meant to care for my mother. A foreigner, however powerful . . . too powerful for comfort for polite society, I'm sure. And then my father appeared, and he didn't let society scare him."

The ghoul picked at Jasper's fingernails, bored.

Martinvale turned an awful shade of red. "You ought to have been my daughter. Your mother took one minor argument too seriously and ran into the arms of the first man who'd have her."

"One minor argument." Tessa felt a chill run down her spine. "You were trying to impress her by calling on a powerful spirit, weren't you? Or were you so jealous you sent this deranged ghost after her until it led to her death?"

Jasper applauded. "So now that you've figured it all out, you know what's coming. This weakling's losing his grip, and I'm ready to have my fun."

Martinvale, having curled in on himself, straightened his posture upon being called weak. "I told you, Miss Preston, you weren't welcome here. This society will never be safe for you until I send him back."

"Don't tell me you've been trying to protect me all these years," Tessa spat. "He's right, you're a terrible medium and you shouldn't have tried to impress my mother. Now I've got to clean up your mess."

Jasper's eyebrow rose.

"Why you?" asked Martinvale.

Tessa met Jasper's gaze, seeking any hint of her Archie behind those clouded eyes. "You know why."

The ghoul chortled. "All these fine and noble emotions are making me chafe. Are you going to play with me, or am I to kill you now?" He grabbed Tessa by the arms, yanking her close. "Or do you want to know what his lips feel like first?"

Tessa thrashed, but couldn't break free of his unnatural grip. His mouth was on hers, and she faintly heard Martinvale's outrage over the angry blood rushing through her veins.

Jasper's cracked and peeling lips scratched hers. She winced at the frigid sensation seeping across her face and arms from where Jasper held her. Her shoulders bucked, but he held firm. His lips pressed further. His dry tongue fought to pry open her mouth.

If Tessa wasn't so terrified of what might happen with such a powerful spirit, she might have gasped with shock and outrage at his insistence. The cold crept further, inching closer to her heart.

In a few moments, there would be no need to fight him. If this ghoul kept up this barrage to all her senses, for his odor was putrid, Tessa would be his new possession. He would discard Jasper for the puppet that he was and use her Sense to do some actual damage to the spiritualist community.

Tessa opened her eyes, glaring at him. He dared *savor* this disgusting experience, his eyes closed. Still unable to wrench away, Tessa brought her heel down on his shoe, followed by a well-placed knee between his legs. She wanted her Archie back. Now.

"I'm a woman of principle," she hissed, "and I'm saving my kisses for someone who deserves them."

Jasper's eyes popped open, and for a moment, he had pupils again. "Tessa," he said in a ragged whisper. "*Run*, dearest."

Then he doubled over before Tessa could grab him, curling to the floor clutching his pants. When he looked at her again, his eyes were clouded and furious. He grabbed her arm, yanking her close again.

"The terms of me contract are to stop the Preston line before they stop me," he said. Everything about him made Tessa's skin feel soiled, in the worst way possible. He licked his cracked and peeling lips. "I'll give you one day to say your goodbyes. No reason to rush this now that we're all understanding each other."

"You're enjoying the anticipation," Tessa said, wiping her lips with the back of her gloved hand.

"That too." The ghoul shooed her away, groaning a little. "Off you go. I'll see you tomorrow."

"I will handle you later," Tessa said, pointing at him and his insolent smirk.

Martinvale gaped at her. "You can't be serious. Your mother was ten times the medium you are, and he obliterated her."

Tessa bristled. "Ignoring your amazing insensitivity, he caught my mother unawares. She had no forewarning, or friends she could trust, apparently."

Martinvale paled, his fists bunching together as his lips pressed into a furious line.

"I've always disliked you, Theodosius Martinvale," she continued. "But I respected you, and your place as head of this society. Thank you for revealing your true nature to me and your board. I can't believe I ever wanted to be a member of this organization."

Jasper's form straightened. Martinvale spun around, mortified to find the esteemed gentlemen of the board watching with derision and censure. He fell to business immediately, repeating his years of disclaimers and explanations why the daughter of the Prestons had no place in the Marylebone Spiritualist Association. Lo, she was even accusing him of killing their most powerful asset all those years ago!

Tessa swept past, finally done with the lot of them. She felt a weight lift. She just didn't need them. "Good day, gentlemen. I hope you don't mind if I keep my appointment with your guest tomorrow," she said, gesturing to the frowning Jasper. "I'm determined to close this case on your behalf. It's long overdue."

The gentlemen of the board stepped aside for Tessa and closed in on Martinvale quickly. Tessa did not turn to watch.

THIRTY-ONE

IN WHICH ONE RALLIES

TESSA REMAINED STOIC OUTSIDE the association's building, maintaining a tight hold on her composure until in the safe privacy of the hackney cab she flagged. She fell against the seat, indulging in a few deep sobs and weeps. She trusted the surrounding noises of the metropolis would sufficiently mask her embarrassingly loud crying.

The worst part about this crying business, Tessa decided as she blew her nose into the handkerchief Jasper had given her, was that the very person who caused her sadness was the person she wanted most to comfort her.

When Tessa returned to the house, she slipped into the foyer a somber mess, having racked her brain for any sort of trick she might play to get the ghoul out of Jasper. She slapped her purse and hat on the side table, and the butler quietly handed them to a maid, who scurried away.

The ghosts in the foyer took one look at Tessa's stormy expression and wisely floated in other directions. Eloise's hasty departure was recent in their minds, and Tessa looked likely to grab any ghost and banish them out of spite.

After pacing in the foyer, her hands resting behind her back on her bustle, she realized there was nothing for it. She stormed into the library, unsurprised to find everyone waiting. Earlier, the newlyweds had postponed their honeymoon trip to Mary's countryside house in shared whispers while Tessa had consumed an alarming amount of wedding cake. Tessa did her best to ignore how they held hands and watched her with grave concern.

Tessa was brief in her recounting. She freely admitted to her uncle that he was right. She shouldn't have gone there alone. Propriety aside, the ghoul and Martinvale could have taken their advantage and no one at Hartwell House would ever have known what became of her.

Tessa knew now, given the opaque strength of the ribbons around Jasper's throat, that whatever Martinvale had done to tie that murderous spirit to his own soul, it must have been an awful blood ritual. Something so heinous that there was no wondering anymore whether he might hurt her. Well, more than he had already. Tessa wiped the back of her hand across her lips and shivered. She managed a small smile when Mary tucked a shawl around her.

Sir Hubert watched with narrowed eyes through Tessa's tale. "I never took you for a fool, Tessa," he said. "Confronting Martinvale at the place where he is most powerful could have easily led to your death. There is power hidden in the association's walls, and clearly he has used it to his advantage for decades."

"Lucky for me, the spirit likes to play with his victims first," Tessa muttered.

The dame's brows rose at that. Hartwell and Mary shared an alarmed glance. Sir Hubert dropped to his knee in front of Tessa, demanding to know what the spirit had done to her.

"Well, I daresay since the entire board saw us, I suppose if I exorcise the ghost, I shall *have* to marry him," she tried to say lightly.

Her tremulous laugh was enough to settle an eerily calm expression on her uncle's face, one that showed how deeply he felt his rage. He pressed his lips together against saying more, but he took her hands in his.

Tessa couldn't convince the others all throughout luncheon, afternoon tea, dinner, and even an outrageously strong nightcap of brandy shared amongst them all that she had to do this alone.

Sir Hubert was determined to arm himself with many weapons. He resorted to rude grunts when Tessa removed from him a letter opener, a fountain pen, a fire poker, a jelly knife, and eventually, the mystical cane.

Hartwell kept asking whether they couldn't find a stronger, more experienced medium to take care of this mess until Mary snapped at him. What, did he think there were medium brigades waiting in the wings for situations like this? Should they call up the volunteer firemen to douse Jasper with holy water?

The ghosts hovering in the hallway, just as nervous about Jasper's possession and return as the rest of them, tittered at Mary's sarcasm. Hartwell refilled his brandy and stopped offering suggestions.

Dame Hartwell was uncharacteristically quiet, sipping her brandy until her eyes drooped and she could hardly sit straight.

Mary asked Tessa what she wanted to do.

"This is my fault," Tessa said, downing the last of her glass, flinching. "And I want Archie back as badly as the rest of you."

Mary took Tessa's hand in her own. "I think, while we'd all like to have Jasper be his irresolute, charming self again, you may want it slightly more."

Tessa glared into her empty cup. "Slightly."

"So then," Mary said, "what shall we do?"

"I don't know," Tessa admitted. "I've never been involved with my clients before. When emotions are involved, things can go a little . . . unexpectedly."

Mary looked to Sir Hubert.

"Tessa almost got herself possessed once because she couldn't keep her emotions in check. They use the rawness as a doorway."

"Well," Mary huffed, "that's not very English."

Tessa smiled. "I'm only half-English."

Mary chuckled. "I meant it seems rather unsportsmanlike to take advantage of the emotions of one's . . . prey, I suppose."

"The dead have their own rules, though we've been slow in learning them," Sir Hubert hiccupped.

"Nothing we've learned has prepared us for this moment," Tessa said.

"This isn't about experience, or knowledge," Dame Hartwell said, breaking her silence.

"Oh? And what can you know about this, my lady?" Tessa asked in a quiet, warning tone.

"I've spent decades trying to reach my husband. Martinvale spent decades trying to clean up his mess. This spirit has spent decades itching to complete his contract so he can roam free. And you . . . Well, you've grown to be a smart, capable woman who knows this is so much more than using your head. Your mother had instincts. Natural talent. She listened to the spirits as if they were people, because they were, once. 'They are our ancestors,' she would always say."

Tears picked at the corners of Tessa's eyes upon hearing that familiar phrase again.

"What are you suggesting?" Hartwell asked.

"When the time comes," Dame Hartwell said, "lean into the fear and trust your natural reaction. This . . . thing . . . wants a fight. Do you want a fight?"

Tessa shook her head.

"And do you really want to do this alone?" Dame Hartwell pressed.

Again, Tessa shook her head, her lip trembling.

"Then stop thinking about how you *should* do this, and just do what feels right. Give a shout when he comes, and we'll be right behind you."

"Doing what?" Hartwell asked.

Dame Hartwell threw her hands up. "I don't know. She'll think of something. She *always* does. Don't ruin my little speech with details. It's rude."

Tessa's laugh joined the others' and the tension released from the room, finally.

"Your parents went Beyond because they knew you," her uncle said. "Your mother could have haunted you. But she knew you were capable, even then, of discovering their work and breathing new life into it. When you were ready."

Tessa threw her arms around Sir Hubert, her smile bleary. "I seem to be crying at every turn these days. Thank you for believing in me."

"I could do no less," he said, his voice gruff. "It's been an honor to represent your parents, and care for you in their stead. You must know you're everything they hoped, and more."

Tessa tightened her hold on her uncle, and if a few tears fell to his silk waistcoat, he made no mention of it. Mary joined them, taking Tessa's hand.

"We will help you, however we may," Mary whispered, squeezing her fingers.

Tessa nodded, staring at their combined hands, a theory forming. She sniffled and pulled away from Mary. Her hand grew cooler immediately. She took Mary's hand again, and though Mary's brows rose, she stayed silent as Tessa studied the tingling sensation.

It was an odd thing to think, but . . . Tessa felt stronger. The brandy was making it difficult to decipher, but she had the distinct feeling that holding Mary's hand sharpened her Sense.

Tessa shared a look with her uncle, a slow grin forming. Here stood the two most powerful mediums she knew in London. And while Mary still hadn't entirely discovered her own method of controlling her Sense, the fact was, maybe she didn't need to. Maybe, just maybe . . . if Tessa could redirect her talents . . .

Hmm. Now that was something to sleep over.

Thirty-Two

In Which a Rescue Begins

It was a late start for everyone the next morning.

They woke red-eyed, with hangovers and rumbling stomachs. They were hardly fit to be seen at the breakfast table, let alone in a battle with a malevolent spirit.

Tessa, having spent much of the night staring at the ceiling wondering whether she was crazy or if she ought to lean into her instincts, took one look at everyone shuffling around and dropped her theory by the wayside. Painfully sleep-deprived, her theory hardly seemed to hold water in the daylight, anyway.

Perhaps she ought to just grab her bag of gems and other tricks, and find the ghoul before he obliterated their still-a-little-tipsy crew.

Tessa was well on her way, having grabbed her bag and sneaked the cane away from Sir Hubert, who had disappeared into the kitchen. After confirming that Mary, her husband, and her mother-in-law convalesced quietly in the back courtyard, Tessa tiptoed to the front door, evading even the butler's notice.

Tessa swung the door open and squeaked when she collided with Jasper, who burst through the door seeming extremely peeved. She grabbed the cane before it fell to the ground.

Jasper caught her arms, preventing her fall and her escape. "And here I thought you were going to roll back into my clutches, Tessa Baby," he drawled. "What a bore to make me come find you."

"I beg your pardon," she said icily, "but I make it a habit to not roll into anyone, clutches or otherwise."

He frowned and shrugged. Tessa wrenched from his grip and backed away, her eyes never leaving his. A soft grin spread across his face, and her stomach dropped. He swung his arm back, winding up to release a punch of otherworldly proportions.

No, she didn't intend to wait around for that.

Tessa dropped her bag and bolted in a clear retreat out to the courtyard, clutching the cane. He shouted and made chase. They were hardly discreet. Tessa knocked over chairs, side tables, anything she could to slow Jasper's advancement. Servants screamed that the devil was taking the Hartwells at last.

Dame Hartwell will have to hire an entirely new staff after all this is done, Tessa thought, distracted.

Jasper took to snarling and tossing the furniture out of his way or at Tessa.

Tessa ducked and maneuvered as she never had, glad she'd decided on the quilted stays this morning. She shouldered her way past her uncle, who had come huffing from the kitchen with a knife.

"I told you," she snapped over her shoulder, "no weapons."

Tessa flinched when a coffeepot sailed past their heads. "The courtyard!" She grabbed Sir Hubert's arm, dragging him with her. They burst outside, startling Hartwell and Mary from a tender moment on a stone bench. "Apologies," Tessa wheezed, "but our guest arrived early."

Mary and Hartwell scrambled to their feet, following Tessa to the center of the little garden. The stone pavers arranged in a circle seemed rather ceremonial now that they gathered upon it, watching Jasper advance.

Tessa bit her lip. Jasper looked ghastly. His skin had taken on a bluish pallor, and his veins were almost black. His hair was limp and greasy, and his mustache knotted and frizzed above his dry, cracked lips. The white opacity of his eyes as he stormed forward brightened until Tessa had to squint to confirm where he was.

Dame Hartwell emerged from the back corner of the garden with a basket of freshly cut flowers. She assessed the situation. With an annoyed huff, she aimed the basket at Jasper's head, hitting him squarely in the temple.

Tessa bit back a laugh as Jasper stopped, stunned. "My lady, you needn't involve yourself."

"Of course I do," Dame Hartwell said archly, joining them on the stone medallion. "He's harassing my protégée."

Jasper wound his arm back. Tessa inhaled and time slowed. She slammed the cane to the ground, the heels of both hands pressing into the handle as she growled words of protection. Time sped up to catch Jasper's fist slamming into the invisible wall she had erected.

He glared at her. Her smirk fell quickly when he gingerly placed a hand on hers.

The shield only worked against forceful motions. Jasper pushed his deathly chill through his touch until Tessa couldn't feel her fingers.

She dropped the cane.

Mary screamed when Jasper grabbed Tessa by the back of her neck.

Hartwell and Sir Hubert reached for Tessa, but the ghoul kept her just out of reach. Sir Hubert grabbed the cane instead, thrusting it forward in a parry that caused the ghoul to sidestep. The movement loosened his grip on Tessa. She grabbed the cane, butting it against his chest.

All movement, all breathing, stopped.

Jasper glanced down at the cane pressing into his chest, clearly aware of its powers. "Do it," he hissed, contorting Jasper's face into a horrific snarl.

Tessa both shook her head and pressed harder, trying to convince herself this was the only way. She had done this once before. She could do it again. Tears in her eyes, she willed Jasper to see her behind the spirit's possession. "Do you trust me?" she whispered.

Jasper blinked, seeming himself for a moment. "I trust you," he whispered, though to Tessa's panicked heart, it sounded like *I love you.*

Tessa fell back as if slapped. This wasn't how she wanted to go about this nasty business. The cane, lacking any real instructions, seemed to have one purpose, and that was to expel unwanted spirits, whether from a captive host or the vicinity, and in as violent a manner as possible. The stronger the spirit, the stronger its force.

Tessa had never encountered a ghost with as much strength as the one possessing Jasper. She was certain the cane would not hesitate to kill Jasper if required, to send the ghost Beyond.

She could not kill Jasper. She loosened her grip. Jasper's eyes glazed over and he caught the cane deftly, snapping it over his knee. "Oops," he chuckled.

"You've broken it!" Sir Hubert wailed. "Tessa, you let him break it!"

Tessa ignored her uncle, all her energy and Sense focused on the fluctuating energy from Jasper. He fought the spirit from within his body. That could be the only explanation. She grabbed his hands, not caring that the chill spread even faster this time down the length of her arms.

Rather than recoiling, Tessa stepped closer, wrapping her arms around Jasper in a tight embrace. She studied his expressions, flickering between concern and outrage. She pushed against the chill, forcing it back into Jasper's body.

"Do you trust me?" she whispered again.

Jasper's eyes cleared and widened, and he barely had time for a nod before the ghoul took over. The ghoul flailed Jasper's head, snarling at Tessa to release him as she held tightly and stepped closer.

"I suppose my Sense, having every intent to be rid of you, burns a little?" Tessa said, taunting him.

"Unhand me!" Jasper headbutted Tessa with a roar. They both fell to their knees with muffled groans.

Tessa heard more than saw her friends rush forward, but she barked at them to stay back.

When the ghoul realized Tessa refused to let go, his face grew still with furious concentration. He shifted his weight, knocking her off-balance. He used the momentum to catch her forearms the way she held him. With a delighted snicker, he yanked her close and began humming.

Tessa gasped at the frigid sensation racing along her fingers, up her arms, stealing toward her heart.

"You dare try to possess me?" she panted, willing the chill to slow its pace.

"For all your talk of amplifying others, who will be there to amplify you?" the ghoul taunted.

They locked eyes. Tessa caught her breath, trying to find her Archie in the clouded, cool blue gaze glaring at her.

Who indeed?

A hand clasped Tessa's shoulder, supporting her without breaking her hold on Jasper's arms. An immediate warmth spread through the left half of her body, and she turned to find Mary kneeling with them.

She is the shield to your spear, Tessa recalled her uncle musing. Theories nothing; he was absolutely right.

"Mary, you're not ready," Tessa gasped.

Mary's responding smile soothed a frisson of Tessa's panic. "I am."

Tessa pressed her lips together, thinking this was hardly the time for emotional feminine camaraderie and yet, wanting nothing more than to burst into tears and crush Mary in an embrace. She nodded and turned to her other side, where Dame Hartwell took her elbow.

Hartwell stood behind Tessa, his hands on his mother's and Mary's shoulders. "We're behind you, Tessa."

Ever the obvious observer, that Hartwell. Tessa laughed as the warmth suffused her body. The heat was now almost unbearable, as if she were storing up all the borrowed Sense from Mary, Alex, and Dame Hartwell.

The ghoul spewed expletives, his spittle raining on Tessa's face even as his voice shook.

Tessa leaned forward, pressing the frigidity back into Jasper's body. She needed to trap it. Demolish it. Mary, Hartwell, and his mother leaned with Tessa, keeping her upright as she brought her face close to Jasper's.

"Ready for another kiss with death?" the ghoul asked with a smirk.

She smirked back. "You won't enjoy it."

Before he could prepare, Tessa captured Jasper's mouth with hers, pouring all the found love, support, companionship—family—borrowed from Mary, Hartwell, the dame, and yes, herself most of all, into the caress.

At first, the heat seared Tessa's mouth. She almost broke free from the sharp pain. Yet something urged her on, and she pressed deeper.

Jasper's icy lips soon reflected the warmth. A roar shook her very bones, and her companions fell back with startled exclamations. Jasper spasmed. She wrapped her arms around him, locking his body to hers.

Dimly, Tessa heard her uncle instructing the Hartwells to surround her and Jasper with clasped hands, forming a séance circle. Once again, she felt an influx of warmth as the circle closed, accepting its aid as tears streamed down her face. She would not disappoint them. She would save Jasper.

Images flitted through her mind.

Their misunderstanding years ago.

That first mortifying embrace on the street, with an annoyed and fearful Eloise floating nearby.

Shared smiles over Dame Hartwell's theatrics.

The unexpected pleasure of joining forces against Mary and Hartwell's teasing.

Jasper's hand at the small of her back, causing a tingle not unlike her first experiences with her Sense. His genuine compliments of her hair. The twinkle in his eye as he raced across the Serpentine, delighted in his element.

Jasper's implicit and explicit trust. His confidence in her.

They were a team, Tessa and Jasper, and no spirit, however strong, would break their bond.

Jasper's body froze. His head slammed back. He stared unseeing at the sky.

"Come back to me," she whispered, placing her hands at his throat and forehead. Tessa opened all forms of her Sense, focusing everything she had even though the roar exploding from Jasper threatened to knock them over.

A tear rolled down Jasper's cheek. He screamed her name.

Thirty-Three

In Which Reinforcements Arrive

Jasper lost all sense of time after the spirit took away the windowpane. He had no clue whether his imprisonment had lasted hours or weeks. Without access to the sensations within his corporeal body, he did not need to sleep or eat. His clothing remained unwrinkled and his cheeks clean shaven.

Jasper crouched, not knowing which way was up, but since his feet were beneath him, he figured he was upright at least. He had spun about for who knew how long, finding no end in sight to the white, barren landscape. There in the distance, though, a dark spot moved.

He raised a hand to shield his gaze, struggling to decipher the dark figure moving toward him in the oppressive bright light. It couldn't be friendly.

Now that it was closer, Jasper realized something chased the figure. How many spirits could a body hold?

Jasper threw his hands over his head as the figures sped ever closer, and then past him. That second figure . . . It looked like nothing more than a shadow to his confused eyes. He blinked, and knew that hair arrangement, or what he assumed was hair. And he most definitely knew that warm scent of vanilla and spices.

"You leave him be," she said. "He's mine. I love him."

Eyes wide, Jasper stood, screaming Tessa's name.

Now so named, the figure took form. Brown arms pumping as she ran, hands clutching skirts, braids and curls frizzled and falling from her careful formation. A beautiful mess of precise energy and determination. Tessa.

Jasper scrambled to catch up with them, not understanding where they were going. He needed something to slow them down, something to let him catch up to their unearthly speed. The ground shuddered beneath his feet. Jasper stumbled to a stop, mouth agape.

Not too far ahead, Tessa's Sense and the spirit possessing him staggered, flailing to not fall over the cliff that had appeared out of nowhere.

Tessa's Sense turned around and grinned at Jasper. "There you are," she said, her voice echoing.

"Here I am."

They grinned at one another.

"Can you do that again?" She pointed to the chasm.

Jasper blinked. Had he done that? By Jove.

He pointed in voiceless warning as the malignant spirit launched itself at her.

The ghoul no longer attempted any semblance of the human form; it had no need of it. The thing was a horrific amalgamation of spider legs and slithering tentacles resembling snakes. Twenty limbs or more shot out to capture Tessa.

She grappled with it, and they fell to the ground, teetering too close to the deep fissure Jasper's mind had created. He ran toward them, wondering what he could do.

"We must trap it, hold it still," Tessa panted, a blurred mess of skirts and dark limbs and the spirit's tentacles. "My uncle—"

The spirit grabbed her by the throat. She gagged. It wound around her, binding her legs, arms, hips, and covering her hair, her nose. Jasper skidded to a halt, not knowing which tentacle to grab. They smothered Tessa until he could only see her wide eyes blinking at him.

Tessa was dying. He was watching her die. Hadn't she warned him that the Sense was, however powerful, a fragile thing? And here was her Sense, trapped with him and this spirit. He couldn't let her die. He wouldn't.

Jasper acted without thinking. He threw his arms around Tessa and the spirit, shouting that the spirit could have him. Just leave Tessa alone. The spirit roared, wriggling within the confines of the embrace. Jasper's hands began glowing.

Jasper touched Tessa's face. The spirit screeched. A tentacle fell back, steaming. Tessa was blinking at him now, trying to tell him something. Not knowing what to do, he kept running his fingers over her face, thinking that while Tessa's Sense didn't need to breathe, she probably needed her mouth to speak to him. He touched her lips. Another tentacle fell.

With her mouth unbound, Jasper stared, trying to understand what Tessa shouted over the spirit's enraged roaring. His eyes roved over her fallen hair, her wide, dark eyes, her large nose and shapely lips. Hang whatever it was she was trying to say.

Jasper grabbed Tessa's face and kissed her.

The spirit, now reduced to an amorphous ball of impotent hostility, sat trapped between them, too injured to move away from Jasper's searing touch. Arms now free, Tessa grabbed the spirit while not breaking away from Jasper's embrace. She leaned into the kiss, encouraging it and him and setting free a burst of warmth from Jasper that made the spirit howl.

The howling made Jasper's bones shudder, and he clung to Tessa as she clung to him. The spirit clawed at them and sprung away. Tessa screamed a phrase and a thousand hands burst out of nowhere, trapping the spirit. Jasper screwed his eyes shut.

A sharp pain caused him to fall away from Tessa with a cry. The world exploded around them.

THIRTY-FOUR

IN WHICH RECONCILIATION OCCURS

THE BRIGHT MIASMA VANISHED. Tessa clung to Jasper, searching his face for any sign of the murderous spirit and only finding his clear blue eyes smiling at her. Tears sprung to Tessa's eyes. She swallowed, hard.

"So you love me, eh?" Jasper pulled curls away from her forehead, tucking them behind her ear. They sprang right back into place, and he chuckled.

"Stuff it," Tessa muttered. She threw her arms around him, embracing him as only her parents had ever embraced her. When a sob broke free of her tense silence, Tessa froze, mortified. Jasper's arms wrapped around her, giving her permission to bury her face in his waistcoat, to let the tears flow.

Rather than feeling stupid or childish when Jasper began shushing her and rubbing the back of her neck, Tessa leaned into him, feeling weeks of tension melt away.

"Thank you for saving me," he said, his breath tickling the curls at her nape.

She shook her head, leaning back to face him, her eyes burning from the sudden tears. "I daresay you saved me."

Jasper smiled, running a finger down the length of her jaw. "We saved each other, then."

He leaned forward, pausing when Tessa tensed. Memories of the spirit's awful kiss caused her breath to catch.

"That wasn't me," Jasper whispered, dropping his arms and leaning from her. "I would never force myself upon a woman. Nothing has changed, Tessa, not for me. But I will walk away if it would make the woman I love feel safe again."

The woman he loved.

Tessa wrapped her arms around Jasper, burying her face in his collar. She felt his quickening pulse against her cheek as he wrapped his arms around her, cocooning her in his solid strength. She turned slightly, pulling away to study the cautious hope in his bright eyes.

The woman he loved. The woman he wanted to stay safe, even if it meant staying away.

A smile dawned across Tessa's face. She took Jasper's stubbled cheeks in her hands, drawing him forward for a sweet kiss. The rough texture beneath her fingers contrasted with the softness of his lips. They shuffled closer, the kiss deepening as their fears and hopes and relief spilled out. His hands moved to her waist. Her fingers slipped into his hair. His tongue teased her, and Tessa, startled and delighted, followed suit.

Only Dame Hartwell and Sir Hubert noisily clearing their throats caused them to sit back to breathe.

Mary and Hartwell, while drained, seemed an unseemly sort of delighted by the spectacle. The four of them remained in their circle around the couple, the exploding spirit having thrown them a yard away, causing minor scratches and bruises.

Jasper pulled back, varying shades of red mottling his complexion. Tessa fell forward, unable to keep her balance with such a heady emotion clouding her sensibilities. She shrugged and looked up at Jasper, her grin inviting round two; who cared who saw after all that happened?

Jasper caught Tessa's shoulders and gave a meaningful glance to her uncle, who nursed an arm while watching with intense interest.

Jasper turned his head to whisper against Tessa's cheek, his mustache tickling her. "Yes, I will marry you."

"*What?*"

"You told that spirit you were a woman of principle. That you were saving your kisses for someone who deserved them." Jasper waggled his eyebrows at her, daring her to contradict him. "Clearly I am most deserving, and I accept. I will marry you."

A bubbling giggle erupted from Tessa. She kept laughing, tears of delight streaming down her face as Jasper kissed them away.

"I look forward to many years of making you laugh, dearest," he murmured.

"Good," Tessa said, pulling him close. "For I don't think I love anyone as I do you."

"That's a relief," he said against her lips. "It would be a damn sight awkward if I had to compete with Sir Hubert."

"Be quiet, you're ruining the moment."

Jasper was quick to comply.

Some minutes later, breathless and grinning, Jasper and Tessa leapt from one another like guilty schoolchildren, turning healthy shades of red and pink.

"Don't stop on our account," Sir Hubert said.

They both stuttered until they realized his body shook with contained laughter.

"I already worked it out with his mother, you silly children." Sir Hubert leveled a glare at Jasper. "Avoid getting possessed in the meantime. I've never seen my niece so nonplussed."

"Even if I had such misfortune," Jasper said, wrapping his arm around Tessa's waist, "I daresay I'm marrying the right woman to remedy the situation."

"Of course she is," Dame Hartwell snapped, "or have you not yet realized this was part of the plan all along? The spirits *told* me."

Tessa smiled, content to listen to Jasper, the dame, and her uncle tease one another as she leaned into Jasper's arm and enjoyed the small thrill from the way he entwined his fingers with hers.

And if anyone noticed a Regency dandy floating in the garden's corner, sighing ever-so-longingly after the healthy pours of celebratory wine now distributed amongst their party by Pomeroy, they had the better sense to stay quiet.

Thirty-Five

In Which the Troupe Recounts

THERE ARE MANY UNSUNG benefits of one's neighbor being an elderly woman with a penchant for minding her own business. One such benefit was her being wholly uncooperative when constables appear, demanding to know what the ruckus was about in her shared courtyard.

In fact, Dame Hartwell's neighbor dismissed the nonplussed young constable on her step with a cookie and a bit of tea. She was firm, saying he ought to investigate far more important things than a bit of loudness in a courtyard.

Thus, Hartwell House remained in good standing with the neighborhood, for if *she* wasn't disturbed, as their immediate neighbor, well then. Everyone knew Dame Hartwell had her eccentric moments.

The first meeting of what Tessa now thought of as the Society of Annoyed and Hesitant Mediums lacked all the pomp and circumstance one expected of the Marylebone Spiritualist Association. In fact, the gathering was so very informal, one might have mistaken it for an afternoon tea amongst a group of exhausted friends.

The Hartwells, Sir Hubert, Tessa, and Jasper sat in the disordered library. Tessa's flight through the house as the ghoul chased her had left its mark. Books lay where the spirit's malcontent energy had thrown them. They sat in piles every which way across the shelves and floor. Chairs and side tables remained overturned except for those in use. The maid had tried to tidy up, but Pomeroy's quiet refusal of letting anyone disturb the troupe left the room in shambles.

Mary had given up trying to smooth the crumpled book pages, choosing instead to sit rather too close to her new husband, holding his hand and glaring at any ghost who dared hover within arm's reach. Hartwell, still nursing an ache in his chest from his near possession, pulled his wife to the chaise, where he might rest his head on her lap. Mary sipped her tea, running her fingers through his hair, her expression tender and content.

Sir Hubert and Dame Hartwell, in strong contrast to this restful energy, maintained a lively debate. Their conversation bounced between which were the cook's best biscuits to serve with tea, to arguing who ought to draft the first charter for their new society, for of course they must begin one. They endeavored to pull their head medium into the conversation, but she was fully engaged.

By saying Tessa was fully engaged, what this author means is she slept in the corner, head resting on the shoulder of her fiancé, whose head lolled back against the top of the sofa. Jasper's arm hugged Tessa's waist, and his involuntary flinches as he suffered a nightmare of endless white caused Tessa to snuggle deeper. Possession nightmares could last for months, even years. She was glad she knew what possession felt like; it prepared her to be Jasper's companion through the lasting effects.

The small snuggling motion soothed Jasper back into a deep slumber. Both he and Tessa missed Mrs. Steele's arrival—Dame

Hartwell had sent for her, of course—so drained were they from their ordeal with the spirit.

Mrs. Steele, though suffering from palpitations of immense joy at seeing her son so entangled, was a little dismayed by this careless display of affection. She was drawn away from the couple by Sir Hubert and Dame Hartwell's entreaties to join them and learn just what had kept her son away from home this time.

After a suitable length resulting in grumbling stomachs, Sir Hubert roused the young people, and they all shared the narrative with a startled and disbelieving Mrs. Steele over a hearty lunch.

Exclamations of, "What, not Eloise Carterprice!"

and, "That girl was always selfish, no wonder you didn't believe her."

and, "Archie, why didn't you say anything?"

to, "That odious man!"

ensured everyone that the recounting to Mrs. Steele hit all the right marks.

Sir Hubert was glad to hear the details of possession from Tessa and Jasper, for it was to be the highlight of his publication, with names omitted for privacy, of course.

"I don't see the purpose," Tessa argued, "in hiding our identities. If I'm leading this society, don't you think your readers will figure it out?"

"But think of the intrigue," Dame Hartwell gushed. "Once his readers decipher your identities, for they shall, they will feel oh-so-clever, and clamor to hire your services. My dear, you might even receive a summons from the queen!"

Tessa's grip tightened around Jasper's hand. He was quick to share two quick squeezes in return. He announced, "If you so much as breathe a word of this before our wedding, you're both uninvited."

The dame gasped outrage, but upon seeing the seriousness in Jasper's stern gaze, settled for drinking her tea, most aggressively.

Sir Hubert slammed his journal shut, his mouth fighting to hide his grin.

Mrs. Steele stared at her son, startled by this protective display. The warm smile that spread across her face as she winked at Tessa made Tessa's heart shiver with unexpected comfort.

"If you're looking for a charming, quiet, and not *entirely* run-down country house for your honeymoon," Hartwell rumbled, turning his head so he might address Jasper from Mary's lap, "I know just the spot."

Mary swatted Hartwell's arm with an annoyed chuckle.

"I don't think that's the place," Jasper said. He rubbed the back of his head, wincing.

Tessa shook her head, smiling at Jasper and his mother. "I think I've had enough of traveling, even short distances. Finding a home where we might run the Hesitant Mediums Society sounds like just the thing."

Jasper threw his hand to his chest. "And rob me of my time with you? I understand your desire to stay always busy, my dear, but there are limits."

Tessa's mouth dropped open as Jasper swooped in to kiss her reddened cheek in front of everyone.

"Never fear." Jasper chuckled at her embarrassment. "I'll find us a little cottage. Away from water stronger than a babbling brook, mind, but close enough to town that we might return on a moment's notice. If I even hear the whisper of a haunting, it's off the list."

Her eyes shining, Tessa raised her hand to Jasper's cheek, whispering her thanks. How wonderful to have someone know her so well.

"What will we do without our cane?" Sir Hubert asked, flipping through his notebook with his customary harrumph.

Tessa rolled her eyes. She would never hear the end of losing the cane to that spirit. "Once our society becomes more well known, there will be many mediums to help us."

And while Sir Hubert continued his grumbling, Tessa caught the amused glint in his eye. She thought back to how they had first entered Hartwell House. Sir Hubert sought a stable income and roof so he might finish his tome. She sought a purpose and belonging.

Knowing her future mother-in-law's eyes were on them, Tessa gripped Jasper's hand, vowing to never let him go again.

His responding squeeze, accompanied by Mary and Hartwell's knowing grins, and the amused approval of everyone else, made it even more clear that Tessa had found both purpose and belonging.

Tessa had never thought to be public with her Sense; yet here sat a room full of people encouraging her to use it. She had never thought her Sense would be more than a way to make ends meet; yet it had brought her back to Jasper.

She had taken the long road around, and the journey wasn't without its battles, literally. Tessa knew the result—her found family and dear Archie—was all the sweeter for her troubles.

"Miss Preston," Jasper whispered, causing a curl to tickle her ear, "I thought I saw a delightful bit of greenery in the back of the courtyard this morning. Might you care to study it with me?"

Jasper's words were as innocent as they should be. His heated gaze, and the grin tucked in the corner of his mouth, promised far more entertaining things than a bit of greenery.

Tessa and Jasper left the library with all the haste of a newly affianced couple doing their best to conceal their intended kissing, and convincing no one.

THIRTY-SIX

EPILOGUE

IN WHICH A SOCIETY FORMS

SOME WEEKS LATER, ON the morning of her wedding, Tessa found herself unable to resist checking on the latest correspondence before buttoning herself into the beautiful gown Mary had gifted for the ceremony. She stood alone in the Hartwell drawing room, staring at the pile of letters on the salver. A ruby wax seal adorned with the Marylebone Spiritualist Association's insignia closed the letter topmost on the pile.

Tessa turned the letter. "Curious."

Jasper, removing his hat as he entered the drawing room, paused at the sight of her bemused expression. "Don't say someone invited you to rid some other unfortunate soul of a ghostly companion. Haven't we earned a day's rest to get married, at least?"

"Aren't you not supposed to see the bride before the ceremony?" she countered, ripping open the seal with a laugh. She scanned it quickly, leaning back against Jasper's chest as he wrapped his arms around her waist.

"Are they begging for forgiveness?" he asked, daring to nibble her neck.

"Something along those lines," Tessa breathed, struggling to focus on the words swimming in front of her. "Really, Archie, we're going to be married in a couple of hours. Contain yourself," she said, chuckling.

"Alright then," Jasper grumbled, stepping back. "For a couple of hours. What does the letter say?"

"Our esteemed friends at the Marylebone Spiritualist Association are rescinding their rejection of my applications. In fact, they are offering me the position of chair of the board." She peeked at Jasper from behind the letter, her brown eyes dancing. "It seems Master Theodosius Martinvale was unanimously voted out of the society as a charlatan, and unfit to run a society of practicing mediums focused on the greater good."

Jasper slapped his gloves against his knee. "Splendid. Shall you take them up on their offer?"

Tessa smiled, reflecting on Jasper's singular way of not presuming to know her answer, or speak for her. A trait she admired in both her father and uncle, and now soon-to-be-husband. "Do you think I should? You will be my husband. What do you prefer?"

Jasper's mustache twisted above a tight smile. "I can't say I'd welcome it, but ghosts are certainly a part of who you are. If you wish it, I'll not prevent it." He combed his fingers through his hair, a mercenary gleam in his eye as he sat at the table. "I assume the position comes with a healthy salary?"

"Ever the pragmatist," Tessa said, crossing the room to sit in his lap. "No, I think I shall stay with my little society just for women like me. We'll be without the biases sure to exist in an established, tenured group of men such as the Marylebone Spiritualist Association. And anyway, I've an eye for managing a team, it seems, or have you already forgotten *your* exorcism?"

Jasper looked askance at her. "If you want me to behave, sitting in my lap isn't the thing to do." He buried a hand in her piled curls, his fingertips kneading the base of her head. "Whatever would you call such a group of women?"

Tessa swallowed a moan as Jasper hit the exact spot that always ached after a trying time with the spirits. "Well, given the first two members would be Mary and myself . . . I've been calling it the Society of Annoyed and Hesitant Mediums. Do you think the dame and my uncle will agree to it, as our social and political research consultants?"

"It's a bit of a mouthful," he said. "What about the Hesitant Mediums for short?"

Tessa let it roll about before nodding. "It will certainly draw the right sort, don't you think?"

They shared a laugh; they shared an entirely satisfactory kiss, and they welcomed the momentary peace before the day's festivities would finally begin.

"Miss Preston?" a quiet voice interrupted.

Tessa and Jasper flew from one another, cheeks ablaze with mortification. Really, having a place to call one's own couldn't come soon enough.

Upon noticing who stood in the drawing room door, Jasper fell back, startled. "Not you again!" He tripped over his feet in his backward escape, suddenly clumsy with fear.

Tessa caught his arm, frowning at his blanched expression, and turned to face the interloper.

There in the doorway stood an all-too-familiar woman with carefully coiffed blonde hair, a somber yet fashionable lavender dress, and a pair of spectacles perched atop her pert nose. She studied the room, Jasper, and finally Tessa. Her eyes lit up in recognition. Though Tessa knew they had never met, the woman rushed forward.

"Don't you lay a hand on her," Jasper warned, scrambling to stand in front of Tessa.

Tessa chuckled, stopping them both. "My dear Archie," she said, neatly ignoring the pleased flush stealing across his cheeks at her sweet admonishment, "just who do you think this is?"

"Eloise returned for her revenge, of course!"

Tessa cradled his cheek in her palm. "Spirits don't throw shadows," she said. "They *are* shadows."

The lady smiled, albeit tentatively, as Jasper gave her an appraising glance. "Just so," he muttered, straightening his waistcoat. He bowed his apology. "Miss Carterprice, to what do we owe this pleasure?"

Edith Carterprice blinked at them, her expression warring between exasperation and amusement. "I'm told you have information about my dearly departed sister."

Tessa inhaled sharply, and did her special blink to lean into her Sense. She poked Jasper with an annoyed grunt. "You said nothing about Eloise being a twin."

Jasper rubbed his side. "You never thought to ask."

Tessa circled Edith, muttering, "The likeness is uncanny."

"That happens with identical twins, I'm afraid," Edith said. "I have also heard you are forming your own society for mediums?"

Tessa's brows rose, and she nodded. "You must tell me your sources, Miss Carterprice. They are unnervingly accurate."

Edith straightened her posture, her expression determined. "I think we run in more . . . *similar* circles than you might think, Miss Preston. I should like to join your society."

Before Tessa could question Edith further, a ghost sailed into the room. He was an elderly gentleman, with laugh wrinkles around his eyes and mouth. He had a slight hunch in his shoulder, and while his clothes hung loosely on him, they had once been of fine quality.

Edith glanced at him, and after a silent exchange, held out her hand. He smiled, taking it with both of his. The effect was immediate. He glowed until he was more light than shadow, finally bursting into tiny snowflakes that faded away to nothing.

Tessa cleared her throat with a meaningful look at her fiancé. "Welcome to the Hesitant Mediums, Miss Carterprice. You must join us for our wedding. We have so much to tell you."

Edith caught her sliding spectacles with a small smile. "If what the spirits say is true about Eloise's escapades, you *must* call me Edith."

Read Edith's story in the next installment of the Hesitant Mediums series: **An Uncanny Bargain**.

Author Note

The Marylebone Spiritualist Association existed, but I was unable to find a Theodosius Martinvale in any of my research, likely because I made him up for the purposes of my story. You can still find the association, which was renamed in 1960 as the Spiritualist Association of Great Britain to reflect its growth and status.

Obviously, I've fictionalized the accounts relating to this story, so please don't take anything seriously about my depiction of the 1888 association. Today's Spiritualist Association is a private charity that offers sittings with visiting mediums, workshops, and classes on all aspects of mediumship. Their objective is to advance, educate, and research the principles of spiritualism, and provide relief to those suffering mental and physical illness through spiritualism.

Some of the most well-known and/or alleged spiritualists include:

- Victoria Woodhull, the first woman to run for president of the United States and 1871 president of the American Association of Spiritualists;

- Charles Dickens, author of *Great Expectations*, *Oliver Twist*, *A Tale of Two Cities*, *A Christmas Carol*, and more;

- Sir Arthur Conan Doyle, of *Sherlock Holmes* fame (who

preferred his spiritualist notoriety over his novels);

- Mary Todd Lincoln, widow of President Abraham Lincoln and a grieving mother;

- Dan Aykroyd, of *Ghostbusters* fame, whose great-grandfather used to run séances; and

- Queen Victoria, British monarch from 1837–1901.

Though its prominence has waxed and waned over the centuries, spiritualism often gains popularity during periods of massive losses of life, such as wars and pandemics, or highly public loss of life, such as the 1861 death of Queen Victoria's beloved Prince Albert. At its core, it is a belief that one can speak with the other side, and that one's consciousness survives after death to bring peace and healing to the living.

Of course, as our Hesitant Mediums know, there is a spectrum to everything . . .

Message from the Author

I hope you had as much fun reading this as I had writing it. If you liked this book, please consider writing a review at one of the locations below. As an independent author, your reviews and word-of-mouth are key to the success of this book and my writing career.

Website https://worderella.com
BookBub https://worderella.com/bookbub
Goodreads https://worderella.com/goodreads

ACKNOWLEDGEMENTS

As with any creative endeavor, one cannot go it alone, even while being an individualistic independent author such as myself.

Thank you to for the many hours of feedback from my beta reader and editor, Jessica Allowski of Cozy Cottage Editing. Your gentle manner in handling introverted writers is perfection.

Thank you to my sensitivity reader, Samiat Baks, who confirmed I didn't introduce internalized racism as I described Tessa and her relationship with Jasper.

Thank you to my Cozy Coterie members, your reactions to the first draft of A Spirited Engagement told me I was on the right track with my snark, humor, and emotion: DJ Smith, Juneta Key, Candace, and Ressdell.

Thank you to my husband for pushing me to take the time I needed to write and make room for self-care.

Thank you to my kiddos for being creative, hilarious, sweet human beings. I'm so glad I'm your mom.

BECOME A VIP

If you would like to be contacted when I release a new work, subscribe to my newsletter or become a member of my community, the Cozy Coterie. Cozy Coterie members read and react to first drafts, receive mailed swag, and are privy to discounts from my store.

Newsletter https://worderella.com/news
Cozy Coterie https://worderella.com/cozycoterie

TITLES BY BELINDA KROLL

HESITANT MEDIUMS

Haunting Miss Trentwood
Miss Preston's Predicament (story)
An Inconvenient Séance (story)
A Spirited Engagement

OTHER TITLES

The Last April
Catching the Rose

Beatrice Learns to Dance
as Binaebi Akah

Haunting Miss Trentwood

Book 1 of the Hesitant Mediums

It is a truth universally acknowledged that father knows best, even after death, and especially about one's suitors.

Resigned to spinsterhood in her English manor house, Mary Trentwood is horrified when her father's ghost crawls from his grave, and struggles as he spouts opinion after opinion about the *most mundane* things.

Mistaking the newly-arrived and quietly handsome Alexander Hartwell as her father's solicitor—for who else would interrupt her mourning?—Mary soon realizes her father is adding matchmaking to his repertoire. Neither Mary nor her father realize Hartwell hunts a blackmailer, and shouldn't waste time seeking Mary's smiles…

Miss Preston's Predicament
A Hesitant Mediums story

It is a truth universally ignored, most principally by the dowager Dame Hartwell, that ghosts and gatherings do not mix.

In this short story, the fashionable and eccentric dowager Dame Hartwell has lured the reclusive Miss Tessa Preston to attend her drawing room séance. If Dame Hartwell can't convince Miss Preston, her former protégé, to return as her medium-in-residence, she doesn't know how she will protect her son and his new fiancée from the brewing storm of malcontent spirits surrounding them.

MISS PRESTON'S PREDICAMENT is a short story between novels. It is a standalone referencing characters and events from the cozy Victorian fantasy romance, HAUNTING MISS TRENTWOOD, the first in the Hesitant Mediums series.

An Inconvenient Séance
A Hesitant Mediums story

It is a truth universally ignored that sons abhor being sent to séances in search of a wife.

In this short story, Jasper Steele has had enough of ghosts to last him a lifetime, so why is he attending a séance? Mostly to appease his mother, who worries about his head and his heart after his summer in the English countryside getting rejected by Mary Trentwood.

Eloise Carterprice has never been one to let a good opportunity escape her, so it's only natural that her ghost appears during the latest séance hosted by her mother. Will Jasper find a bit of romance? Will Eloise have her bit of fun? Read on, dear Reader, read on!

This is a short story bridge between HAUNTING MISS TRENTWOOD and A SPIRITED ENGAGEMENT. It is a companion story to "Miss Preston's Predicament."

A Spirited Engagement

Book 2 of the Hesitant Mediums

It is a truth universally acknowledged that ghost brides are annoying romantic rivals.

Making her reluctant return to London after a ten-year absence, Tessa Preston cannot hide her dismay at her employer's friendliness with Jasper Steele, the man who chased her away. To make matters more annoying, he's haunted by a *most insistent* ghost bride.

Determined to prove her indifference to the charming Jasper, Tessa realizes the entitled ghost demanding his attention may not be all she seems. Meanwhile, unaware of Tessa's enmity, Jasper is delighted to have a second chance at her affections, and will let nothing, not even her cold stares, dampen his enthusiasm.

A SPIRITED ENGAGEMENT is a standalone romantic fantasy featuring characters from the cozy Victorian fantasy romance, HAUNTING MISS TRENTWOOD, the first in the Hesitant Mediums series.

The Last April

An Ohio Civil War Novel

Spontaneous, fifteen-year-old Gretchen vows to help heal the nation from the recently ended Civil War. On the morning of President Lincoln's death, Gretchen finds an amnesiac Confederate in her garden and believes this is her chance for civic goodwill.

But reconciliation is not as simple as Gretchen assumed. When her mother returns from the market with news that a Confederate murdered the president, Gretchen wonders if she caught the killer. Tensions between her aunt and mother rise as Gretchen nurses her Confederate prisoner, revealing secrets from their past that make Gretchen question everything she knows about loyalty, honor, and trust.

THE LAST APRIL is an entertaining, thoughtful slice-of-life novella of Ohio after the Civil War, meant to encourage teen readers to reflect on themes of fear and hope in uncertain times.

About the Author

Belinda Kroll writes sweet and cozy Victorian fantasy and fiction. Think Jane Austen-lite vocabulary meets modern sass. She is a user experience design professional, hobbyist photographer, and lindy hopper.

Kroll is obsessed with eyeglasses, Korean dramas, home renovation and cooking shows, and petting every dog that allows her to do so. She has a line of stationery for writers, readers, and creatives at Bright Bird Press. She lives with her family in Ohio.

Website https://worderella.com
Instagram https://instagram.com/worderella
Membership https://worderella.com/cozycoterie
Bright Bird Press stationery https://brightbirdpress.com